Scars of Sea & Sky

J. M. Gordon

Published by J. M. Gordon, 2024.

SCARS OF SEA & SKY

First edition. September 6, 2024.

ISBN: 979-8227501431

Written by J. M. Gordon.

Table of Contents

To Mom:

You were the first one to believe in my storytelling skills and let's face it, you're where I got those skills from. Thank you.

Love you!

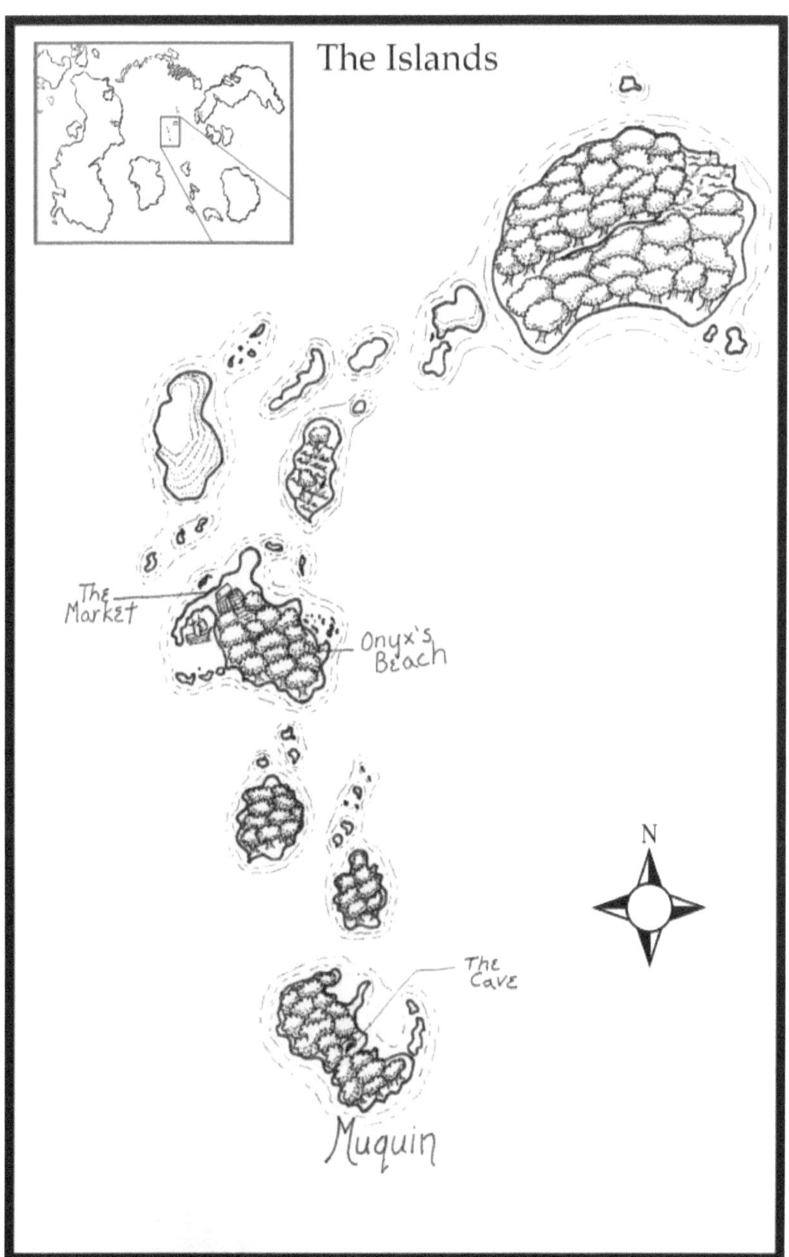

The Islands
The Market
Onyx's Beach
The Cave
Muquin
N

<u>Prelude</u>

Strange, really, how the smallest of choices create the largest of changes. It can make the difference between a king or a peasant, a good meal or bad, or even the difference between life or death.

Those were my first thoughts as water closed over my head and ropes dug into my flesh. I couldn't remember if the wave or the rigging had been what had knocked me overboard; though, neither option changed what now was. I fought for the surface.

Salt spray air, half-liquid breath and the ropes were dragging me under again. Too much weight for man or elf to fight against. This time I let them pull me down, tired beyond belief. The days leading up to this moment had been wearying, a storm that had rolled on for so long. For a moment, I just wanted to close my eyes and let the seas take me. For a moment, life was calm, the choice was easy. I would never have to fight again. That moment passed.

Dragons are made of fight.

Heartbeat, slipping from one form to another, wings pushed me up and I broke the surface, gulping air with a snarl.

Not this way.

I refused to let things end this way.

Ropes jerked, cut flesh, tangled and pulled me back. I surged against the waves, trying to break free. The battle was endless.

By the time I felt sand and shoreline beneath my feet, I had lost the ship, lost count of the hours, lost the feeling in every limb and lost every last bit of fight. I returned to human form and lay half in and half out of the water. A change in tides could kill me. I heard the gravel crunch. Friend? Foe? Whichever, my future was now up to fate.

Chapter 1 - Bad Manners

"Lady deAvaric?"

The air inside the palanquin was stuffy and she played with her skirts, alternately smoothing and scrunching the fine fabric in her hands as she ignored the call from the outside. She noted a loose thread and had to hold herself back from picking at the embroidery.

"Lady deAvaric?" A guard she'd long ago forgotten the name of spoke. Forgetting hadn't been on purpose, but because her fraternization with them had become so limited.

"I do not wish to be here." The thought barely became a whisper before she sighed and spoke aloud for the ones waiting outside. "I am ready."

She unfolded herself from the palanquin that felt like a wooden cage as gracefully as possible - she was tall for a woman - and listened to the whispers among the staff scurrying about to move her luggage to their lord's chambers. Some assumed she couldn't understand them because she avoided speaking unless necessary. The truth was that her accent left her self-conscious and she already felt awkward enough. The chatter at least kept her distracted from the chill spring breeze. She turned her face towards the sun to soak in the light. If she'd been allowed to have her wings out, she'd have turned her back and let them soak up the light. Another frustration.

Gossip had settled into two camps. Her being a scandalous harlot that had their lord under some thrall was a common one - because it was decided that was the only way such a pale ghost of a woman would ever be considered by him. Amazing how soon some chose to forget. The second group was made of more than a few servants scolding the others that this strange auburn-haired woman was High Lord Bryndagr's REAL wife and the current Lady Bryndagr was the interloper. Others didn't correct it directly, but sternly shushed gossip that was insulting to her. Still others listened, some taking in the corrections, others brushed them aside without a second thought. Well, at least gossip was consistent no matter where you were. Truth fought tooth and nail to be heard while the juicy and salacious spread like wildfire.

High Lord Bryndagr finally entered the courtyard, flanked by his two younger brothers. The gossips fell silent, whether in respect or because their lord was handsome was debatable. Sleek black hair, the rare grey eyes - known as Bryndagr grey - and sharp cheekbones. Handsome. Even knowing what she knew, he was still handsome.

A low bow and she was more aware than ever of the spring breeze blowing across her back, drying the sweat from being cooped up in the palanquin. Custom, custom, cursed custom. Customs of his land did not want to let a lady ride a horse all the way here. Dragon custom was to expose the scars to prove the match. Funny how he didn't seem to feel the same applied to him, but a lord in the Dawnlands couldn't parade around shirtless in front of his servants.

Introductions, formalities, all the normal necessary irritations commenced and passed in a haze as she held her head high and stared at him. It wasn't polite. Courtesy dictated a demure maiden with lowered eyes, or at the very least, one that didn't look on the verge of challenging the master of the house. Her nails dug into her palms even though she was sure she was holding her skirt. She softened for a moment when a small boy was introduced. Nails drew blood from her palms once he was led away. She followed Lord Bryndagr to an inner - far more private - courtyard filled with early spring blooms. It was a beautiful place for a most civil war. They faced each other as the servants withdrew.

The smack of her palm against his face was loud and satisfying, even as she felt the welt rising on her own cheek. He sighed.

"I will remember to stop you from that one day. You hurt yourself more."

"It would be preferable if you'd remember I don't want to be here first."

"Aislinn, please. Can we attempt civility?" He was so calm, composed and even. Why did that always make her feel so much angrier?

"Every year, spring and fall, you call me through this bond. If I ignore, you tug and pull and wheedle until I can't ignore it anymore. I'm sorry, but it wears away all civility."

"I miss you." He took her hand and laid a kiss on her fingertips.

She exhaled and looked away. His eyes were too honest when he voiced those words. She was aware that she hadn't pulled her hand back.

"Kaienar, I miss you too. A part of me always will miss what was. Always. But I'm only here because I can't dissolve this bond. Maybe you would keep it no matter what, but I would get rid of it if I could, and you know that. What you are doing is neither right nor fair."

"Is it fair for our son to grow up without his mother?"

Space loomed between them now; she had snatched her hand back. That was a low blow, if he was going to take the fight there, she'd meet him.

"Just to remind you, his mother died. That's what you tell him, that's what you told the new Lady Bryndagr, at least until you had to explain my reappearance." She held up her hand to stall explanations, shaking now, "I know, I know. Marriage of politics, not love. I've heard it before; I don't care. It doesn't change that you have a new wife and replacement mother more palatable to your court for him. Doesn't make it so I can live peaceably as second wife or first wife or whatever you would install me as. Either way, I wouldn't be the only wife and we know what that leads to."

"She is not his mother, he does not accept her as that, and she…" His voice trailed off and Aislinn pushed the red hot jealousy down. Dragon instincts insisted Kaienar was hers and only hers and she hated that feeling. She wanted to hunt this woman down, it was hard to hear him when he spoke again. "We are strong, we can make it work."

"If we were strong enough to make that work, you'd be strong enough to not call for me." She stroked a branch laden with cherry blossoms and softened her voice. "Besides, the time for that passed long ago. Our life together was as fleeting as these blossoms. Doesn't matter what customs say. You gambled my life for your house, you can't fix it, Kai. You can't undo what was done and every time you ignore my wishes, you prove you don't want to."

"We all make mistakes, Aislinn."

"Very true. But some of us try to fix them while others layer mistake upon mistake in their pride." She broke a sprig of cherry blossoms off the tree and watched the petals scatter as she did so. The remaining twig and petals scattered like shattering glass when the sprig hit the ground. She sighed, accepting the inevitable as always. "I'm here, you know you can't make me peaceable, and I know you will try. Either way, I'm here. And I just wish for this to be over with."

Kaienar leaned in to kiss her, sighing when she turned her head.

Aislinn sat in the garden that night as the moon rose, shame and frustration being her only companion. She rolled her head from side to side, trying to release tension. One more night. It hadn't taken long to see that one night was too short, Kai would attempt to call her back again almost immediately. Two or three nights and she could spend half a year away. A week was useless, as he'd still call again in half a year. There was sound, a sense of a dragon's aura, a realization she was no longer alone.

"I know you're there, I can feel you." She spoke in the tongue of the Dawnlands.

"My apologies, Lady deAvaric." The boy was endlessly polite and much older than his five years. Tutors and strict etiquette would do that, she supposed.

"There is no need for apologies, little one." She didn't bother to tell him to call her anything other than Lady deAvaric, there was no name he could call her that would improve the situation and the child was almost certainly incapable of dropping the honorifics. Besides, she didn't want to hear him call her by her first name.

She watched as he stood in the shadows at the end of the garden. He was fascinated by her every time she came - she vividly remembered the wide-eyed toddler with his fist shoved in his mouth as he stared at her - but after the first few visits, she'd been forbidden to seek him out. Her heart twisted and her mind whispered treacherous thoughts, urging her to stay here. She knew he was following a half-remembered scent, she could always sense him in the shadows, never quite disobeying his father. Just like his mother. But tonight... no. She let the boy come closer.

"Papa says you knew my mother."

"I do. Very well." She doubted he'd see her present tense as anything more than poor language skills.

"Will you tell me about her?"

"No. Your father does not wish it, he has his reasons." Her heart twisted as his face fell, she softened the blow as delicately as she could. "She and I are very alike though. Keep your eyes open and you may learn something about her."

"Is that why Papa has you as a mistress?"

"Yeeeees, among other reasons." She was cringing and trying not to laugh in the same breath. He had her lack of tact.

"What is a mistress? Nurse and tutor say it's a companion for my father, but I think there must be more because he has lots of companions… and you aren't really here much to be a companion." Her son was now standing right in front of her, hands resting on her knees, earlier shyness forgotten.

"A mistress is…" she paused, debating the wisdom of being blunt like her brother, Damian, had always been, then decided she may as well drown in the ocean depths instead of playing in the shallows. She would rather he have something close to right instead of whatever they would fill his head with trying to avoid it. "Well, to be honest, you are too young to be told the whole thing, but a mistress is someone who is physically intimate with his lordship, like a wife, but she does not have the status or station of the wife. I am not currently considered a legitimate lady and if he were to treat me so, it would cause shame and embarrassment to his wife."

"In-ta-met?" His pronunciation was close enough, she did not correct it. Her pronunciation could be off as well. Besides, it was sweet, and she had a feeling it was not the only word he had questions about. All parents had to feel something like this, but she suspected being raised by her brother and his lack of sugar coating made it worse in ways for her. She paused for a long time while considering the best way to explain.

"Have you ever startled his lordship and his wife in the morning?" She was gambling that he had. They had barely managed to keep him away from her and Kaienar before.

"Oh! Adult play!" Her son indeed had her inappropriate timing.

"Yes." She tried to keep her face straight. Was that really what Kaienar had called it?

"What's that like?"

"That's a lesson for when you are older," Aislinn said hastily. She had her limits. He must have seen something in her face because he only pouted instead of asking more. She changed topics. "Why are you out so late? I doubt your nurses know of this."

His guilty face told her all she needed to know. She was struck again in that he did indeed have her eyes, at least in hue. The famed Bryndagr grey had not been able to subdue her stubborn brown, even though other browns had failed through the ages. Kaienar had remarked upon it before, but Aislinn had never fully realized it. The first few times she'd seen Enar there had been too many held back tears, and his eyes were the blue of most children. Once he was old enough for the brown to come through, she'd only been allowed tormenting glimpses. She wished she could run away with the boy, but was too aware that was ill-advised, so she stared at the trees until she could school her expression.

"Why risk it? I'm sure you'll be punished if caught." She turned in time to see his face turn white and rushed to reassure him. "Oh, don't worry. I won't tell."

"I want to learn magic."

"What magic do you seek on such a night?"

"Any kind. Uncle is really, really good at magic, and when he comes home at night, he'll always have a plant or something to show me and he'll tell me what it can be used for, even if it's not somethin I'm sposed to know," Enar was getting excited and his words were beginning to melt together, "and it's really, really interesting. Did you know that foxglove..."

She let him babble for a bit, correcting him only when she found it necessary and finding his enthusiasm for the subject enjoyable, even if some of his knowledge was slightly macabre, but then, her education hadn't been much better. With the content he had learned, he confirmed which uncle was the source: Eingeir. That particular brother of Kai could teach the child far worse things, but so could she. She had a feeling Eingeir's tutelage was his peculiar way of rebelling. He had disagreed with Kai's handling of this situation, despite never saying so aloud. At least not to her. His deep loyalty to his brother had a double-edged twist: if Kaienar went against what Eingeir thought he should be, Eingeir would seek to correct the issue, or failing that, he would eternally remind Kaienar that he had failed. Aislinn was pleased someone caused Kaienar some inconvenience. And that someone not aligned with her saw this as wrong.

"You know a lot. Do you know magic?" The boy stared at her, she could see the sudden realization he may have found another source of information spark in his eyes.

"Yes."

"Can you teach me some?"

"I need to know what you know first. Have you learned of the elements?"

"Yes. There's light, dark, fire, earth, wet, and air."

"Very good." Aislinn let the small slip she was certain of pass, he had the idea of things. "What are they connected by?"

"Spirit."

"And?" Aislinn had always found Kaienar's clan to be oddly weak on parts of the basics. They were focused on lineage and dignity and honor through the ages, but always skirted the oddest of things regarding magic. They shied around their long distant origins and never focused on the why of protecting humans specifically, only that it was the duty they were created for.

"Spirits?" Enar grinned, trying to charm his way out of ignorance. She smiled and shook her head at him, removing her necklace as she did so. Two triangles with sides that curved gently inward had been hooked together to form a star. The tips of the lines forming the triangles extended slightly past the corners and between each pair was caught a tiny stone that represented a different element. It was backed with something that looked to be mother-of-pearl, but in reality was a scale from a long forgotten member of her clan. She pointed to the scale.

"All things are interconnected. Light. Dark. Everything. Spirit binds it." She tapped the scale, "This represents that. And all are made of a variety of these elements, in different balances. There is the minor balance." She traced delicate lines etched in the scale between pairs of elements. "Light to dark, earth to air, water to fire. The opposites. All contain a grain of their opposite and you would do well to keep that in mind. Then there are the major balances." She traced the triangles. "Elves tend to light and air. Light. Air. Water. These make up one triangle. There are the stone folk of the mountains that tend to fire and earth."

"The one of dark, fire, and earth." He smiled up at her proudly, she couldn't help but smile.

"Correct. Elves and the mountain folk are made of elements that do not need to fight for balance as they are elements that follow the same path. That's why they are so long lived. And then there are humans," she put her arm awkwardly around him as he snuggled into her side. "Humans combine all the elements in one ever shifting mass, which is why dragons came from them."

"We came from them?" He was trying to sniff surreptitiously now, wanting to know this stranger's scent.

"Yes. Long, long ago. In days forgotten, we came from them." She pretended not to notice his actions.

"How'd we do that?"

"It's said a man prayed to the spirits in the old days when there was more power in the world and elements were raw. He prayed for something to protect against the ravages of the wyverns and from the greatest warriors in the tribes the dragons were created."

"How do we live so long if humans don't?" He accepted it with the ease only a child could. She had actually argued with adult dragons on this point. Some believed dragons to be shaped from the raw elements and separate from the humans they were charged to protect, never mind all the connections between the two.

"In very simple terms, the ever shifting balance of the elements works against humans as they have a fixed form. We do not. That ability eases the battle. That is also why all shifters originally come from humans - selkies, the wolves, dragons, all of us."

"Can I be a selkie when I grow up?"

Aislinn laughed.

"It doesn't quite work that way." She fastened the chain around his neck. "This necklace was your mother's. I want you to have it."

Enar glowed with delight, but the moment was ruined for Aislinn as the air grew heavy with a familiar presence. It wasn't long before Kaienar cleared his throat.

"Papa! Look what she gave me! It was Mama's!"

Kaienar was appropriately appreciative, but firmly ushered Enar out of the courtyard. Aislinn waited in the courtyard. She knew he would hunt her down if she left, so why delay the inevitable?

"We had an agreement."

"He sought me out. I won't turn him away if he does that, Kai." On the inside, she petulantly screamed that their 'agreement' was more a dictatorship. Voicing that never helped.

"You bring chaos wherever you practice magic, I'd prefer you not bring him into it."

"I bring chaos? Why? Because I learned to control my power without being bound to some school or master? Besides, I was not the one that ignored the rules of old magic and nearly caused two deaths. That was you."

"Your brother-"

"Is not a part of this. None of them. And you know that. Rin and Daren do not practice most magic except in very rare, very controlled, or very desperate instances. As for Damian, his mistakes are in the distant past; that he will be paying for them eternally only makes him more cautious in the now. And you conveniently forget that to become any kind of a master, one must make mistakes. And he is an undisputed master of magecraft. The number of apprentices he turns away for that is astronomical. And whatever they have done is not what I have done." Her jaw clenched and she looked away. It was so hard to hold back once he decided her family was open to critique. "You have always known who I am. What I am. What. I. Do. I dare say you knew it better than I when we decided to have Enar." At the last she stared directly into his eyes. He dropped them to the side almost immediately. No matter his words, his entreaties, his explanations, he knew who was wrong in this.

"He will learn limited magic when he is of age, it is not necessary for him."

"If you truly wished to avoid accidents, you would start him early. The worst accidents always come when someone plays with something they don't truly understand. Like a half known tale of magic." She ripped cherry blossoms off a branch, half angry with herself for the destruction of the tree but more angry at this situation. She was trapped like a caged animal and words and petty destruction was her only respite. Even then, she had to keep her voice low; she knew how some of her accusations could play out in Kai's court. "Maybe you're afraid his tutors won't lie? If he seeks out skilled mages... or books... there are far too many paths that might lead him to the truth. And what if he's a conduit? What then? Do you plan to wish his magic away? Or were you planning on locking your own son up?"

Kaienar growled and swept out of the courtyard. It wasn't long before her nervous maids appeared, requesting she return to her room. She could see a pair of guards nearby, waiting for the word to move in if she refused the maids' request. Foolishness. She liked Lily and Rose and had no desire to get those ladies in trouble, even if they did spend hours subtly trying to convince her to forgive Kaienar, or at the least overlook past wrongs.

"No worries, the honored prisoner will return to her cell" She spoke aloud and caught a brief scowl on one of the guards as she passed. She noted his features as he was not familiar to her, she'd need to find out his name later. It was good to keep track of who could understand her, especially if they had not an ounce of loyalty to her.

When she returned, the room was empty. She considered destroying the furnishings to vent her frustrations, but that did little for anyone in the long run. Instead, she leaned against the windowsill and slept, wrapped only in her thick travel cloak. One more day, one more night. She would survive.

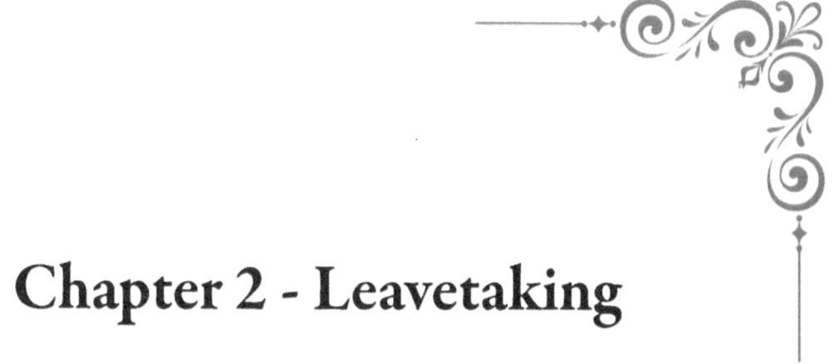

Chapter 2 - Leavetaking

Onyx boosted his pack up on his shoulders.

"You know, there are those that have been eyeing you. You could stay, enjoy the season. Get a wife." Mer was following him as he helped Onyx tidy up his rooms for the season.

"And so could you." He smiled up at his friend as he finished packing another bag.

"We were talking about you, elder brother." Mer ruined his use of the honorific by sticking his tongue out. "Besides, your brother misses you as well because he can't run away or enjoy the season."

"I thought we were talking about potential wives and Dojaek understands my reasons to leave better than most." Onyx paused, considering, and then packed a few more whale teeth he'd scavenged from a washed-up carcass. Similar items had proven popular with traders and sailors on his last trip. "Besides, I'm trying to find something for him."

"I know, but some day you'll need to stop running. And your family won't let you keep running forever. You do know this, right?"

Onyx glared at his friend. Mer raised his hands.

"You leave earlier every year. And come back later. Even your rooms get lonely."

"So does my other house. I have to keep both company. Ah, the difficulties of a double life." Another smile, this one more forced. Onyx wanted his friend to stop making this trip more difficult. He couldn't stay here. There was too much weighing on him. Selkie customs, family traditions, old failures, all too much.

"I think I'll follow in a few weeks." Mer locked Onyx's door for him and reached up to tuck the key between roofing tiles. Onyx narrowed his eyes when he realized it was likely slightly out of his reach. He would repay his too-tall friend at a later date.

"Some day you'll need to stop running. You know that, right?" Onyx tossed his friend's words back at him as he slung his second bag over his shoulder and wondered if there was anything else he should bring.

"Some day. The bright squids rose from the deep early this year." Mer was looking down the road towards his home. With his words, Onyx realized why his friend had been especially irritating as winter began to break. They had done the same in the spring Mer's wife had drowned.

She'd been a beautiful cow, but so delicate. Most of the bulls had been off hunting, working together to herd and capture the early bounty of squid. Nobody was certain if she'd been craving fresh food after a winter of preserved fish or attempting to surprise her husband with his favorite treats when he returned from his hunt, but whatever the reason, the result was the same. Her body snagged in rocks near a well-known clam bed, the changing of the season mixed with the early shift of currents had created dangerous cross-currents.

Onyx had only just begun to prepare for his trek when it happened. That year was to be the first time he made this trip.

He had been the one to recover her from the tangle of rocks she had been caught upon; he was one of very few willing to risk it. Obstacles were less dangerous when a selkie was able to switch between forms as quickly as him and he could not stand and watch his friend's pain while others held a frantic Mer back from the dangers.

Onyx could never forget the moment he laid her on the beach in front of his friend. To him, he was delivering misery to a good friend. To Mer, after the initial grief, Onyx was a friend of friends he could never quite repay. Onyx had remained weeks longer than he intended for Mer and the tragedy had become a strange and irrevocable bond between them.

Onyx glanced up and realized he was far from the only one remembering that moment. He tossed a pair of cloth-wrapped whale teeth at Mer who jumped in surprise when they smacked him.

"Those should get you some fine Dark Moon wine. It will be good for celebrating your arrival and I don't have time to make a side trip for it. Bring no less than two bottles." The quality of the teeth was worth at least four, possibly five with Mer's haggling abilities.

"I will not forget them, elder brother." Mer picked up the bundles and nodded his thanks.

Onyx turned towards the road to the sea. Time to leave home for a few months. Maybe this year he would find some of what he'd been seeking.

Chapter 3 - Unfond Farewell

Aislinn sat up in the middle of the night and watched the moonlight play along the floor. She breathed deeply, trying to ignore the silence that always felt louder here. The air was heavy with the scent of flowers, mostly cherry blossoms and early lilacs. She missed the sweet scent of the lilies of the valley that would be blooming at home. The hardy plants she had planted had failed to thrive here, much like her. Kai was asleep on his stomach beside her, she let her fingers trace the pale claw marks trailing down his back.

"Hurt me never again, lest you hurt yourself." She murmured the half remembered words and rose from the bed. The fine dress could stay on the floor, she'd find another. It was late enough she could eschew custom and return to port on horseback. She could also smell rain in the air, it seemed far away, but she hoped it would break over her on the ride to port. She could use the cleansing sensation it would provide.

Either way, if she left soon, the ship could easily catch the morning tides and be far away by the time the sun reached its peak. Sneaking away burned her pride, even though she was trained to be covert, but singed pride was better than any alternatives available. Her scars tingled as she began to dress; Kaienar was reaching out through their bond.

"I was hoping you would remain asleep." She spoke without looking back.

"I was hoping you would stay."

"I know, but I want to catch the tide and the port is a bit of a ride and..." She pulled her shirt over her head. She was babbling. Kaienar had managed to charm her during the day. A book of poetry he'd found and thought she'd enjoy. A gentle sparring match in the inner gardens - their bonds unfortunately kept them from more vigorous practice. He'd done a variety of little things like that; reminding her of old times and making everything harder. She almost felt guilty leaving, but the little voice of truth in the back of her mind would not let her stay. She trailed off for a moment when she realized she'd run out of explanations. "Why am I bothering? We both know why I'm leaving so fast."

"Polite force of habit?" The slightest smile came to his face as he spoke and her heart twisted for a moment.

"Yes, I am unfailingly polite, High Lord." She made a mock curtsy in breeches and boots, then found a shirt. He chuckled at her before his expression saddened.

"Our lives are long. Will you ever forgive me?"

"Maybe, but I won't forget. And I'm not sure you'll change. And that's the true problem." She slung a bag over her shoulders. It contained money and the few items she'd brought with her or bought here for those back home. The lavish trunks that had greeted her with the palanquin would remain. It was a part of this farce. He showered her with gifts, she came here and returned them. She'd keep only a few things; either to placate him or because it was something one of her siblings could use. She wished that in return for the refused gifts she could take back the bits of herself that this arrangement stole. Aislinn straightened her spine. Best not to wish for what could not be. She would leave this place as much herself as she ever was.

Kaienar followed her to the stables, cat quiet, but she felt his grey eyes on her without even looking back. She kept her back to him and saddled a horse in silence. To be fair, he could make leaving a thousand times harder.

He could make her walk or wait for a palanquin or declare the horse stolen and have soldiers go after her. She was one part grateful that he wasn't and one part angry at her gratitude. The small kindnesses could never make up for him ignoring her will. She led the horse to the outer courtyard, feeling relief - and anger at her relief - when she didn't hear a second set of hooves. He wasn't going to attempt to ride with her this time. It made it much harder to board the boat when they rode side by side and conversed. She mounted the horse, back stiff, fighting the urge to turn back.

"Goodbye, Aislinn, my heart."

"Fare thee well, High Lord Bryndagr. Long may your kingdom last." She threw out the formal farewell and urged the horse forward as quick as she dared in the moonlight.

Chapter 4 - Delays

A islinn reached port long before the night reached the grey hours that were neither night nor day. She felt the knots in her spine loosen a slight bit when she recognized the ship she'd arrived on. A few coins to a night hostler to care for the horse until it was picked up by Kai's people and she bid the animal farewell.

She pulled her scarf up to cover her face as she walked along the docks. Without it, the smell of fish and the heavy tang of blood thick in the air was almost overwhelming. Whaling ships, new to port, was her first guess. Or perhaps a cargo of seals; possibly worse if the port authorities could be bribed enough. Though skin-hunting would be a risky trade here; bringing shifter carcasses through Minado was punishable by a long, slow death as dragons ran this port and had little tolerance for such trade. Perpetrators caught here would be skinned inch by inch or spend a moon cycle locked in cells near the tideline - repeatedly near drowning til the highest tides finally came and finished the job.

She was relieved that the scent died down closer to her vessel. The captain was awake and leaning on the railing, carving a whale's tooth. He looked up from his scrimshaw as she hailed him.

"I cannot for the life of me figure why they can't let you stay a few more days once you've delivered the diplomatic paperwork and lovely bribes. Very undiplomatic, if you ask me." His neatly trimmed and curled mustache accentuated his frown.

"I didn't, Hanjib, but if you knew lords better, you'd want to run as well. Stay too long and you might say something undiplomatic, or worse, become a lord yourself, and then where would we be?" She grinned at him and he shook his head. He'd run this trip enough times to be more than vaguely aware that it was more than the claimed paperwork, but he never asked beyond that. Despite his teasing, they both knew he was happier not knowing. Captain Hanjib Lascore was a professional. Part of why her brothers hired him repeatedly. He had a point though, even with a skilled windworker, it was nearly a month gone with the round trip. "Any word from the twins?"

"Not by glass or wing. No orders or errands, and the way the air is feeling I'll not be changing my path once we leave port. Leastways, not for them." He looked to the sky.

"Duly noted. I'll do my best to stay out of the way once we've set sail."

"You're useful. I've crewman I'd rather stay out of the way more than you." He delivered this high praise and was back to scrimshaw by lantern.

"Thank you."

He grunted in response as she passed.

She went to the tiny cabin that was hers on these trips and dropped her bag on the narrow bunk. As far as she was concerned, her cabin was heaven. It was just her in here; no lords, no gossip, no customs to observe. She let her body rest for a moment, inhaling the sweet scent of fresh reeds filling the mattress. Despite the short time in port, they'd managed to freshen her bedding. She realized the room smelled of lilies of the valley as well and turned her head to look at the tiny desk. A sprig of white flowers was in a tiny glass vial with a wax seal on a ribbon around its neck. Two dragons pressed back to back, fierce and ready for enemies from all sides; the deAvaric crest, her crest. She fumbled with the drawer beneath the desk and withdrew a silk and sheepskin wrapped bundle. She unwrapped it carefully, revealing an obsidian mirror.

Aislinn cut her finger on the jagged edges of the mirror and streaked the blood across the surface. As it soaked into the glass, the dark surface turned clear. An image of her brother, Damian, appeared in the glass. He was bent over a book and barely nodded to let her know he was aware of her. She remained silent for a moment while he completed whatever he had been reading. She didn't question the nearness of the glass to him. Damian was amazingly prescient, it would have been more surprising had no one been waiting.

"Another season completed?"

"Yes, unfortunately it does not look to be the last," she sighed and worked another kink out of her neck.

"High Lord Bryndagr will someday realize he is no match for your stubbornness. He is not a complete fool."

"I wish I were stubborn enough to ignore the pull."

"Even you cannot stop the tides, little one." As he spoke, he laced his fingers together to rest his chin on and leveled his gaze at the glass.

"I can fight them with my last breath."

"And likely would. Have you news?"

"My return may be delayed, there is a storm moving in. Thank Daren for me?" She held up the vial with the lily.

"As long as you thank the captain for me. I am certain our dear brother's request caused no end of difficulties for him."

"I will, and I'll also thank him for finding whatever oddities I'm sure you requested." She smiled what felt like the first real smile in ages. "Have you any orders?"

"I thank the captain for the tasks he completes for me by compensating him generously and sending other patrons his way." He fixed her with an irritated stare as he said this, then paused for a moment, considering. "And no, no work of note has come since your departure."

She released the spell after a few more minutes of pleasantries and dozed off, only waking once they were underway. She strolled up top for air. The sky was calm, but oppressive; she could tell it was a false calm.

The promised storm hit mid-afternoon with a sudden fury that was far worse than expected. Driving sheets of rain cut straight to the bone with a soaking chill as waves tossed the ship about like a bit of driftwood and turned the deck sideways and back again. Aislinn was pressed into service when a member of the crew was knocked unconscious after being dashed against the deck. He was fortunate not to be washed overboard, he probably wouldn't feel fortunate when he woke.

Her first assignment was to right a double foul up - cargo that should not have been secured topside was and it was secured in a manner that wasn't recommended even for cargo meant to be on deck. Crates and barrels threatened to break loose and break other, more necessary things. Captain Lascore's earlier comment now seemed less of a compliment to her and more an indictment of some of the newer crew, especially as she knew Hanjib had been driving them all day to prepare the ship for the storm.

There was a pause, merely a moment's lull in the rain, but it was the only warning she had. Aislinn felt more than heard something off in the creaking of ropes and wood behind her and jerked back, narrowly avoiding the loose boom that hit the crates with the force of a battering ram. Unfortunately, cargo could not jump out of the way as well; crates and barrels tumbled over the railing. Ropes, netting, and chunks of railing whipped about like living things, snagging Aislinn and dragging her down with them. There wasn't time to untangle herself from her work before she hit the water.

Some part of her registered the shouts when her head broke the surface the first time, but the crewman had to save themselves and their ship. The tangled mass of flotsam wasted no time in pulling her under again. It was hopeless, she wanted to give up, but by sheer instinct, she switched to her dragon form. The snarled mass jerked her back. Wet ropes refused to tear under her claws and instead tore raw patches through scale and skin as she fought with them. Sometimes the bits of cargo would help in her battle for air, other times they rolled over her, pushing her down until her lungs nearly burst.

Afternoon must have passed into endless night, but there was little change in the darkness to her. Muscles screamed with fatigue until she could barely force her limbs to move at all. She was still fully dragon when her feet touched bottom. A brief rush of energy and hope drove her a little further shoreward, but it did not last long. She was further from land than expected and her right hind leg was no longer cooperating. Her body gave out a few feet from a pebbled beach. A wave pushed the flotsam the last few feet and Aislinn was dragged with it.

She rubbed her face against wave-smoothed rocks as she crawled on the beach and let herself drift back to her smaller human self. Skin hunters were out and about. Not the season to be not human. Her hands drifted down her legs along the ropes and tried to push them loose. She only succeeded in scraping the skin on her hands. She was aware that her wings were still out as she drifted on the edge of consciousness, but no longer cared. Shadows crossed above. After a few moments she felt a sharp beak. Gulls. They took off after a moment.

Pebbles gently clicked against each other. Footsteps. Light. Cautious. A hunter?

She didn't have the energy to raise her head to look.

Words she didn't understand. The tone didn't sound dangerous. Maybe she would survive this morning.

Hands rolled her over.

"Continental? Amarantine?" the voice had spoken again. She hoped it wasn't looking for an answer. "Are you badly hurt? Hey! Hey!" She was dimly aware of being shaken as the darkness closed over her.

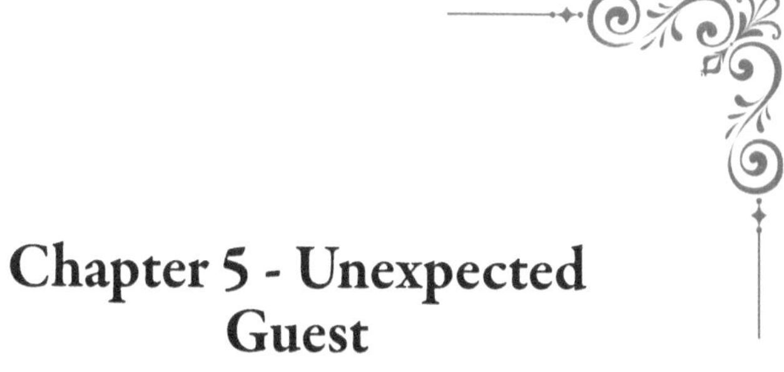

Chapter 5 - Unexpected Guest

A sleek bit of mist separated itself from the waves and edged onto a rock. It was a seal and he kept his dark eyes trained on a speck along the horizon, disliking its return after the storm. He kept low in case they had a spyglass on board, knowing a lone seal watching so closely could pique their curiosity. He relaxed only slightly when they appeared to be headed for the trading post that sprung up on the far end of the island once the waters were safe to travel in the spring. He was almost certain he was not the only one of his kind hiding from the upcoming season in this cluster of islands, though he hadn't seen any other selkies. With that possibility, a ship pausing at the trading post was the best outcome, if it didn't pass all the islands completely.

Onyx slipped backwards into the sea once he was satisfied with the course the ship was taking. He danced among the currents, a sleek silver shadow snagging fish and mollusks and cephalopods and tossing them high up on the shore. A nosy tern examining his treasure trove backed off when charged by the very loud and irate seal, but not before snatching a small octopus. Onyx shook his head and let it pass. He had more than enough food for now.

He laid on the beach for a moment near his feast, nibbling a couple of delicacies as he let the first rays of the sun warm him. A long stretch and he was laying on the beach in his human form. He rolled over and stood up. He carefully pulled the woven willow creel he had tucked among the boulders just below the waterline loose before filling it with his remaining catch. He found the rest of his things high and dry, where he'd set them atop the boulders. He slung a leather bag over his shoulder and strapped a sturdy knife to the thigh opposite the hip the creel rested on. He paused to gather a few fronds of rarer seaweeds offered up by the waves and tucked those into the creel as well.

A pair of gulls were lazily circling a spot a short way up the beach. Something had caught their eye. He debated the rewards of exploring their find and decided for it, playfully concluding that stealing from the birds would even out his morning. Along the way he quietly picked up more bits of flotsam and jetsam strewn on the beach that he thought useful, worth trading, or simply interesting. Storms, for all their dangers, were harbingers of plenty for him in this little cove.

He cleared the last few boulders between him and the gulls' patch of beach and came upon a mess. Rigging, wood, and even part of a sail had washed up on the shore. The gulls were ignoring him in favor of something in the midst of it. He cautiously removed his bags hoping to get close enough to grab one and scare them. It almost worked, and he laughed silently at their surprise as they hurriedly took to the air. He stopped laughing once he realized what the birds had been after.

Tangled in the wreckage was a body. It looked to be a woman, lying face down. He felt a hollow certainty that she was dead, but called out anyway. His eyes caught a slight twitch in response, but it was impossible to tell if it was her or the waves pulling the ropes and her with it. As he came closer, he took in the reddish hair and pale skin. She was a foreigner - or at least foreign to his homelands. Everyone was a foreigner here. He changed the language he was speaking to Amarantine. Still no response. He tilted her head slightly and let his breath out in a rush when he realized she was still breathing.

Onyx edged around her carefully, realizing now that some of what he had taken for ropes and flotsam was a mane running down her spine and a tail. Part of the "sail" was actually her wings and there was a smattering of scales across her body.

He had found a dragon. She would be worth a fortune to hunters, especially with the addition of her hair color - he doubted red hair meant much in reality, but if they could label something as rarer for more coin, they would. He wasn't sure how she'd gotten here, beyond the obvious answer of 'washed up by the storm', but he was certain she was someone fate oddly favored. He found her first and he found her before the chill air killed her.

He carefully cut the ropes from her body, wincing at the sight of the mangled flesh around and beneath them. Had the tears gone much deeper, he doubted she would have survived, he swore he could almost see the pulsing of the artery in her right thigh. Onyx groaned again once the debris was cleared and he saw the full extent of her injuries. He was glad she was unconscious. The hip was clearly dislocated and without the debris covering it, her leg looked more like a piece of raw meat.

It took several tries before he found the leverage needed to force the hip back into place, hands slipping on the mess several times as he did so. She gave a tiny squeak that was more air being forced out by the motion than a response to the pain.

Onyx was sweating and exhausted, but still took his time examining the rest of her. It was easier to do this when he was right next to the water than to wait until later. Once he was satisfied that nothing else was dislocated or broken, Onyx edged her back out into the water.

He supported her limp body and kept her head above the waves. Once he was waist deep, he laid a hand on the worst of the wounds.

Water around them turned to slush as he drew energy from it to heal her. He ignored the temperature drop until she shivered; he let the waves repeatedly clear the slush away so he could continue healing her as much as possible.

Back on the shore, he used bits of rope and the sail to make a stretcher that cocooned her with the best protection from the cold he could offer at the moment. He swayed and nearly collapsed as he picked up his other bags and returned them to their places on his body. Not the time for this. Later. He'd rest later. He wasn't exactly sure where he was going to keep this dragoness or how, but he would figure something out. He was too curious where this was going to lead and how it came to be to leave it be. Besides, he had already entangled himself in her story.

The trail home took much longer than his journey to the beach. And even though he was always proud of his handiwork and pleased by the sight, he could only recall a handful of times he'd been quite so happy to see the little home he'd built. The hut was small, well hidden in the seagrass and the roots of a fallen tree, but it was cozy and functional. It took him only a few moments to lay out bedding that had been tucked away for the day and stoke the carefully banked fire. He stripped the dragoness of her canvas cocoon and dove into his stock of rags and rushes to dry her off before tucking her in his bed.

The sun was high by the time Onyx could finally rest for a bit. He lounged in the doorway, soaking it in with his eyes closed. A thin barley porridge slowly cooled by the fire, he would see if he could get some in her once it was done. The warm scent of salty broth overlaid the earthy porridge and the nose-tickling scent of herbs he had used for poultices mixed with it all. He was not surprised when he dozed off for a moment.

The sun was lower when he woke; the porridge cooler and the broth richer than intended. He stretched and glanced towards the bedding, frowning when he realized his companion was showing early signs of fever. He put that worry aside for a moment and fed her, stroking her throat and carefully coaxing her to swallow first water, then broth, and finally a bit of the porridge. Food for himself next, then he washed her down and cleaned the bedding. Then a little more sustenance for both of them, healing, fresh poultices – he quickly created a rhythm. He had found this mysterious lady who had managed to battle the sea until she reached land, he would take the battle from her now. Nightfall found him almost too exhausted to sleep.

He awkwardly tucked himself beside her. Once she was well, he would figure out other arrangements if need be. Until then, he would doze beside her like he was on the beaches back home. If her temperature changed, he could sense the changes and act as a heater in the chill of the night or do whatever else was needed. He woke several times as her body heated and cooled. The final time, slightly before dawn, he found it difficult to return to sleep and lay staring at her face, wondering what this dragoness was like and if her eyes were blue, or gold, or maybe something entirely unexpected. He was attempting to be patient, but he was curious. A part of him wanted to use every last bit of power he possessed to wake her so he could have his answers. The only thing that held him back was the knowledge that every last bit of his power would still not be enough.

He continued his care that day and the next as the fever rose. It broke shortly after nightfall the second day and he collapsed in bed beside her. He needed rest, at least a few moments, before any more healing. He hoped she was out of danger for the moment. He closed his eyes and slept the next several hours.

He woke in the predawn chill, body feeling as if tides battered him against the rocks. Onyx rolled and stretched and then checked on the patient. Her leg looked worse than Onyx felt, but he realized that even with his extended nap, he did not have it in him to work any more healing magic. He stoked the fire and dug sleepily through jars scattered about, as well as some still tucked in the drawers of his apothecary cupboard. He was working mostly by smell and feel, eyelids too heavy to keep open. He sloshed water into a pot along with his choices and swung it over the fire.

He then lightly dozed until the pungent smell alerted him that the mixture was ready. Mash it together, boil it down more, strain it, cool it - the sun was rising by the time he was ready to pack the mush around the worst of her wounds. He rested his forehead against hers for a moment and was relieved to feel no sign of the fever.

He worked water down her throat once that was done, knowing that he would need a more efficient method of feeding her if she did not wake soon. He then wiped down the pot and tossed dried seaweed and fish in it along with a generous amount of water. Onyx rummaged through his other supplies and frowned. He didn't want to leave his charge, but if they were to eat anything other than rice, barley, and the poor soup he had heating, he would need to. They both needed more. His hunt when he'd found her was only meant to last a day or so for him, and he'd burned through it. There would be no way for him to continue healing her or for her to heal without more.

He stumbled out to the beach, not really waking until he reached the water. He dived into the water, letting the crashing waves clear his head. Between one breath and the next he flexed into his seal form.

Onyx chased clams today. Not his favorite, but simple, slow moving, and very abundant in a nearby patch of water. He knew where to dig and soon had tossed a pile on the beach that would be enough to last several days, even if the newcomer woke up ravenous. At the thought he practically ran back with his catch and poked his head in the hut.

He was relieved to see that his guest was fine, but extremely disappointed that she hadn't woken up ravenous. He left the clams in a bucket to soak while he ate rice drizzled with soup broth. It was soon gone, and still no sign of movement from her.

Herbs. He could find some outside nearby, and even some early root vegetables to eat perhaps. He dimly realized some part of him was hoping the aromas of his cooking could bring her out of her slumber. At the very least, it wouldn't hurt.

She was still not awake when he returned with an armload of plants. He dutifully cleaned her, fed her the remainder of the thin soup, and changed her poultices before slumping down beside her.

"I wish you would wake. I wish you could tell me how you washed up on my beach." He pulled the bucket towards him and cleaned a few clams, eating a few raw to sate his hunger. He really hadn't been paying attention to how much he was wearing himself down healing her. He focused on chopping up vegetables and making a new broth for the clams; it kept curiosity and loneliness at bay for a few minutes.

He sat beside her once everything was in the pot. He noted a delicate tattoo on one wrist and traced the air above it before realizing that she had not had her arm that way earlier. Perhaps it was a hopeful sign?

He started working on a trinket he'd been making for market and soon realized that distraction was hopeless. His focus was on his mystery guest. There was no more normal care he could attempt at the moment, but her hair was a mess he hadn't truly dealt with. Despite everything else he had done, brushing it seemed almost too intimate. But he could no longer ignore that the freshly dug clams had carried less grit than her mane did now. And it was something to do. While he waited. For the soup. For a wake up that might never come.

The motions of untangling and smoothing were calming, and he found himself humming to her as he worked. He finished by tying her hair back in a simple braid. The soup was done by then and he discussed the flavor and his cooking techniques with her while he ate, voicing his belief that there were radishes in his islands that would make it taste much better than what he could make here. He promised to let her taste the few pickled ones he had brought along when she woke.

More rote tasks and early to sleep, feeling a little like this would be a pattern until the dragoness faded away.

Chapter 6 - Ignorance
Was Bliss

Aislinn was in a haze, she smelled pungent herbs and went to find their scent, winding up in a memory in her own mind instead of the waking world.

"Damian, you haven't been listening to a word I've said."

"I am not the only one incapable of listening." Her brother carefully placed several vials in a small wooden case, preparing for the trip home.

"I am more than capable of carrying the paperwork through the Dawnlands, you know this. I'll be quick and you and Daren can get back to Seacove." She paused as Damian raised an eyebrow dubiously. "Yes, I will stop on the return and see Kaienar. That is part of why I wish to do this. He's... you know his family is pushing for him to marry."

"That is part of why I wish you not to go. Better to end it now." He was buckling straps and packing things slower now.

"I love him."

"I am aware." He wasn't looking at her. Whenever Damian didn't look her straight in the eyes, there was something more. Something that he felt he could not or should not say.

"Order me not to see him."

"Aislinn." There. A harder edge. She was getting some reaction from him.

"Order me and I won't. You know I wouldn't." She was half crying in frustration.

"I will not." Damian's expression had been unreadable at the time; looking back she realized it had been profound sadness.

"So he's not that dangerous, because if he was, you would have no problem ordering that, but you don't want me to see him. Why?" So childish. She wished she had stopped and trusted him.

Damian looked to the ceiling and closed his eyes.

"Damian, why?" her voice dropped to a softer, pleading tone.

"If you wish to see him, I will not stop you. I know well the pangs of love and what they may lead to." He lightly tapped the burn scars on the side of his face with a pair of forceps he had picked up from a table. "I wish you only happiness, Aislinn, and this way will lead to sorrow. High Lord Bryndagr is as aware as I am of the reasoning. Ask him. His words hold more weight for you right now."

"To ask him, I would have to see him, and we're leaving before his family returns. For all I know, they might return with a marriage contract signed and date set. We don't have much time left together, if any." Aislinn stared at her brother until he met her gaze. She refused to drop her eyes, even though she could see an unnamed fear in his.

"The documents are in Daren's trunk." Damian turned back to his work and Aislinn felt like the air had left the room.

She kept her pace calm and measured as she left the room. She needed to show him she was capable of calmness and restraint. Also, Daren's trunk had a half dozen complex and mostly unnecessary locks, she would need to focus. It took her a few minutes to find the lockless, camouflaged drawer he'd placed the documents in. She was absorbed enough by her task that she nearly jumped from her skin when Daren cleared his throat behind her.

"And what are you doing?"

"I am to carry this paperwork to the fiefdom that borders my Lord Bryndagr's land. Damian has agreed to it."

"And I suppose you'll visit '*Kaidarling*' on your return?" He pitched his voice to falsetto when mentioning Kai.

"Why brother, what bit your groin? You ought to get that checked. Also, yes, I will. And have I mentioned you are the most annoying of all my brothers?" She attempted to move past him and he blocked her way with one arm.

"Thousand and two times just this quarterday. I don't think you should go. I *order* you not to go."

"Daren, you've ordered me to not to go outside before because a ship docked that'd been out to sea for more than a few days." She lifted his arm and ducked under.

"Rowdy sailors! Some have appetites most unhealthy for little sister." He spoke with earnest conviction. She tried not to laugh.

"Dearest brother, we live in a seaport. I am an adult. And you get up to far worse." She held up the documents, half to show him what she had been searching for and half to cover her attempts to hold back a smile. "I am delivering these. Damian has given me permission and if you wish to argue, you can take it up with him. He has also suggested that I have Kai tell me why the pair of you are so determined Kai and I are a poor pairing. So if you *honestly* wish me well, you'll let me go."

Daren opened his mouth and then closed it, his usually witty banter suddenly gone. He had to force the next words out. She felt that same unnameable fear from him.

"I know Damie is right, but... be careful, Little One. He's dangerous to you. No matter what you or he intend, Kaienar can hurt you."

"I'm not sure why you think that, but I'll keep it in mind. Hopefully, I'll figure it out soon enough." She felt off balance at his use of 'Little One' - he didn't use nicknames, not like that - . but he lifted the heavy feeling before she could dwell on it.

"I liked you better when you were small and worshipful and listened to everything we said."

"I liked you better when I was small and thought you knew something." She waved at him with the papers as she tossed the remark over her shoulder at him.

"I know everything!"

"Everything except that you're a fool, but it's fine, I know that!" She laughed and closed the door quickly behind her. It wasn't the best of comebacks, but she wasn't going to leave room for him to make another.

That memory faded into another, and another. Fragmenting and fading until she was beneath the cherry blossoms with Kaienar; blood dripping from both their claws and then it faded to black as her mind backed away from the moment.

Chapter 7 - Rhythm of the Waves

Onyx woke to his new companion slightly tossing and turning. It was a hopeful sign in his mind, even though he now needed to immobilize her injured leg better. He still had trouble focusing on anything other than his companion, but forced himself to work on jewelry and oddments for sale at the market. He would definitely need better trade goods with the added mouth once she awoke. He kept up relentless banter throughout the morning as if the dragoness could hear him.

He apologized for leaving her and let her know he would only be gone for a short while while he went to gather on the beach. His intentions of what 'a short while' meant changed when the beach had far more interesting things than expected. The remainder of things dredged up by the recent storm had washed up in the night. The flotsam and jetsam and sheer potential of what he could gather moved him further down the beach. Netting, rope, fishermen's floats, all kinds of things that could either be repaired or be used to repair other things. He excitedly dived into the water after a bit of wood jammed in the sand below the surface of the water. It looked to be, and was, a perfect size for replacing a nearly worn bit of shelving in his hut.

Once in the water, he was tempted by a small shoal of flakefish. Their flesh melted in one's mouth when prepared properly, and he knew exactly how to prepare them properly. He quickly filled his creel with the tricky little fishes before turning back to the plethora of shells and creatures not normally seen on the beach, keeping to his seal form as he dropped the creel among some rocks jutting out in the water. Keeping the fish in the water would keep them fresher longer.

He was distracted by more fish before he completely reached dry land, but this hunt was disturbed by the distinct squeal of oars. His normal response would have been to find a rock to hide behind and watch, but this day he found himself turning to face the approaching dinghy.

Two men. They tossed out nets over the school of flakefish and pulled them back in. Onyx impulsively rushed at the nets, grabbing the weave in his teeth and tugging sharply. The pair swore at him and yanked their nets back. They checked for holes and one shook his fist at Onyx, but the movement held no real menace, the man's threat was more in jest. Not hunters, not by a long ways.

He relaxed and playfully chased fish towards their boat. The men made their haul quickly, whooping and yelling directions at him once they realized that he wasn't chasing the fish away. Once done, they tilted their hats at him and tossed a fish his way. He caught and swallowed the offering, watching closely as they left. Only sailors out fishing. Nothing more, nothing less.

Onyx returned to shore and toted his bounty to the hut. Still no signs of her waking, at least not fully, but the new items had him distracted enough that he felt less disheartened over it. She would wake when she woke, until then, he would tell her tales while he worked. He cleaned the replacement shelf and let it dry in the sun as he turned to sorting out the bits and baubles. Repairs were first. He had neglected the house in favor of his guest and that would not do, winter had left more than a few marks. He boiled seaweed outside for a plaster mixture to repair any damage to the walls and while waiting for that, he patched a few spots in the thatch and began to repair the small chimney atop his roof.

Over the past few seasons spent here, he had pushed his hut a little deeper into the roots of a fallen tree. He checked over his work and patched anything that might lead to the roots or house falling into decay.

He hummed as he worked and nearly forgot his companion. The hut was small, but it was the closest thing Onyx had to a home and it brought a certain comfort to him. He visited other islands and even northern Amaran in the winter, stopping only to overwinter in his homelands, but this area drew him once the spring came and he could feel the waves calling him. It felt safe.

He began carving a delicate pattern of vines along the edge of the new shelf, carefully shaving down bits that he would later add shell inlays to. He let the work absorb him for a bit. She did not exactly wake when he tried to feed her, but less coaxing was required to get her to swallow. Tiny hopeful signs. He squeezed her hand, hoping she'd feel some comfort in the gesture.

Care for her, care for his home, go to sleep, wake, repeat. From the day he found her, the moon passed a full quarter cycle this way. Every day he knew he should hope less and detach himself from her impending death, but every day and every little victory of feeding made him that much more determined and entangled in her tale. Sleeping beside her wasn't helping him detach either; it was unfortunately putting different distracting scenarios in his brain. He tried to find a better way to sleep, but the hut had only ever been made for one and he did need to be near her in case anything changed. She hadn't had any more fevers, but she'd thrashed about one night and almost re-injured herself. He didn't mind sharing a bed at all, but he could only hope she wouldn't be angry when she woke.

One night he awoke to lips weakly tracing their way up his jawline and to his mouth. He willingly responded, having barely enough cognizance to avoid her injured leg, at least, as much as possible, and pleased that he was not the only one who did not mind sharing a bed.

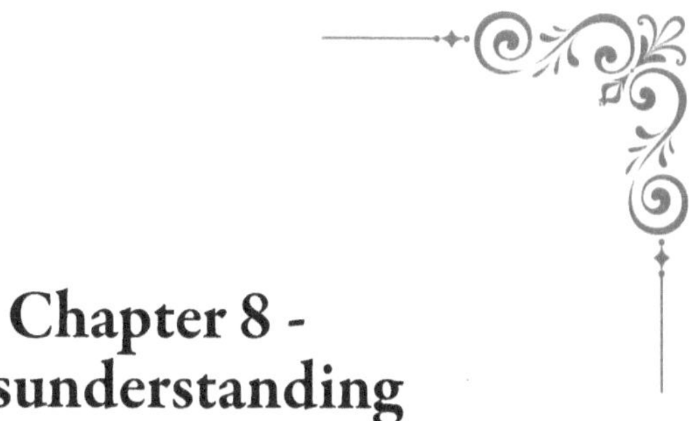

Chapter 8 - Misunderstanding

Aislinn's eyelids were warm with the after-traces of illness when she woke. She wasn't sure where she was, but it was dark, and she could hear deep breathing. Kaienar? All she was sure of was that the form curled up next to her was as naked as she was and male. She didn't make a habit of taking bed partners, so Kaienar. She nuzzled into him, nothing clear in her head at the moment. Mostly, everything hurt, up to and including thinking. She tried resisting temptation, but a need for even the slightest bit of comfort overruled pride and dignity.

She kissed him, and he sleepily responded. His kisses lacked their usual desperation, they were almost languid, as if they had the whole of time for kissing alone. Hands slid over her body, slightly hesitant, as if this were all new. She could smell the ocean and the pair soon found a rhythm that reminded her of the drawing and fading of waves upon the sand. The rhythm was soothing, but unfamiliar. It took a moment for the collective differences to sort themselves into meaning. This was not Kaienar, nor anyone else known to her.

She shoved the stranger away from her and pushed herself as far as she could in the opposite direction, wings flaring out as she hit the wall in a too small room and knocking what sounded like a full apothecary's worth of jars to the ground. A low rumble could be heard from the far side of the room, which with the limited space was far too close. She focused on the area the noise was coming from, waiting for her nocturnal vision to come to the fore so she could see who and what she was facing.

Black hair gleamed in the light of a dying fire - longer with a clean but well-oiled sheen to it and tied roughly back from a surprisingly delicate but unquestionably male face. It was a face she could not look away from, not because of his attractiveness - though in other times that could hold its own fascination - but because of its sheer feralness.

Elegantly shaped and luminous black eyes reflected the firelight, no signs of whites, not this close to his wild self. There was the hint of sharper than human canines between his parted lips. And a look of fairly raw frustrated desire was etched over the whole thing - that part she tried to ignore. By themselves, his features could have belonged to a variety of peoples, but together...

As she neared her conclusion, the surprisingly deep grumble altered and became a low soothing hum. He edged forward. Her eyelids drooped. The soporific effects of that voice confirmed his lineage. Selkie.

She flung the first thing her hand touched, hitting him on the shoulder with a shallow metal bowl. The hum broke off and she braced for battle. Springtime. Selkies were becoming more unpredictable now, especially the males. He stared at her for a long moment as the ringing sound of the brass bowl slowly faded from the air, then sat back, rubbing his shoulder.

After a few more moments, the selkie tilted his head quizzically to the side, feral look completely vanished. He spoke and she tried to edge back, wary of a selkie voice. She didn't have to understand his language to fall prey to the mesmeric tones. He tilted his head to the other side and spoke again, this time in a language she understood. Amarantine. Despite being named after her homeland, it was a mishmash of a language for traders that started with an elven base and threw in splashes of every other language about these seas. Over time, it had evolved into its own language, with multiple dialects. His was different to what she was used to, but still understandable. She chided herself internally for her distraction and refocused on his actual words - this was not the time for linguistics.

"I dreamed you kissed?" The way he spoke it reminded her of a northern port in the Dawnlands. They sometimes called it Seal's Cant. More proof of what he was.

"I... no. I did, but it wasn't you..." Aislinn fumbled for words, and he looked down and covered a smile, his response made her feel, if possible, more embarrassed. It was also disarming. Perhaps this wasn't what it seemed to be.

"Who are you, why am I here, and why are... were we..." she gestured. Somehow, the idea of saying it made it more real and more mortifying. Not saying it had the effect of making her feel childish and in the back of her mind she reflected that there was no way to win this. She wished her mind was fuzzier again, she might not notice how foolish she felt.

"You did not have clothes when found. You washed up on the beach." He offered the explanation gently and edged towards her, not looking at her eyes. "You had a fever, chills. I was afraid spring chill air would kill you if I did not stay close." He paused in his advance, retreating and rummaging around in a trunk. She tensed until she saw what he was getting. Clothes. He turned to put them on. "Very sorry, I forgot customs."

One worry eased in her gut. Clothes could be more optional to these shifters as they tended to live in their own communities and slip in and out of the seas, at least from what she understood. With dragons it depended on the culture of the humans they lived around. The entire situation now felt less ominous. His eyes flicked to her again as he turned back and she narrowed hers in return. Why was he staring at her thigh?

Thinking of her body had the effect of reminding her of the bashing given by the sea; fear and adrenaline from moments ago was now ebbing away and leaving only pain and exhaustion. She realized why she hadn't been able to draw her legs up under her and her body swayed, rejecting even her current half-sitting position. A warm shoulder pushed against her and arms steadied her.

"You must lay down. You are not well."

She let him help her, mostly able to swallow squeaks and whimpers of pain in her throat. Mostly. He laid her down and turned to stoke the fire. She blinked off the sudden influx of light and let her eyes adjust before looking towards the pain. Her right thigh, the one he'd been staring at, was a mass of half-healed rope burns. To a far lesser degree, it was the same with her palms. As bad as her wounds were, with the degree of healing, it was clear they had been far worse to begin with.

"How long was I out?" With everything she dimly remembered, the wounds should have been deeper, worse. Even with healing and a day or so of rest.

"A quarter cycle of the moon." He sat down beside her with a bowl of water. "I have no clothes to fit. Your..." He gestured at her back in frustration, clearly hitting a language wall. "Sails? Back fins?"

"Wings?" Sea Cove's Amarantine, the most heavily elven of all, would have to suffice on her side. She lifted one of her wings to be certain she understood what he meant. And regretted that small movement.

"Wings? Wings. Wi-ings." He played with the word for a moment. She could see him continuing to turn it over in his mind. He was much less threatening in this light. "Yes. I have nothing to fit your wings."

She drew them and her tail in, returning to a fully human form and feeling grateful someone else hadn't found her like this. He turned and dug for another shirt then went outside for a short time to allow her privacy to change. He returned a few minutes later, damp and with the fresh scent of the ocean trailing him. He kept his eyes lowered to the side, the faintest tinge of red on his cheeks.

She knew without asking the why for his abrupt cold swim and felt the corner of her mouth twitch even as she saw his do the same. The situation felt more and more ridiculous by the moment. He turned his head and caught her watching. She couldn't hold back her laughter when she saw it echoed in his eyes. The selkie tried hiding his smile behind his hand and schooling his face back to calmness.

Aislinn shook her head as she watched the struggle and what began as a giggle in her throat became a full-bodied laugh.

"It's not funny." She was having trouble speaking through the laughter. "I'm sorry for... molesting you and then attacking you... for doing exactly what I asked."

He gave up trying to fight his own laughter at that. She stopped sooner than him only due to her body demanding she not laugh because everything hurt too much. Aislinn watched him laugh until he was laughed out and when he was finished he dabbed tears on his sleeves.

"It is fine. I thought I had..." he paused, looking for a word, "I thought I dreamed and confused awake and asleep."

"No, I thought you were-" She looked away, laughter suddenly gone. "I thought you were someone else. Someone who was dear to me a long time ago."

She could feel the weight of his eyes without looking. She finally turned back and met his steady gaze. Dark eyes were full of curiosity and sympathy, the two emotions seemed to be at war. He pursed his lips, then looked down to the basin of water he had brought in after his impromptu bath.

"Your leg." He knelt, soaked a cloth in the water, and laid it on her leg, hands resting gently on top of it. She was going to say she could wash herself when the covered area grew warm. He pulled a rag stiff with ice away and repeated the process with a new rag in a slightly different spot.

"You're a witch of the salt brush." Her voice filled with admiration. She'd heard of the selkie healers, but she'd never before met one.

"No, I do not have the training to be called that." He smiled a shy, pleased smile as he shook his head. He paused to pour a mug of water from a kettle and handed it to her. When her hands shook trying to raise the cup, he wrapped his hands about the cup to help her drink. "My skills are very basic. Everyone is taught this if they any talent. Besides, only cows are witches of the salt brush."

"Ah." It took her a moment to realize what was meant by 'cows'. Females. The wondrous qualities of water did only so much for her thinking, and the water was hot. It was still wonderful, even if there was someone far too close to her, which was also distracting. She longed for another mug, but was disappointed when he didn't offer her more before continuing healing. Though, it was hard to argue that his healing skills weren't needed more than a second cup of water. She doubted she could hold the cup on her own now that she was fully awake and all adrenaline had drained away. She tried to distract herself from the thirst and pain as he worked and chatted at him.

"I knew that. Or at least I'd heard that. I've been to places where the opposite was true: only males were taught healing. Or only very special people, who are very full of themselves and actually know nothing about anything. My brothers are more practical with that, if you had the knack, you learn. Damian always says that a bleeding wound doesn't care who heals it so long as they have the skill." She was babbling now, she knew it, but it almost kept her mind off the cold heat and the itch of healing. And the pain. And the thirst. And the proximity of a still strange male.

"Mother wished me to learn more, but father felt... bulls fight and defend, cows heal." He stared at her leg, frowning. She was uncertain if the frown was directed at the condition of her leg or stifled dreams. "It is slow to heal. The burn and bruising run deep. Was not even in place when I found you." He saw her confusion and mimed the motion of popping a joint back in place. She was relieved she had not been conscious for that.

"Then you've done well." She leaned back, pushing away the urge to itch. And the new urge to find food. Sleep would be best, but the hut was small, and she wasn't quite sure how to avoid a repeat of earlier. There wasn't really room for two sleeping areas. Although, being fully aware of how bad and deep the pain was might slow her troublemaking down a bit now. The selkie finished his work by placing an acrid-smelling poultice on her leg that eased the pain. He then offered another mug of water. She took a sip and realized it was broth.

She moaned slightly, near tears with how amazing food seemed at the moment, and almost knocked the cup out of his hands. She calmed down, doubly embarrassed. First by her reaction, second by her lack of observing that he'd drawn this cup from a second pot by the fire - it could have been anything and she'd drank it without thinking. She didn't bother to sort out what part was worse and focused on draining the cup with his help.

"Let this rest. I'll give more in a bit." As he spoke, he held his finger up to pause her.

She nodded in reluctant agreement and tried to relax as she watched him bustle about the place. He put a few things away - including the bottles she'd knocked over earlier - before pulling dried plants and other items out from a case of drawers on the far side of the hut. She couldn't make her eyes focus enough to recognize more than a few. He would glance her way, sometimes nod, sometimes frown, and then pull other items out or put something he held back.

Her eyelids drifted further down as she watched the routine, comforted by the familiarity of the motions. Damian was a doctor and a mage - the purpose of her host's work resembled that most of all - but there were parallels to Daren meticulously preparing delicious meals for the household and Rin precisely blending pigments and inks to paint the most accurate record of any one of the many things he studied. It wasn't only the selkie's movements, his demeanor held that same blend of passion and duty that her siblings brought to their tasks. The familiarity and exhaustion made her defenses nearly non-existent and the rhythm of the mortar and pestle grinding whatever he'd chosen left her somewhere between awake and asleep. She didn't even startle when he shook her gently to wake her.

"Was food okay?"

She nodded, trying to make her mind work a little better. The cup he held helped, she could smell more broth.

"Careful." He helped her drink. She tasted a slight hint of medicinal herbs, but he'd blended it well as it was only a hint. He sat back on his feet. "Sleep now. No more food."

"Probably best. I don't need to get sick." She laid down, slightly more awake as he finished putting a few more things away. She realized she wasn't sure where he was going to sleep.

She was trying to figure out how best to ask about sleeping arrangements, when he suddenly slipped out of his clothes. She turned away, mentally noting that she would need to solve the intricacies of selkies and their clothing customs and trying to talk herself out of the panic his actions caused. She turned back when she heard an odd shuffling sound and where the man had been was now a sleek gray-white seal. A small part of her mind noted that she would have expected a sandy brown or perhaps chocolate or even a black like his hair instead of the rich speckling of all the grays of a bright foggy morning. He harrumphed into the spot next to her and gave her a questioning look as he bobbed from side to side. She was left with the feeling he hadn't exactly thought this through and was only realizing that when he was unable to actually talk with her. To his credit, this was a better idea than the no ideas she formulated.

"Well, it is your home. If you insist."

His head tilted further, eyes narrowed in concern, and he pointedly looked about the room.

"I'm not kicking you out of your own bed. Yes, I think it will be fine to have you as a seal and me fully clothed and do you realize that I'm feeling slightly insane talking to you like this?"

The sound he made was nearly a laugh.

"You're a bit of a brat, aren't you?"

Eyes wide and dark and far too innocent to be believed.

"I'm not that gullible, brat." She carefully rolled over, her back to the mound of gray fur, flesh, and muscle behind her. She was glad he seemed a little on the small side for a selkie bull seal, especially once he leaned against her back and let out a sigh like a contented cat. "Yep, you're a brat. Flippers to yourself and come mo-" her yawn cut her off, "-orning, I need to know your name."

A squeak, part protest, part curious.

"Aislinn. Aislinn of the clan deAvaric."

Chapter 9 - Hunters

Onyx dreamt of childhood and the terror of hunters. In his dreams, they were drawn by his rare coat, but instead of taking him, they took everyone around him while he watched, helpless. He woke as a hunter raised a club to take Mer out. He shakily checked that the dragoness - Aislinn - was still alive and safe. It took awhile for sleep to return, but finally, her steady breathing lulled him to sleep. He felt the slow transition of night as morning drew ever closer, but lingered in a light doze until the sound of oars creaking reached his brain. Instantly alert, he swiftly moved to the waterside, remaining in his human form for silence of movement. As the water embraced him, he returned to his seal form, coat blending into the water.

The minor disturbance was caused by two men in a dinghy. Spearing fish. They were hunting food, one man was clearly focused on that, but the other's eyes darted about, looking for more. Onyx had seen that emptiness before. Nothing was ever quite enough. Endless greed.

He dove deep and carefully swam under their boat, wanting to confirm his suspicions. He rose until he could make out the studding on the bottom. Anything trying to tip or upset their boat would be slashed and stabbed. Only one type of boat would have that. Only one type of sailor would need that protection because only one type regularly hunted something clever enough to purposefully tip a boat and small enough to be slowed by such injuries.

Skin hunters.

He didn't bother looking to see if there was a gap he could use to tip the boat, instead he swam along the bottom back towards the shore. He was glad the cooking fire was so small that any frail wisps of smoke blended with the morning mists. His home's overall appearance also blended into the surrounding terrain, and that was not accidental.

He stayed low once back on shore, nearly crawling back to the hut. Once there, he pulled out a dagger he kept near the doorway and slunk into the grasses nearby, senses on high alert. He could almost envision what would happen if they found him. Many hunters either had enough skills or magical ability to guess what he was, or had lost enough care for the lives of others that they'd test the odd loner to be certain they weren't passing a payday by. And if they discovered he was a selkie, they'd presume Aislinn was the same.

He would die long before he'd let them drag her to the water to be drowned. That was a hunters favorite way to force selkies to switch into the desired form before murdering them. Aislinn would fight, he knew that much, but he also knew her condition. He'd once rescued kittens a farmer had attempted to drown. The man tossed a bag into a creek and walked away, not a care in the world. Aislinn, injured as she was, would be about as difficult for these men as those kittens had been for the farmer.

The oars creaked again and one of the men swore. Onyx felt lucky that the oarlocks had not been thoroughly oiled. Most of their strokes were silent, but ever so often that warning squeal came. The sound was slowly fading away, but he held his spot until the sun burned off most of the fog and he had a clear view of the water. The boat was gone.

He relaxed, shook out stiff muscles and dove in for a few more fish before returning to the hut.

Aislinn was stirring, but still asleep. He hummed to her to soothe her back into deeper sleep. He tried not to think about how alluring she looked in his spare shirt with her hair slowly escaping the braid he'd tied it in. Or the brief moments before she had realized he wasn't... whoever she'd thought he was. The way she'd felt...

Food! Breakfast! She would be hungry once she woke and so would he. Gutting fish was needed work that was not at all appealing. And if that didn't work, he would soak in the sea again.

His switch in focus worked, mostly, but he was still glad she remained asleep until nearly midday.

Chapter 10 -
Acquaintances

Aislinn slept deeply. The chill of predawn didn't disturb her slumber, though around then she was vaguely annoyed as the bed had been warmer earlier. She opened her eyes a crack and saw the selkie was gone. The warmth mystery was solved and the mystery of where he had disappeared to took too much energy. She closed her eyes again.

The hut was warm with sunlight and the cheery fire when she opened them again. It was also filled with the smell of food. She sat up and smoothed her hair down to attempt to look presentable, and with vain hopes she could smooth away any lingering embarrassment from last night.

Her host was present and leaning over the fire, focusing on fish on a grill and flipping them with a practiced skill. The sleek dampness of his hair and the freshness of the smell of the fish said he must have plucked them from the sea shortly before laying them over the fire. He glanced over when he heard her stirring.

"How are you? Food is almost done." He flipped one onto a simple wooden plate and sprinkled salt and some cut herbs over it. "Eat, you need your strength for healing."

"Thank you." She took the plate and nibbled at the fish. Very fresh, very simple, absolutely delicious. There were smaller dishes and shells with a variety of herbs and preserved vegetables. She carefully tried a couple and made a mental note that the bite of them was not something her stomach was up to. Not yet.

"Onyx," he said as he flipped another fish off the fire and moved the remaining ones to the cooler edge of the grill. He salted and seasoned his once that had been completed.

"What?" She paused in mid-bite.

"I am called Onyx, Aislinn of the clan deAvaric."

"Ah." She hadn't been expecting a name like that and felt oddly stupid. He watched her face.

"It is a good name?" He seemed to be looking for reassurance. "A trader gave it to me when I was little. She said to my father that his son had eyes like onyx, and it has been what I have been called ever since."

"Oh. Yes. A very good name... just not what I was expecting."

"Outsiders have too much trouble pronouncing my selkie name." He said it matter of factly; Aislinn was only mildly insulted at the slight. She could pronounce it, or at least try, if he'd let her. He didn't seem to notice her irritation though. "Have you heard of the Clans of the Moon?"

"Yes... I'm guessing you are from the clans of the Crescent Moon?"

"Yes! You know them?" His face had lit up.

"Not really, but a friend is half selkie, so I've learned a little about selkies."

"What clan is she from?"

"Not exactly certain, her mother left her with her human father." Slight lie, but no need to prejudice him against someone he'd never meet. Laira had never asked to be born a part of the Dark Moon. "She's not Crescent Moon though. Looks nothing like you. She could be Poised Moon?" The Half or Poised Moon clans had a variety of selkies, some looked to be of Onyx's clans, others more like Dark Moon and if Laira ever went north, it was possible one could take her in, she understood that happened with some of the Dark Moon children. Clans of the Full Moon were not a good suggestion, their kind looked quite similar to the Crescent Moon clans from her understanding. Not that he was likely to ever meet Laira, but stranger things had happened.

"I would like to meet her," he replied after a long pause and Aislinn was almost certain he knew she hadn't told the full truth.

"She's far away from here and she's of the traveling folk; that might be extremely tricky."

"She sounds interesting." He was brighter now and he placed another fish on her plate before she had completely finished the first one.

"She is. I'm sure she'd love to know more about her selkie side. She'll be jealous that I got to meet one and she hasn't," Aislinn replied. Onyx blinked and Aislinn again had that feeling that he knew she was lying about Laira's clan. Odder still, it felt like he understood. Either way, Aislinn's gentle prompt was all it took for Onyx to start chattering about his kind. He did so with a mix of pride and politely hidden exasperation that only love could bring. The fondness made her wonder why he was so far from home. He did not talk about himself, just selkies in general, and a few stories of friends, but she left that alone. She had no need to know that much about her host. He was safe and would not hurt her, that was all she needed to know.

She finished the second fish and leaned back, basking in a sunbeam from the open door. He cleaned up the breakfast mess while talking and put a kettle on for a rich, herbal tea. Despite his chattering while working, he paused when he sat for his own cup of tea.

"Why are you here?" The question left Aislinn's mouth before she could stop it. She'd broken her internal promise not to pry into her host's life with surprising rapidity. To stave off frustration and introspection that she didn't have energy for, she decided to blame it on exhaustion.

"I'm avoiding the beach." He stared into the distance, she would bet his face was directed towards the islands he called home, and she wondered what – or who - he was missing. "I do not wish to settle there anymore. Not this moment."

She did wonder why he was avoiding the selkies' mating season, but she let the moments where she could ask more pass in silence and he did not elaborate any more.

"You are awake, you should try a walk, test your other limbs." He ducked outside the hut and returned with a staff of driftwood. "I found this on the beach shortly after I found you."

She nodded, happy to be able to get away from a place that seemed filled with emotional traps. Onyx helped her to her feet.

The ocean breeze was brisk, but the sun was warm and she felt it melt pains she hadn't known existed. Unfortunately, it couldn't melt away the injuries in her leg. She could not, even if careful, rest her weight on it for more than a split second. To be honest, she could barely stand on her good leg, even with the staff. She had been oblivious to the damage the previous night when she was kicking and crouching, and now she wondered how much damage that panic had done. Terror made people do amazing things, but could also destroy things amazingly fast.

Her hair was caught by an errant breeze and blown across her face. She hadn't had a chance to properly rebraid it yet, and now it was causing problems. She attempted to hold the staff, push her hair back, and stand. She nearly toppled over and it left her feeling absurdly weak and vulnerable. The difficulty of what was normally such a simple task had her near tears and she was trying to pull herself together to figure out a solution, when she felt a pair of hands brush the back of her neck.

She didn't have the leverage to jump or she would have. She hadn't been fond of unexpected touch for a long time and this was in far too delicate an area. Her skin twitched, attempting its own escape, before calm flooded her body. She realized Onyx was humming softly, barely audible under the breeze. He stepped back the instant he had her hair roughly tied back.

"Thank you."

"I can fix it better if you want." His offer was gentle. "Or you can sit and try yourself."

He gestured to a fallen log and helped her over to it. She contemplated his offer as she settled in, wanting to take the brush and do it herself, but holding her arms up long enough to properly braid her hair felt impossible.

"I'd like that. If it's not too much trouble."

He disappeared inside the hut and returned with a brush and a small jar of oil. They sat in silence as he focused on his work and he soon had her hair brushed, oiled, and smoothly rebraided.

"Thank you. You're good at this."

"Sisters." He shrugged, went back into the downed tree, and returned with some dried fruit. He pressed a larger portion on to her, but did nibble some himself. They sat in comfortable silence for a bit.

"You are very lucky," Onyx said.

She stared at him, blinking several times in an attempt to make her ears work correctly. Had she misunderstood? His Amarantine was good, but not perfect, she doubted he lived in a trading city. There was also the potential that 'lucky' meant something entirely different in the selkie dialect.

"Lucky?"

"Yes, you survived the storm. I wasn't here for more than three nights before you came. If you had been shipwrecked earlier in the season, you would have died on shore." His earnest expression told her he meant what he said. Then he pivoted, looking out at the sea.

She followed his gaze and saw a pod of whales rising in the distance. When she looked back, he was focused on her, with an expression of someone trying to solve a puzzle.

"Why were you on the waters so early in the year? Mostly hunters are about this early. Traders, too, but most move later in the season." His black eyes seemed to be looking through her and she could tell he was weighing the likelihood of her being a hunter of any sort. A good eye could tell she was built strongly for a female, so that occupation wasn't out of the question with her, even if she was a shifter herself. She was preparing to fight him off with words or the strength she didn't have, but he shook his head after a few moments.

"You aren't a hunter, so what were you doing?" His words were half declaration, half question.

"How do you know?"

"You don't look like one."

"Don't be fooled, I'm not weak and they come in a variety."

"No, not how you look. How you *look*. To the sea." He gestured at the fading movement of the whales. "You weren't weighing them for coin."

"That would be foolish to do so, especially since I don't have a boat or a crew to catch them." She countered his words, mostly because his logic was on the cusp of making sense to her.

"But hunters still do. Even if it's something they don't hunt. They calculate what whales would be worth if their hunt is bad that day and they must make do."

"Dealt with a lot of hunters?"

"I have seen my lot." His eyes narrowed, but the fury was clearly not directed at her.

"If you know of hunters, you must know the risks - why stay here alone?"

"I don't tempt them enough to risk the tides, they push towards the rocks here. It is difficult by boat and hut is well camouflaged."

"Yes, but why be here at all?" She had to admit, he had her curious, though she knew better than to fall for mystery.

"Why be on the water early in the year when you are not a hunter?" Question countered question, he was polite, but something underlying his careless tone was sharper than she'd thought him capable of. She realized she wasn't the only one slightly wary.

"I was a courier. I had diplomatic papers and greetings to deliver and gifts that the sender wished to arrive before certain festivals, so I had to take to the sea early in the year."

He held her gaze for several moments and again tilted his head quizzically, as if she were a puzzle he couldn't quite solve.

"Why can you tell that lie so well? I understand you don't want to say your friend is Dark Moon, I don't understand this lie."

The shock felt as if she had been dragged beneath the cold waves again. She knew how to keep a straight face, she truly did, but could not completely in a moment like this. He blinked slowly, having caught the flicker in her expression and she looked away.

"Don't answer with another lie." His tone was firm, almost angry, but at the same time, very sad.

"Why I'm traveling is not your concern. I do swear that I'm not a hunter and no one is hunting me."

"True. You are welcome to stay here until you are well." He stood.

"Thank you, I'll try to heal quickly, so I don't disturb your solitude for too long."

"I like company. Lies make me lonely even when others are about." His voice was tired and he gazed out to sea as he spoke. The whales were long gone.

"Understood. I'll do my best not to lie, I don't really care for it either. But there are things that I cannot share." She wished she could say more, it seemed a poor offer to someone who had saved her life. And the tale of Kaienar was... complex.

He tilted his head, weighing her words again. He seemed to see the sincerity in them, as he nodded and extended his hand to her.

"Come. I will help you back to the hut."

The remainder of the day was quieter and Aislinn took that space to nap. When she was awake, he did not allow her to do anything, but he worked at a variety of tasks. She did not have the energy to argue, so resolved to watch. Some tasks he did made perfect sense - tidying the house, airing the bedding, scouring the pans. Other tasks, such as cleaning and sorting items he had found on the beach were slightly more incomprehensible. Not so much the task itself, but the how of his sorting. One pile held mostly larger objects such as boards, but a smattering of smaller items like shells were mixed in as well, some tucked away in a pouch. A second pile held a fisherman's glass float, along with a pouch that he'd filled with things such as wave smoothed whalebones, odd-shaped bits of rock, a silver spoon that he polished up, and a completely intact pearl necklace. The third pile and bag contained a broken oar, a cracked cup and plate, two seashells, and a handleless knife mostly covered in barnacles and muck. It was a mix of oddities that seemed to have no similarities.

Her questions only gathered that there was a market on the far end of the island. She guessed the market, coupled with a sharp eye for the debris that came ashore, was how he made his living while here. The tension between them had evaporated by the evening when it came time for him to heal her again. Then, despite a brief argument on who would sleep where, the pair ended up sleeping together again. Selkie seal leaning against Aislinn's scarred back.

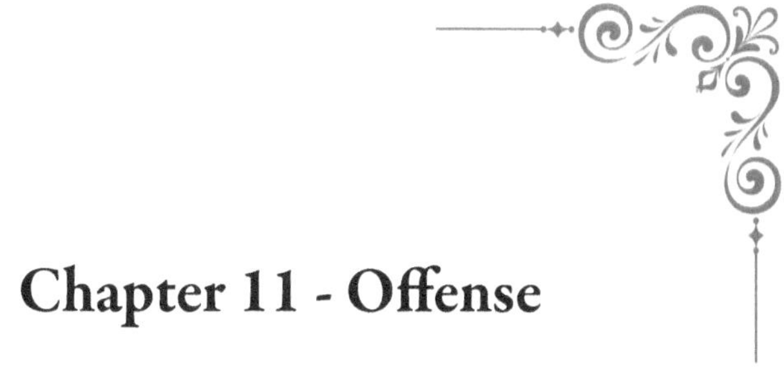

Chapter 11 - Offense

Onyx woke first the next morning and realized that the wrappings he'd placed around Aislinn's leg were loose. He sighed. Extra healing, better immobilization.

He stoked the fire, setting a pot of water and mixed grains beside it before turning his attention to healing.

He carefully eased up to her side, hoping not to wake her. It was working well enough, she was hovering on the edge of awake, but not fighting as he removed previous wrappings. He paused, letting her slip back into a deeper state of rest. To pass the time, he tilted his head left and right, trying to see the tattoo that shimmered on her hip. He squinted and could barely make out the intricate lines. He doubted anyone would ever see it if they weren't looking as close as he had to. It was an enigma: a carefully crafted mark almost nobody could see. Another enigma came in the form of the old clawmarks on her back, the scars seemed almost too neat to be from a fight. He pushed his curiosity aside and returned to the leg.

He decided to use a more direct style of healing and left the basin of water aside. His palm had barely come to rest on her hip when she jerked away. The sound she made was a twisted moan of pain and fear. Her eyes opened, focusing on him before she slumped back, now trembling. He suspected she'd wrenched the leg slightly when she started awake.

"Onyx." Her tone sounded as if she was telling herself, not speaking to him. Her breathing calmed. "What are you doing?"

"Healing. Your leg needs to be immobilized better."

"Carry on." She nodded, but her body tensed; clearly steeling herself for something. Her skin flinched under his touch and the next thing he knew, her hand was on his, her claws digging in. He could see the whites of her eyes.

"Aislinn?" He was confused and not sure what was happening. He was almost certain his touch was not causing pain - he was barely touching her - but her reactions said otherwise.

"I'm fine. I'll be fine. Just... just do what you have to do." Her breathing said otherwise.

He hesitated, but this was needed. He began humming softly and felt distressed when he had to lean into his selkie skills far more than normal to calm her enough so he wasn't afraid she would jump and injure herself more.

He considered using the rag and water approach to healing, but he was better with fine adjustments using his bare hands. The leg was so deep into healing, he wanted to be sure it was healing perfectly, and he was afraid her movements of late had reinjured her and he couldn't sort out new from old without touch. He decided to attempt it.

The twitch of her skin flinching beneath his palms almost physically stung him. He could not understand how he could be hurting her. There was the idea that his touch could simply be that repugnant, and that also stung a little, but that was easily pushed aside. His pride wasn't important, not when this change did not make sense. None of this did, and he was having trouble maintaining an outward calm for her.

Aislinn's breathing had slowed. She was still awake, but bizarrely drunk on his humming. He realized he would also have to work on being more restrained with his voice. He - and most of his kind, now that he thought of it - generally avoided using their vocal tricks on non-selkies unless needed, so he'd had precious little practice around them, even traveling about. By selkie law, they weren't supposed to use their voice on those without it, unless in dire need. Healing Aislinn was close enough to that, in Onyx's opinion.

Onyx switched to talking to her, hoping to keep the effects more even. A few moments later, her skin flinched particularly hard at a touch, and he pulled his hand back.

"I am sorry you don't like touch." It wasn't quite what he meant to say. He meant his touch, not general touch, but it was close enough. He didn't bother correcting himself as the apology was more to the air. He *was* sorry, but she was a little too dazed for an earnest and complete apology. His words had an odd effect though.

"I don't. Didn't. I liked it once." She suddenly rubbed her face against him like a cat and somehow shifted position to lean her weight against him. The mood became entirely too intimate. She truly was drunk on his voice.

"Hush." Onyx could not follow her shift in thinking and did not want things to go beyond what they should. He edged away slightly and let the moment pass before laying his hand on her hip. She hissed in pain. "Does this hurt?"

He hoped to get an answer that made sense as he could not read her right now, but her answer was another puzzle.

"No." Her eyes were sad. "It's only a messenger, warning me to surrender or face the consequences."

"No consequences here. Only healing." He kept his voice light and moved forward with healing, deciding he would have to use the rag after all. He could attempt a more thorough healing when she was completely awake. Never again would he attempt to let her sleep if this needed done. She was far too confused in the moments between sleeping and waking. When he came back, claws dug into his hand again, despite the barrier of the rag. He let them and stopped all movement.

She was agitated enough now that he wasn't certain if going forward or stopping would be worse. She could injure herself worse if he didn't finish and get the leg immobilized, but in the process, she might get injured anyways.

The claws suddenly released.

"You are not his *most exalted* lordship." She spit the honorifics portion out like it was poison.

"I am not." He could agree with this, even if it did not make sense. The claws dug back in for a moment.

"You have no right at all to anything and never have. You are not my mate. No claims." Her eyes narrowed, calculating. Her fangs were slightly bared. Onyx was still very confused, but agreed. She stared at him for a few more moments, her eyes softened and cleared with recognition. "You are not him."

The claws completely released this time. Onyx's hand spasmed slightly as the blood returned. His fingers accidentally brushed her skin and she did not twitch. In fact, she was finally back to sleep.

Onyx finished healing her and carefully wrapped and stabilized her leg. He avoided thinking of what had occurred while he finished making food. Once he was sitting in his doorway, he finally gave himself a moment to piece together the last little bit of time. His bowl of porridge with pine nuts sprinkled atop it was half ignored as he mulled over this new mystery. He wanted to uncover the truth of the near disaster.

She had a mate, or it sounded like she did. He was not surprised. Her first night awake had shown that was a distinct possibility. And the scars on her back now made sense from the very little he knew of dragons - which was in total a pile of hearsay and one poem about a warrior dragoness with back "claw-marked by deepest love". That part had always confused him. He wanted to ask more about the scars, but wasn't sure it was allowed. He refocused on the current question and not on dragons in general.

She did not sound fond of this possible mate and had not mentioned him while awake. He knew she had brothers, and possibly nieces and nephews, so family had been mentioned, but not this mystery mate. Onyx was completely confused by her words about the messenger and her vehement assertion that he held no claim. He watched her sleep, stretched out and calm again. He attempted to understand, but his mind ran in circles and tangents, so he gave it up. He leaned back against the doorframe and closed his eyes. He absently rubbed his hand and healed the clawmarks she had left. One thing was certain, she had been serious about trying to stop him from doing something.

Lungs emptied in a whoosh. He knew why she had been so agitated. He pictured it in his head before he could stop his imagination. A faceless mate yanking her close by her hips, taking what he saw as his. The Aislinn in Onyx's head was not *physically* fighting for some reason - he could not picture the fierce creature who made it to the shore after battling the waves failing to tear a single opponent apart, so something had to keep her from doing so. But fighting or not, it did not matter. He could remember the white of her eyes, and her terror from earlier. He could feel the wrong in what he pictured and wondered how the shadow man could not.

He rubbed the back of his hand and watched her, uncertain what action to take now, lost on if he should even mention his new knowledge to her. She stirred and he found a temporary answer. He would let her rest, for now. Rest could at least heal the physical wounds. It took him two tries to find his voice and he sang a lullaby to her in selkie before returning to tasks to busy himself and keep his mind distracted.

Chapter 12 - Obligations

Aislinn woke late in the morning. She stretched and rubbed her temples, trying to get rid of a mild headache caused by uneven sleep. She'd had dreams, she thought, but they were lost to the sunlight. Probably better that way. She lay there for a bit, soaking up sunbeams and fresh air that flowed into the hovel, letting them remove the ache in her head. She noticed a splint on her leg that hadn't been there when she'd fallen asleep. It surprised her, but it made sense. She'd been having trouble keeping it still. She imagined she hadn't moved much when she first arrived, so it had been more of a nuisance with needing to heal all the cuts.

When she finally looked for her host, he was sitting right outside on a woven cushion that had seen better days. His back was to the hut and she crept forward as best she could.

"Mooorning." She kept her voice low and spooky, hoping to startle him and was surprised when it worked. She could have sworn her crutch and the noise of her struggling with the leg brace would have been enough to wake the dead.

He blinked several times before looking up at her and his eyes were a mixture of surprise and concern. He held the beginnings of a pendant in his hands.

"You should not be up yet."

"I'm stubborn and easily bored. I never sleep as long as folk think I should." She maneuvered so she was sitting with her back leaning against the side of the hut and her leg at an awkward angle. She realized that move was likely most of her energy for a day. "Or I sleep too long. I have no in-between. Star of spirits?"

Onyx glanced back to the item in his hand and nodded. He was smoothing fine slivers of bone against a coarse stone. She watched his technique for a bit, approving as he smoothly switched to different spots on the stone depending on how much polishing was needed.

"Do you bring the stones with you or are they just something you've found?"

"Found. Stones are heavy. Better tools are home." He was distracted, focused on his work. Aislinn noted notches in the white shards and watched, wondering how exact his skills were. He laid the pieces down in the rough star shape when he was not working with them.

She picked slightly at the cushion while waiting for the next step. Fabrics were obviously not his forte, she'd noticed a few roughly patched items about the house. Her eyes rested on a piece of bark with a crude charcoal diagram of the pendant. It had notes, and she recognized the writing, even if she could not read it. She'd heard of it in the Dawnlands, and from her understanding it was peculiar to Crescent Moon selkies. She would have to see if he was willing to teach it to her.

Wax and what looked to be a wax and charcoal paste were warming in small bowls beside a charcoal brazier. He smoothed the mixtures across the bones, three and three. Then he attempted to fit the delicate pieces together in a star form. They looked a loose mess, with no hope of actually fitting together. Any passerby would say the last piece was far too awkward to thread and complete the shape, but Aislinn was engrossed, waiting to see the outcome. He pushed ever so carefully with his thumb, then a slight wedging and twisting with a fine awl, and the bones were a beautiful six-pointed star. One dark triangle, one light, looking like the bone had somehow grown or been interwoven like ribbons in those shapes. And even more impressively, the black wax hadn't smeared all over the place. Aislinn clapped in delight and giggled slightly, it took her a moment to calm down.

"Apologies. I love watching artisans at work. It's magic." She smiled at him. He shyly smiled back. His way of accepting the compliment.

He looked behind her to the house and excused himself to get breakfast. Aislinn pushed aside her embarrassment at her reaction and leaned forward to examine the star, being careful not to touch it.

"You can hold it." Onyx spoke, reappearing next to her unexpectedly. It was her turn to jump slightly. She was almost certain he was hiding a grin as he set down a bowl filled to the brim with food.

"Are you sure? I don't want to accidentally disassemble it." She found herself half reaching towards it as she spoke.

"The fit and wax holds it together for now."

She lifted the pendant, still cautious and feeling like her breath would break it.

"This is fine craftmanship. You would have a steady business if you sold something like this in a stall in Seacove." Aislinn set it down after a moment, still nervous about its delicacy, even though she was certain he was right about its sturdiness.

"I will remember that. I want to visit someday."

"If ever you do, consider my family's hospitality yours." She ate, noting that this morning's offering was a bland but filling reddish brown porridge with pine nuts scattered across the top. Her host obviously had multiple skills. "I think you would like the great library. Not everyone can see all of it, but... I know some folk who could give you access to whatever parts of it you wished to see."

The questions came quickly then, and Onyx was almost tripping over his words as he asked about the city and the library. She gathered from some of his questions that his island also had a library, but he was excited to see what another library in another place would hold. She answered his specific questions, but when he asked her of Seacove in general, she could only find a few words to speak of it.

"It's... home. You turn down a street and suddenly, even though you are a step from the market, you're in a charming row of little cottages with laundry strung between them. Next turn, you might be dockside, or by the waterfall. It's always changing." Aislinn felt this was the best description she could ever give of her city and she missed it in that moment.

Once she finished her food, Onyx took a look at her leg and splint.

"Wear this when needed. Always at night, you thrash since waking."

"Sorry about that." She winced, guessing what was making her thrash. "Especially sorry if I've hit you."

"No trouble. Your leg has worse." His expression said that she had definitely hit him.

"Can I make it up by helping with anything?"

"No need. Rest and heal." He gathered the dishes, clearly making sure to keep the thing called 'work' away from her. She asked for a needle and thread. Onyx looked at her questioningly, but brought some to her. It came in the form of an embroidery box, complete with threads, needles, clippers, and fabric patches. Perfect. Aislinn stole his cushion as he was clearly and audibly scouring the dishes and re-working breakfast leftovers for their lunch.

"You don't need to do that! Rest!" Onyx had caught her in the act.

"Do you like your cushion torn like this?" She was oddly used to getting around excessive politeness and fussing. She would do something useful.

"No, but- You-" He cut himself off. She felt she'd addled the poor selkie's brain somehow.

"I can fix it. It will take only a moment and then you can focus on your jewelry making. Do you have a preference of these scraps for a patch?" She was never certain if it was her tone or her expression that made people give in. Onyx shook his head no and huffed, a sound that was more seal than human, before disappearing back into the hut.

Aislinn focused on the cushion, actually little more than a worn fabric cover over a layer of reed mats. She had seen a pile of reeds inside the hut, she would see if these could be used once the outside was repaired. She knew she was being somewhat rude and stabbed the needle through the fabric in frustration. She'd dealt with enough good-hearted people who refused to let others help, it usually came down to telling them that they were receiving help or resigning herself to twiddling of thumbs. She had proved horrible at thumb twiddling.

Onyx came back out after a short while, she could feel him watching her as she wove and stitched pieces to patch the holes in the cushion. Once she had it patched, she showed him and asked for rushes to work on the inside. Onyx looked conflicted, but brought out the requested materials and returned to household tasks like airing the bedding.

Her task was almost mindless and Aislinn was done before lunch. More porridge, a little bit of a spiced fish broth drizzled over it this time. Once lunch was done, she worked the mats into the fabric and closed the edges.

"There. One cushion repaired. And a lesson: if you don't let me be useful, I will search for tasks to do myself."

"You make fine stitches." Onyx was turning it over, examining her work.

"A lady must know her embroidery." She actually did start work on a minor bit of embroidery on a larger scrap of cloth. She planned to fold it over and make a drawstring pouch. It was calming, and she had a feeling she was going to have to fight to assist him with other work.

He sat on the cushion and returned to work on the pendant for a little. Aislinn looked up when she realized the tools he used were silent.

"How do you know what you are sewing?"

"It will be a bag. Small purse. I'm just… improvising." She shrugged. She was mostly stitching vines and flowers, easy enough to shorten or twist them to fill the needed space. "Sometimes I plan, but right now… I need something to do."

Onyx brought out bags and carefully emptied them out on a cloth. Aislinn stirred through the bits and baubles.

"I find things and sell them at the market. If you can use any," he motioned for her to take them.

"Are you sure you don't need any of this?"

"Everything I planned is elsewhere."

Aislinn stretched out on the grassy patch, laying on her side to sort the things Onyx found on the beach. It was a very simple task, not enough to wear her down for sleep. At least, it wouldn't have been if she weren't injured. She dozed off, waking when he set their dinner in front of her. She pushed herself upright and a blanket slipped off.

"You looked peaceful." He sat down on the cushion again. The pendant was as he left it. She saw the rest of his blankets on makeshift frames nearby. It looked like he had rinsed and aired them out while she slept. Likely had done other things as well. He seemed to be in constant motion, like the waves on the shore.

"Thank you." She stretched and stared at the items on the cloth while she ate. It was the group with the broken oar and the dagger.

His sorting system she had been confused by suddenly made sense. The first pile had been for his use - she'd seen some of the boards in use already. The second pile had been for quick sale at the market. The intact glass float she'd seen would be fine pay for the quick work of cleaning it up and trading it to a fisherman who could use it. The odd stones had indents or holes that would make them fine weights for fishing lines. This, the third pile was more or less his curious self, not sure what he wanted a thing for, but interested nonetheless. She focused on the blade, seeing a hint of the metal beneath. As she suspected, once the muck was removed, the metal underneath was almost pristine.

The way the metal survived the waves and made the blade alone worth a bit, but with a handle... Aislinn searched through the other bits and the pair focused on their respective projects until nightfall. Onyx refused her help in preparing the bedding and by the time he had laid it out, fed her, and examined her leg, he was clearly spent. The selkie was a lightly snoring seal seconds after snuggling in. She absentmindedly patted his head and wished him good dreams, feeling slightly guilty that she was taking so much of his energy.

Aislinn lay there for a few minutes, hanging peacefully on the edge of blissful rest. The scars on her back started to tingle, then almost burn. She dragged herself from beneath the blankets and furs, to the squeaking protest of her sleeping pinniped companion, and limped to the shore with the help of her staff. Along the way she grabbed a scrap of cloth. The intensity of the feeling increased the closer she came to the water.

"Finally realize I've had an accident, my lord?" She spoke aloud to no one, her bitter tone matching the chill in the air.

She stumbled and shoved her body in the waves, keeping the scrap of fabric held high. She focused on it, and it took a moment to light aflame. One leg in the sand, the feel of the wind, waves about her, fire in her hand and light and shadows thrown by the flames. She focused on using the blend to boost her skills. No words could be passed through their bond at this distance, but emotion could. She was fine, stay away. She felt the tugging ease, replaced with gentle concern. She repelled that with a very clear surge of her almost ever-present anger. The attempts at comforting soon stopped, ending with one last pull on the bond. She growled and stabbed the crutch in the sand to hold her if the waves changed. She needed to reach out to someone who could make certain she was left alone.

Heartbeat slowed, breath deepened. She slipped into a half-slumber.

She was home, or near enough, her soft boots treading the polished wooden floors above The Velvet Glove. Someone was guiding her here, that much was certain, she never had the skill at this to find home on the very first try without help. She paused her steps as she felt eyes on her. She half turned and caught a glimpse of a dark, curly head, ducking behind a door and then peeping back out. A very serious child giggled and Aislinn smiled.

"Caeda, why are you hiding?"

"Uncle's been worried, so I've been waiting here for you when I sleep. I knew you were okay, I saw you all coming home." Caeda grasped her aunt's hand and led her towards Damian's study. Aislinn wondered what else she had seen, but didn't press it. Her niece's visions were sporadic and often nothing more important than how the eggs would turn out that day if her uncle Damian cooked instead of Daren. Trying to interpret the multitudes of outcomes often led to more confusion.

"Uncle, she's here!" Caeda's joy made Aislinn feel slightly guilty for not reaching out sooner.

"What day is it, Aislinn?" Damian was ever practical, eschewing pleasantries for trying to locate her in time, as dreams often wove their own path through it.

"Not certain, but it's between a quarter and a half a cycle since I set out from Minado. The moon was just past full then, and now it's passing to dark. Have you heard from Captain Hanjib?" She crossed her fingers, hoping the ship had made it through the storm safely.

"Near enough to time, that is well. As are Captain Lascore and his crew. He reached out to us once the storm had passed. He would be scouring the isles for you, however his ship was not as fortunate and he is held up by repairs. Are you well?" Eyes fixed on her, he would spot a lie a league away. Not that she would lie to him, but any idea of skirting the truth and minimizing her condition was out the door as well.

"Injured. I was torn up by the rigging and flotsam. My leg suffered the worst from it. I have a selkie assisting me though. He's a healer."

"Selkies do not have male healers. Not of high skill." Damian was suspicious, his statement asking questions.

"He's gifted in it, they taught him the basics, and he's very curious, so I believe he taught himself more. A waste really, not to teach him beyond it. Onyx of the Crescent Moon clans."

"Please, tell me you have not washed up near a selkie colony at this time of year."

"No, he's off by himself. Hermiting. Honestly, I'm not certain where I am. Other than in one of the many clusters of islands between here and Minado. There's a seasonal market on one end of this isle. The whole place is large enough to have woods and be more than a stone above the sea." She sat in a chair, enjoying the free range of motion her body here could manage. Caeda sat on the floor beside her, resting her head on her lap. Aislinn stroked her niece's dark hair. "I came to let you know I'm safe. Enough. Also, so you can let the High Lord Bryndagr know it. My sleep was disturbed earlier tonight by him."

"Likely one of his people in the isles reported how stressed the Captain was. I will see to him. Reach out immediately if anything is needed. We will come as quickly as possible."

"Aw, you'd use a portal for me?" She teased her brother. Portal magic was complex and delicate to set up, but Damian had one he maintained for use at a moment's notice. To keep it stable, only one could exist in his workshop at a time and once that was used, it would take months to construct a new one. He had been searching for a suitable site for a secondary one since she was a child, but yet to find it. Despite all of that, she had no doubt he would sacrifice it for her, a certainty that warmed her. Unfortunately, Damian was unamused by her levity, his extreme lack of humor emphasizing his worry.

"Youthling, you are aware I would burn down cities to protect my family?"

"Yes, brother. I was teasing. I am fine. And it would be pointless to waste a portal, I don't even know where I am, so you would have to locate me first and- stop frowning, I'm only reporting the truth as you've always taught me to." She stuck her tongue out and the gesture received a small smile.

"We would be there already if we knew your location." He looked exhausted, even in the dream. She wondered how long it had been since he last truly slept.

"I must go. To reach you, I had to use the sea as an augment. I'll return once I have more information or if I need assistance." She looked down to see that Caeda had already faded away, lulled into a deep and true sleep. The room and her brother faded as Aislinn willed herself back to the islands. She felt waves surrounding her as senses slowly came back to her. Things like sound, including the bark of an excitable seal. Getting closer and closer. A panicked squeal and Aislinn was fully aware and back in the islands as pain stabbed her arm.

Onyx had his teeth firmly clamped around her upper arm and was frantically dragging her up the beach and out of the water. Aislinn noticed the tides had shifted somewhat, but nothing too drastic. She scrambled to get her good foot under her, but Onyx somehow threw her up the beach with an incoming wave before she could. His shape formed a bulwark behind her to keep her from washing back down the beach as the water drew out. She was sputtering, spitting sand and water out as she washed back against him.

"Onyx! Stop! I am fine!" She turned to face him and realized that 'small' for a selkie bull seal was still a very large animal. She froze when he bellowed in her face. The sound began while he was a seal, but before his bellow was completed, he was human. He was swearing, his tone left no doubt. It was a mix of his clan's language, straight up seal, and Amarantine, but Aislinn recognized the cadence and emotion all too well. Cadence, unfortunately could not explain the why, and it took him a moment to find words she could understand.

"Don't you understand tides? And why would you rest in the water with an injured leg? Do you wish to drown? You were lucky to make it past the rocks the first time!"

"I am sorry I scared you, but I am fine. I needed the cold and the water for a spell." She held her hands up, showing the now-charred scrap of fabric. They also formed a very inadequate barrier against a raging bull seal.

"You could not wait until first light?"

"No. I couldn't... I... someone was calling to me. Via magic. And I had to answer. I've taken care of it, they'll leave me alone."

Onyx looked away and snorted. He was silent for a few moments as water formed droplets and rivulets that ran down his body. Some was evaporating, leaving him wreathed in a fine mist. A distant part of her mind noted that he should have been shivering, like she was.

"I thought you'd fallen in the water. I thought you'd drowned. You should not even be walking," he said.

"I'm like a stray, aren't I? You've found me, you've nursed me back to health and if anything happens to me now, you'll blame yourself," she said before she could stop herself. Her tone was detached, not accusing. The idea was sweet, but potentially problematic. Onyx looked away, his refusal to meet her eyes confirming this suspicion. She shook her head and stared beyond him, focusing on her crutch. The water was slowly lapping at it. After a moment, he looked at her, then turned to see what she was staring at.

"Oh."

He was in the water in a moment, less than a heartbeat between man to seal. She appreciated the smoothness, even as she pondered what to do about this new revelation. She did not have the energy to deal with a selkie with potential delusions of romance, even if he was polite about it. Onyx returned quickly and dropped the crutch from his mouth before switching back. He then helped her to her feet and assisted her with the uphill walk to the hut.

She collapsed by the embers of the fire, cold and pain suddenly overtaking her, shivers wracking her body. Onyx leaned forward and touched his forehead to hers, mumbling something softly in the selkie tongue and then she felt warmth flow through her. He shook his head and said something else as he turned to stoke the fire.

"Did you just call me an idiot?"

"You know selkie?" He was either too pleased at her knowledge to be embarrassed at her knowing the insult or he didn't care. Either one was a mix of charming and irritating.

"I know a variety of insults. In a variety of tongues. One of my brothers taught me an interesting stash of knowledge. Idiot?"

"Injured, laying in cold, cold ocean, not even sun to warm… idiot." He grinned, eyes sparkling and daring her to refute it.

"Not an idiot. Just do idiotic things sometimes."

"What spell was so important?"

She paused. His words had given her a way to stymie his apparent fondness, but she wasn't certain she wanted to take that route. The silence stretched out. She opened her mouth a few times to speak and closed it again. Onyx focused on the fire. She wished he would start babbling, something to fill the void. She did not trust her mouth in this moment.

"My... mate... was calling to me. We're dragons, so if he came to find me... well, we're territorial and we're each other's territory. He'd attack you. Rip you to pieces." She looked away as she said this, even calling Kaienar her mate rankled. She looked up and met Onyx's eyes.

They were dark and full of pity, a reaction she didn't understand. Even if it was the correct response to Kaienar. She tilted her head up and defiantly met his gaze. The staring match lasted for only a few seconds and she looked away first. The silence grew stifling again.

"Why don't you want him?"

"I never said I didn't want him." She couldn't bring herself to meet his eyes. She heard the gentle clink of dishes and the swish of water. She felt relief, he was going to leave it alone.

"I need to travel to market."

"I can manage for a bit by myself."

"I could stay away long enough your mate could come and get you." He gathered the rags with his back to her. Clever. She felt she should have seen that trap, but Onyx was trickier than expected.

"I..." she paused, then remembered his talent with spotting lies. "I would rather be flayed alive by the rocks than call for him. Satisfied?"

He turned to face her, head tilted in a manner she was becoming all too familiar with. Onyx's curiosity had been piqued.

"No. Is he who you thought I am?" Bastard. He was too clever by far. His words were a question, but she could tell he knew the answer. She disliked him catching the connection as well as the disconnect, but she was not about to clarify why she might reach for someone one night even though she vehemently refused his help the next.

Her eyes narrowed at Onyx and this time he dropped his eyes first. It didn't feel like a victory to Aislinn though, more like the victor mercifully disengaging. The tense silence remained as Onyx worked on her leg and hands. He did not ask any further questions, but brief calculating glances told her he was mulling over this new information. They returned to bed with no more words spoken between them.

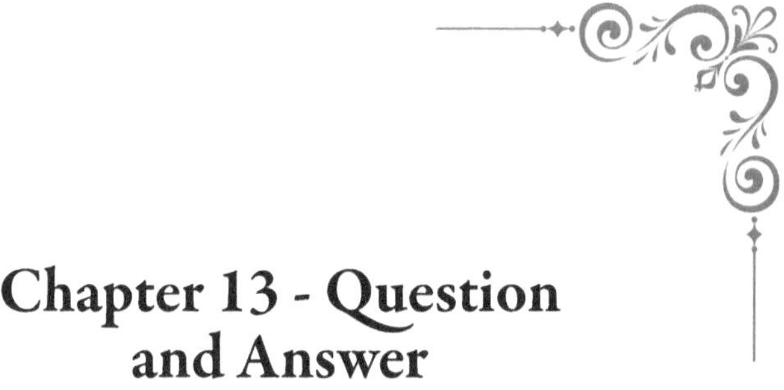

Chapter 13 - Question and Answer

Onyx did not lean against her this night, leaving her space, however Aislinn found herself pressed to him in the chill of predawn. Frustrated at her tendencies to seek warmth, she crawled out of bed and began to stoke the fire.

She felt eyes on her within moments. She turned around and Onyx was laying on his back, pale belly up, nose now towards the fire. She was impressed he had moved so silently. He exhaled loudly in exasperation as he stared at her, expressive even in his seal form.

"I'm not going anywhere. I was just cold."

He rolled over and eased himself beside her, leaning against her. She found herself smiling despite her frustration. They sat in silence watching the fire and listening to the crackle of the logs. It was an easy, comfortable silence. When Aislinn broke that silence, she surprised even herself.

"He chose his court and his lands over my life. I survived, but I can't forgive him. Even though a part of me understands, I can't forgive him. And twice a year, in the most glorious and beautiful seasons, he calls to me through this bond because he misses his mate. And he calls. And calls and calls. And it's like tides resisting the pull of the moon. I go. I have to. And some things I used to love, I hate because of it. And I know he cares, or used to, but the way he cares cripples and crushes me and..." she sighed, frustrated and so very tired, "Forever sounds so romantic when you're young and foolish, but when betrayal occurs, it's a drawn out death sentence."

She paused and used her thumb to wipe tears that had managed to sneak past her pride. "Remember the lie? That's why I'm so good at it. I have to tell it repeatedly. And probably forever will. Satisfied, curious sea-cat?"

Onyx touched his nose to hers, eyes wide and whiskers full of concern. The simplicity of the gesture caught her in a way that others' words of wisdom and comfort never had. She relaxed against him, shaking slightly with shadows of old sobbing. Somewhere, in the midst of it, Onyx changed to human, humming and singing under his breath as he rocked and held her.

She calmed as the soothing selkie tones sunk in, then looked up at Onyx and laughed. Despite his calming tones, his face was a mask of panic.

"The possibility of crying females is universally terrifying?"

"I... my sisters..." His eyes were wide as he shook his head. "It is never smooth."

"Believe me, the tears weren't coming. I'm not sure I even know how to really cry over this anymore." A hiccup of a giggle bubbled up in her throat. "I swear, I shall not cry unless there is a death. Or I hit my finger with a hammer."

"Thank you?" He released her and backed away slightly, calming once he was satisfied that she wasn't going to burst into tears. She could see a thousand new questions building in his eyes. Eternally curious.

"How can he reach you at a distance?" Onyx had breakfast ready in a moment and was now focused on her. "I thought- I know mirrors can be enchanted, but..."

"It's complex. We're bound. He can't reach out to me as well as he would like, because I don't cultivate it any further; but being bound, neither can I refuse him as well as I like. And before you ask, there is no way to undo it." She smiled sadly at him. He looked into his bowl, fiddling with his food. His mood was off, she wasn't certain why and tried to reassure him. "Don't worry. He can't tell you're with me. It's not like he sees through my eyes or anything. That would be an entirely different kind of magic. Or a much stronger bond than we have."

She was surprised when Onyx did not ask about the magic. He was slurping his morning porridge quietly, not looking at her. She felt she had done something wrong and wasn't certain what. She let the silence hang.

"Healing your leg last night," Onyx paused again, "I was trying not to wake you."

"I don't recall being woken, so you did well." She was surprised he'd woken up again to do so after pulling her from the waves.

Onyx shook his head. "You did wake. Your mate is a lord?"

"High Lord Bryndagr." She remembered the leg brace and now suspected he meant the night before last. She wondered what else she had said. "He actually has a longer title, but that has generally been the maximum of respect I give to him."

"You panicked. Thought I was him." Onyx raised his hand and she could see the pale scars of recently healed skin. He did not look her in the eye, she had the sense this was half confession and half question. "I'm sorry. I calmed you too much, you were confused." A long pause. "You were terrified."

She wrapped her arms around herself, considering the wisdom of leaving the hut for a moment. Falling on her face while attempting a quick exit did not seem like it would ease the awkwardness of this situation. She fell back on honesty - it had always been her preferred method.

"If I thought you were him and you were touching my hip, I was terrified." She forced a bit of porridge down. It did not calm the sick feeling in her gut. Nor the anger that even stranded on an island, she could not escape Kaienar's shadow. She added, "that would be one of the things I used to enjoy that I now hate."

"Why-" Onyx started with questions and she cut him off.

"Complex. Leave it at that." Her tone was sharper than she meant it to be. Onyx merely nodded in acceptance of her answer. The silence was back and much more uncomfortable.

"I was not sure how to tell you. I was going to pretend I had not heard, but I know some lands..." He was now looking at her apologetically. He looked trapped, clearly not sure what he was supposed to do. His head suddenly bobbed in apology. "I am sorry."

"Apology accepted. In the future, probably best I'm awake, but I understand why you did it. And on pretending not to hear, believe me, most in my country like to sweep such unpleasantness under the rug as well." Silence returned and she searched for another topic. "So, your voice. Is that trick you do with the humming natural or do you have to train it?"

"Any selkie can. How well they can, practice and skill." Onyx shrugged.

"How skilled are you?"

"I have practiced hard." He had that shy smile she was becoming accustomed to and she could tell he was being modest.

"How does it work?" She had Damian's fondness for deconstructing magic, and this was a much happier subject. "Can you... make an enemy walk away and forget about you?"

He laughed and thought for a moment. "No. Make them still if they are not a strong mind, but not control them. Perhaps attract?"

"Show me," she said. Onyx looked dubious. "You've already hummed at me, is that the extent?"

He paused, then switched to his native tongue, singing softly. She had heard him singing softly while he worked, and he had a lovely voice, but this had an entirely different weight to it than the singing he'd been doing then. His voice sank into her bones. She realized she could not run if she'd wanted to and she had absolutely no desire to bolt. He was lighting a candle and marking it as he sang and she found herself curious, but in a languid and distant way. His voice was all that really mattered. He came closer to her, eye contact and proximity strengthening the feeling. He broke eye contact and leaned close to her.

Aislinn woke in his arms, disoriented.

"Look at the candle." His voice was clear of the tones.

Aislinn glanced over at the candle confused.

"You've only been out a moment."

It took a few moments to realize that the candle hadn't even burned down to the first mark he had made.

"I take it you've gotten in trouble for doing that before."

"I'm not always alone on my travels. I wasn't used to others' reactions at first. Selkies…" He hemmed and hawed for a few moments. "Push and pull. Humans, not as much. Now, I avoid it."

"Nor dragons apparently."

"I told you to sleep. You barely did." He pointed to the lowest mark. "The first I accidentally did that to a human, the candle went this far."

"But you say you can't command me?"

"Sleep, calm," he paused, making an embarrassed sound in the back of his throat, "Seduce." His smile was annoyingly charming.

"So what you can get me to do is limited?"

"Yes. That is how it works. Also mood. Your mind. Language."

"Language?"

"I told you to sleep. A selkie who did not know your language may only calm to near sleep." He paused, looking away. "Precision is hard. I wanted to calm, but did too much last night. You were neither asleep nor awake."

She nodded, both in understanding of his description and in certainty that time was not translating correctly. She wasn't sure if it was due to her unfamiliarity with his dialect or limits in his Amarantine. The bad dreams of the night before were coalescing into vague and confusing memories. She would figure out the grammar later. Common sense said not to trust someone who could restrain her with his voice, but his caution and concern at her distress overrode that warning.

"Can you sing me to health?" Aislinn missed her brothers the moment she asked. She felt that question was either Edorian or Damian speaking through her. Her bookworm brother Rin's thirst for knowledge in general was only matched by Damian's desire to test and know exactly how something worked. She was now trying to analyze Onyx's skills, one part for her curiosity, one part so she could tell them about it.

She suspected Onyx's healing was water-focused, and by default, connected to light as that was life and growth. Attempts to test him with other elements in his healing would be more dangerous than it was worth. For her. Damian could probably come up with a thousand small tests. Fire could be an excellent thing to use a touch of in healing, it could also result in combustion. Earth could strengthen or stiffen. Air was... highly unpredictable in her opinion. Testing his music and healing was an avenue she could examine though. She watched Onyx's face as he contemplated her words and was struck by the notion that he would feel at home among her brothers and would love to explore the intricacies of magic.

"Lay down."

She did as he asked and he began to undo the makeshift brace stabilizing her leg. His hands weren't as sure as usual, she guessed the other night was playing on his mind.

"No need to calm, I'm awake. Just... coax more healing." She took his hand and placed it on her hip. She flinched slightly, but that was more reflex than anything; she trusted Onyx.

He began to sing softly after a few moments and fingers ran across her hip. She was surprised he chose selkie to sing in, but didn't comment. He was attempting something neither of them had a clue how to do, the choice made sense. Besides, now that she thought of it, him powerfully telling her to heal would either not work or might work in ways entirely counter to the intention. Healed hip, rest of the body destroyed attempting to make it so.

She could feel the song sinking in again. This time the sensation was coiled in her bones, starting very near pain and edging into real pain after a few moments. She bore it until her lungs began to lock up, but then the pain was gone before she could protest and her body was suffused with calm. Onyx was waiting to re-wrap her leg, she could feel him testing it slightly. She was more than satisfied with the results of this experiment, she could feel the difference in her leg.

"If this keeps healing so quickly, I may be able to hunt soon," she caught his glance when she said this. The smile he flashed was uneasy and she was unsure if she'd offended him by insulting his host skills somehow or if he was not pleased at the idea of her healing and leaving. Either one could be problematic. "I don't like inconveniencing you. I would like to do something to assist."

He smiled again, this one more genuine and warm. "You are no trouble."

"You're hunting for two instead of one. Your hut is set up for one instead of two. Everything is double what it should be and double what it's made for. Hunting is something I can do – more than sorting a bit of bric-a-brac."

"I need to travel to the market soon. The trip will take a full day." His face twisted in a frown. "I think... if you heal like this for a few days, I can prepare food for you and you can take care of yourself for the day."

Aislinn suppressed a laugh. He really did not seem to understand the concept of her taking care of herself or assisting him, but she would take this small victory.

She worked on whatever minor tasks he allowed her the next few days, trying not to show when pain inevitably came and resting frequently. Their conversations became more lively and they shared tales to pass the time. She found herself wishing he would return to Seacove with her, and told herself it was only because he would enjoy it and she owed him

In this time she also worked on finishing the bag she'd begun and crafting a new handle for the blade. She handed both to him the night before his trip.

"These will sell well." His words were practical, but his eyes were full of praise as he tested the knife on a few veggies and ran his fingers along the embroidery.

"I hope they do. Use the coins to pay for whatever I cost you and keep any excess for yourself, you've more than earned it." She watched as he turned back to the blade, fingering the texture of the simple wood and leather hilt she'd added. "It's elven made. Specifically those of the southern isles. I'm not sure how it came to be here, or with such a poor hilt as it originally had, but it will hold an edge like no other and you need not fear it rusting. If you have use for it, I'd suggest you keep it."

"This is your money." His eyes clearly said he wanted to keep it.

"You've more than earned it with your care. Please, keep it."

"Thank you." He set it aside and stared at it almost reverently.

"Take care of that blade, it will take care of you."

"I will." He stared at it for a long time. "Have you met elves?"

"I'm... I am part elf." She felt a stab of pain as she spoke.

"I thought they had pointed ears and some had-" He put his hands above his head, mimicking the antlers and horns that some had.

"Some have horns. They wear them like elegant crowns. I don't take after my elven side much." Not at all anymore, but she wouldn't say that. That was too hard to explain.

"They sing a lot? I know there is elfsong."

"It's not a real song. They do sing, but the Elfsong is more..." She tried to dredge up the memory of it, she didn't want him to ask why she was sad. "It's like all your senses are sensing something extra. A sound the ears can't hear, or a sweet scent that's tasted instead of smelled. They call it a 'song' because it's the closest thing to describe it."

"It must be wonderful. Where does it come from?" He was lost in the thought of it.

"Everything. Everything has its own music."

"Living things or things like rocks and water?"

She laughed. She couldn't help it.

"That's... there's a lot of elves that would say rocks and water are living, but in a different way. But to answer your question, they all have music."

"What do I sound like?"

"I said I survived. I didn't say he didn't damage me."

It took a moment for Onyx to catch on and he looked horrified.

"See why I don't want him near me?" She laughed to keep from crying. "I never heard it the clearest, but it's gone now."

"How?"

"Please." She was trying to find words to apologize for bringing the topic up and stopping, but that one word was all she needed to say.

Onyx leaned forward and briefly touched his forehead to hers.

"Rest now?"

"Yes. I think that'd be best."

They prepared for bed in silence. Aislinn snagged a few of the preparatory chores to assist him, but precious few. Once they were beneath the covers, she stared at the ceiling, unable to sleep. Onyx let out a sigh. She wasn't the only one awake. He twisted about and she looked at him. He lifted his head and looked back with his darker than dark seal eyes.

"Don't worry, Sea-cat. I can't sleep either." She patted his cheek and drew her hand back. "Sorry. You're too easy to pet when you're a seal."

Onyx stuck his chin forward and she laughed.

"I'm not gonna scratch your chin." Despite her words, she found herself playing with his whiskers and scratching his chin.

After a few moments of this, she guided his chin to rest on her shoulder as she stroked his head. For once, she was the one humming. After a bit, he countered with his own humming, or the seal equivalent thereof and sleep soon claimed them.

Chapter 14 - Trading

The next morning, Onyx checked and rechecked every aspect of the hut, his pack, and the weather before leaving. They had breakfast and Aislinn crawled back under the covers with a vague promise not to overexert herself. When he gave one last glance, she was sleepily watching him leave, hair loose because she hadn't yet rebraided it. He waved and turned away, trying not to think of how he'd rather be next to her. He was aware the intimate way they'd nestled together the prior night was a fluke and likely wouldn't be repeated, but he craved the possibility.

Normally he had a variety of spots he would stop at to gather the sea's bounty from before reaching the market, but today he only paused for items that could be found along his path. The one exception was a quick side trek to a lookout point where he could get a clear view of most of the waters on this side of the island.

From this perch he spied only a handful of ships and those looked to be trading vessels as they had neither the cut nor build he associated with hunters. These were larger, sturdier and more stable ships. None were suited for chasing down prey that might seek safety in shallow waters. He relaxed, but only slightly. Just because they weren't around now, didn't mean they wouldn't be. And there was always the possibility of a ship anchored someplace out of sight.

He reached his destination well before noon, but the market was already in full swing. He bartered with various traders, some he knew, some he didn't. Some had their wares on blankets spread across the sand and pebbles near the rowboats they used to get from ship to shore. Others had set up crude sheds and shacks that would remain as a skeletal ghost town once the trading season ended. Still others simply had a cargo crate or barrel opened for patrons to glance into. He stopped or was stopped by many of the other patrons of the market. When someone saw something they wanted, the rule here was to make an offer, even if it seemed like the person wasn't selling. One never knew until they asked.

Aislinn's pouch actually garnered a simple dress, shirt, and pants from a merchant looking for something a little more detailed and intricate to offer clients at his next port - Onyx talked up it being of elven make to sweeten the trade. The silver spoon became a fine, if lightly worn, spare blanket. The glass fisherman's float was exchanged for extra medicines a fisherman had brought along for his journey and so on. Onyx had obtained all the necessities and was idly fingering a length of luxurious fabric when he felt fingers brush against his side. Pickpockets were surprisingly rare in this market, the same questionable laws that allowed it to thrive also allowed for violent retribution to those who were caught thieving, but the sensation set Onyx on edge, even if it was nowhere near a spot a thief could take anything from. He went back to examining the cloth, senses on alert for the culprit. Another brush.

This time he caught the offender's wrist, spinning around to face them in one smooth motion. He found himself face to face with another selkie. Blue eyes, dark brown hair. Skin like cream. She nudged up against him, eyes all affection. Despite her masculine dress, his senses were definite that she was very much a female and very much a selkie. He could practically taste the seas on her.

His emotions were divided. One part was genuinely curious about what the cow was doing in such a comparatively remote place. Even though the western clans were far different from his, few selkies wandered far from the colonies once spring came. Another part was attracted by her and growing increasingly distracted by the sound of the nearby waves. That part began to fantasize about the wild tumble of the beaches during the season. He quickly returned to reality when he realized he was not picturing this cow with him on the beach. That was when the final and most sensible part told him to move away, she was looking for a mate and that promised only trouble for him, especially in this place.

He moved to another vendor and she followed, making tiny little chirrups in her throat that most humans could not hear, but selkies could. He patently ignored her while bartering for spices and a few other oddments that caught his eye. He traded the strand of pearls for a variety of semi-precious stones and had them bundled up before it occurred to him that he was buying components for amari nodum - the wedding jewelry. The season had not even come and all it took was one mildly persistent cow to throw him off balance and make him start designing amari nodum. If he didn't watch himself, he'd be weaving a set and trying to call a cow – ANY cow - to the beach.

Even as he berated himself, he felt the lie in that statement - he had someone in mind. He shook his head to clear it and was about to run from the market as fast as his feet could carry him when he spotted a new set of vendors and a new blanket being spread near the exit. They offered a lovely chocolate-colored sealskin and what looked to be seal bones and slabs of dried seal meat. Humans would need to test it to be certain of its authenticity, but a selkie could see it was real. At least, he could see it. One of many oddities he had. All the items held a sheen that he had never witnessed on seal meat and fur. The whole blanket was covered in it. He schooled his face to neutral calm and tried to locate his pursuer.

She was nearby. He let the softest of responses past his throat. It took two tries before he got the volume and pitch right to catch her attention. The instant he did, she was right by his side, arm looped in his, masculine disguise apparently forgotten. Warm, inviting, open to whatever he had in mind.

Onyx led her out of the busy market by a side path. By the time they were out of sight of the market, she had already left a mark on his neck and they were both giggling like they were slightly intoxicated. Which was not far from the truth.

Onyx kissed her slowly and deeply, remembering recent kisses with another. It would be so easy to give in to the instincts screaming in his blood and take her, right here and now. Then he imagined this lovely cow on the beach and his ardor cooled; remembering brightly colored beads scattered across the sands, like obscene alien drops of blood. Not now, and never this one. Lovely as she was, something about her reminded him strongly of Neha.

She was confused when he pushed her away. "What's wrong?"

"There are hunters in the market. Be wary and be gone." He gathered up his bundles, trying to school his breathing, focusing on the memories of scattered beads, and trying not to focus on someone he couldn't have. She mistook it as a ploy and brushed up against him.

"You can protect me." Her voice was layered with the selkie trill.

"I already did by getting you out of there. Now go, before they catch you." He gave her a flat look when she rubbed up against him again. "Was I not clear? I'm not interested, find another bull somewhere else." He hoisted his bundles on his back again.

"Oh. I see. You're a walrus, not a selkie." Her voice turned the spring back to winter.

He sighed and ignored her. He wished he was not as used to this as he was. She moved around him and stood in his path.

"Need to get home to your bull, tusk-tangler?"

"Yes, so sorry I mistook you for him." He stepped around her in the moment she was processing the insult, not feeling like fighting. She could assume what she wished. He wondered, as he often did when he heard selkies stoop to such insults, if they remembered how often lines were blurred or if they just ignored how similar blurring occurred on the bachelor beaches where cows and bulls spent the seasons isolated from the other sex when they weren't quite old enough for the beach. They had to be extremely oblivious to forget cheerful bachelors living together and spinster aunts that gazed adoringly at each other. Or friends who wedded the same bull and the rare cases where two bulls took the same cow. It wasn't a large population, but there was always a handful in every village he had visited. Clarifying this was random pointlessness he preferred to avoid at the moment, if a selkie didn't see it, they usually didn't want to see. Her slurs and yells faded into the distance as he wandered towards his home.

It was too late for his mood by the time they fully faded, he was bleeding on the inside. He should have been used to insults, but they never ceased to cut, even if he could present a calm facade.

The road stretched long before him and he was left alone with a pack digging into his shoulders and his mind digging into the past.

Chapter 15 - Hunting

Aislinn lay beneath the blankets after waving Onyx off and counting the number of times he turned back to check on her. Easily a dozen. She smiled despite herself.

As soon as his silhouette disappeared on the horizon, she rummaged around the shelter, knowing she had seen both a bow and materials for snares tucked away. Despite his warnings, she would do her best to test her leg later in the day. She found and laid out the items needed before re-braiding her hair and laying down for a bit.

After a brief nap, she used her crutch to hobble away from the seaside. She stopped once she was deep into the scrub. She was wrong about how much her leg could handle, but it would do. The next part was easy enough: wait.

The creatures forgot her presence and a few quail-like birds came out of the woods. Aislinn edged an arrow back and carefully raised her bow. Pause and shift, pause and shift. She was pleased they had not moved out of sight before she could loose her arrow. She was even more pleased that the weeks without practice had not spoiled her aim. Unfortunately, getting to the downed bird took a bit longer than she was used to. She used a knife Onyx had left for her to dress the bird and was exhausted by the time she was able to return to the hut with her kill.

The meat was tossed in a pot along with a few herbs she recognized and some rice. It was nowhere near her best culinary attempt, but she needed more rest. She slept the afternoon away only rising as the shadows were lengthening into evening.

She slung the bow over her shoulder again and made her way towards the beach, her leg mostly tolerating what she considered the mildest of use. She felt a few fresh shellfish or something else gathered from the tidepools would not go amiss and the walk could help stretch the kinks out a little more. She had barely started poking about when she heard Onyx roar. She hobbled in the direction of the sound as fast as her leg would let her.

The slowed pace chafed. She knew that whatever forced that sound from him would need to move or she was going to destroy it. And if it hurt Onyx before she could reach him, she would hunt it down.

Chapter 16 - Reflections of a Selkie

Onyx wished he could trace his troubles to an exact moment, but the moment that came to mind was only the culmination of years of being a little different from the others.

From childhood, he'd stood out because of his different coat. Many selkie's seal forms were darker, nearly black-coated, especially when wet. There were also a variety of brighter browns like a sandy beach or dirty brown-greys. But Onyx was a silvercoat - a pale white-grey that almost shone speckled with darker steely grey spots. Silvercoats were rare. Even in Haseu, the beautiful and bustling capital city of his homeland, he only knew of one other, and she was a very old lady. And his coat had caused him no end of trouble.

He was told to be cautious on the open shore when others were not, or at least were not told as often as him. Many pups followed their parents' lead in politely shunning him when possible. Silvercoats were said to be a sign of being spirit-touched, which was considered extremely auspicious or a sign of misfortune, depending on the individual. Neither public opinion or attempts at reading his fortune had been clear in regards to which he was, though he had his opinions. He barely minded this, he had not been wary of strangers and always tried to befriend visitors to the capital of their homeland, so it wasn't exactly a lonely existence. And it was all he knew.

He was overjoyed when he was around ten years old and his family visited the southern port city of Sanno, the only port in his homeland open to trade with non-selkie outsiders. He sought out all the strangers there - selkie and otherwise. Curiosity drove him to be first on any trading ships, examining wares and chattering at the sailors, as he devoured knowledge of the trader's tongue to ask questions about the world outside. His father was run ragged trying to keep track of him.

His curiosity was another thing that set him apart. If he was home, he was sneaking about trying to learn from watching the witches of the salt brush. When not doing that, he could be found in libraries, both the public one and the private ones of several families. He soon felt he'd memorized all the books that pertained to anything other than his homeland. He'd felt far too familiar with the entire population of Haseu after a while to bother looking for new friends there. He knew the instant there was someone new in town and the older he was, the quicker he was able to figure out if someone could be a potential friend. If he was in Sanno, he had no end of things to research, and new people to meet.

Thirteen had been a pivotal year. His brother announced he would never take to the beaches, so it was up to Onyx to carry on the family name. It wasn't a surprising announcement, but added pressure on him to marry well. But that seemed far away.

The more immediately impactful event was learning why he was shunned by many. He'd understood it in abstract, but a day on the beach truly brought it home. A bold hunter landed on a beach full of youngsters slightly south of Sanno. Onyx was playing with several other pups there. There was no question the others were selkie; many, including Onyx, were in seal form, but the man made a beeline for him. Onyx turned, expecting a potential new friend as he had not yet seen a hunter at work. He could still remember the club striking him and his mother appearing from nowhere and driving a long hairpin through the man's eye and into his skull before the guard arrived to stop him and the rest of his crew.

The part that he remembered most clearly, other than his mother's fierceness, was the space. He had been playing in a cluster of other youngsters, fighting and flirting and laughing. After the man came, there was space. A space not limited to a few days. It was a space present every day thereafter. He had been enjoying a life of friends and fun. Sanno had given him a taste of normal and then it had disappeared. His family had returned to Haesu, as his father's business had been completed and Mother was no longer pushing to remain in the south.

Over the years he'd found a handful of friends, those who either tolerated or enjoyed his oddness. But he could not forget that emptiness. And then he lost some of those to his first - and only - midsummer trying to claim a mate on the beach. That year had been the peak of folly.

To outsiders, a selkie colony at midsummer looked like a wild, tangled orgy with no rules and excessive violence. To a selkie, there were layers of delicate rules that had a plethora of shifts in nuance, especially between clans, but were overall similar throughout all of selkiedom. Follow the rules, win a mate, win respect. Break those rules, perhaps you could gain a mate, but there was a cost: the face you would lose in your community could be worth far more than the match you made. And community was important when storms easily cut off trade routes and winter meant no outside help at all.

First, a bull had to find their cow. This part happened off the beach, so the proper wooing and exchanges of gifts could take place. Then males competed for the best spots on the beach. An ideal location would have some protection from the weather yet be highly visible. The stronger and quicker the male, the more likely he would be to win these pre-contests.

And then the real season began. A moon cycle of battles to prove one's fitness. Most were sparring matches, mere formalities, really. Others were more desperate. Some parents tried exercising more control in matching their children than others, to varying results. More than one pair of star-crossed lovers had used the rules of sands to change whatever match had been decided on against their wishes. Once the season was over, if a bull had defended his chosen mate, she was his, as were any offspring conceived, no matter what their true bloodline was. In some ways, it was a straightforward system. Like many things in life, it had intentional and unintentional consequences and nuances. And despite the possible complexities, it was something most looked forward to once they reached a certain age.

That desire to win on the beach was an aspect in which Onyx was no different from his peers. His path, however, took a route somewhat different to that of his peers. He was a dreamer, more focused on the beautification of the home and the crafting of the amari nodum for his potential bride than the fighting. In looks, he'd been called pretty as often as handsome, a truth that sometimes vexed him, and in seal form his speckled pale grey coat stood out against the sea of darker bulls. He was considered lightly built for a bull and in either form this played against some tricks taught young males. Though he was very quick, he would not say he had the lightning speed possessed by some of his friends and rivals.

What he did have was a careful cunning, and he coupled that with some surprising strength in his body that he had worked hard to gain. He could not always overpower the other males, but he could hit at weaknesses to overwhelm and bring them down when they attempted to attack what they suspected was a weak rival. Few saw his tricks coming, even among his friends. He was almost certain Mer was the only one who had any idea of his true skillset before the beach. Most assumed Onyx's first few seasons would be marred with losses, exactly as his practices were. That was something that held little shame, overall, but received sadly knowing nods amongst the elders and some of his worried friends. They were certain he'd have a hard time winning in any season.

Mer had countered some naysayers, having long ago noticed that Onyx seemed delighted even when he lost. He was right. Onyx never fought to win in practices - every loss, Onyx learned another opening, or another limit to a trick or idea. The older he got, the more he kept track of others' skills and weaknesses, determined to win whichever lady he set his heart on.

He had also been cautioned against the idea of choosing purely for love, but his dreamy and romantic streak refused to be curtailed. 'The heart cannot fill the larder' was a common bit of wisdom for selkie parents to pass to their offspring as they attempted to guide them to a suitable match. The islands could be rough, and, in theory, part of the reason for a strong male was to have someone strong enough to battle the tides and chills for food in the deep dark of the winter, even though they had functioning markets and not everyone did that any more. Cows had their tasks as well, they were trained in beachside foraging and ways to effectively keep and cook food, along with the arts of healing. They bandaged and cared for their potential mates between fights, showing their skills and beginning a bond of partnership that would benefit both the couple and their families.

Parts of this made sense to Onyx, but he had also seen many odd couples thrive that did not fit this mold. He also felt the roles were somewhat antiquated, maybe for small groups of the wild selkies of the Dark and Poised Moon clans it was needed, but his people had cities and villages. And another side of the beach was clearly showing off the beauty and desirability of one's potential mate, which did not add up to being at all useful. If beauty was needed, why not love? Onyx had been certain he could have it all, a bride that would please his family, please himself, and perhaps a bride that would somehow bring him some new level of acceptance.

He became convinced he was in love with who he thought was the most beautiful cow of all. Her name was Neha, she let him call her Ha, and when she caught his eye, he set about wooing her with all the skills he possessed. His gifts for her were not the richest, but all were carefully crafted and filled with whimsical and beautiful touches. His amari nodum were the same. Unfortunately, competition for the beautiful Neha was stiff, including another of his closest friends, Otarii.

Otarii was quick and controlled; his skills in hand-to-hand were nearly unmatched. Onyx knew of his friend's one weakness, a spot on his right knee that had never correctly healed after falling from a rocky height as a child. It was hard to spot, and harder to leverage, but in a lead up to the beach proper, the two fought viciously for Neha's favor. Onyx repeatedly struck Otarii's knee, from every angle he could manage. His final move was not a strike, but to move out of reach just fast enough so that by following him, Otarii overextended that knee. His friend collapsed, lost the cow, and due to the injury's severity - his chance at the beach at all that year.

Onyx lost his friend.

Mer had visited Onyx that evening, warning him that his desired match was not all she seemed and nobody was worth the friendships they had built, but Onyx rebuffed him. Neha had been wavering over which of her suitors she would choose, but with Rii's defeat, she accepted Onyx's jewelry and Onyx was blinded by desire. Mer left, shaking his head. Onyx wished he had listened.

Neha was his everything, and he saw signs, but was slow to realize he was not her everything. She had encouraged friends to fight friends, he'd not been the only one to lose a friendship trying to win her favor. It left all her suitors desperate to have something to show for their losses.

On the beaches, he won battles, but she was not pleased at how he won. Trickery often looked more subtle and lacked the explosive finish of the other males throwing each other around. For her glory, she goaded him to fight in ways that his body could barely tolerate. And she was neither highly skilled, nor overly concerned with healing him or helping him heal himself. He did as best he could after bouts, wearing down more quickly than he should have because he was carrying all the burden of the beach.

But Onyx had a stubborn heart and kept fighting. Another cow might have fallen for his mettle alone, or kindly convinced him that they were not to be so both could slip off the beach in the dark of night and go their separate ways. Neha was as shallow as she was beautiful, and vain. Quietly leaving the beach did not befit her status, so they continued on. With no assistance from her, Onyx was forced to ignore more cosmetic injuries, such as a black eye, for healing cracks he could feel in his ribs. She practiced her wiles on other males while convincing him she had eyes only for him and he saw through the lies, but convinced himself it was so he could better prove himself with more challengers. She drew in more suitors and created more battles as the season continued to mar his face and wear down his body. Still, he kept fighting, and to the surprise of all, winning. She revelled in the glory of the fights, certain all eyes were on her.

She finally found a bull she decided better suited her idea of a mate and lured him in. The two males tore up each other as well as the beach. Most fights lasted minutes, this lasted hours. They were bloody and torn and they would pause and break apart with sides heaving, but then would attack again, seal form to human form to seal and back again. The pair finally fought to a stalemate. Onyx had no more to give and neither did the interloper. By rights and rules and respect, Onyx won. He limped to his mate, head held high with pride, but when he went to nuzzle her...

Neha stepped away.

Everything faded for Onyx in that moment: sounds, colors, the pains of his body. According to bystanders, the beach went eerily silent. Anyone who wasn't completely tangled in their own affairs had been caught up by the ferocity of the earlier battle. No one could tear their eyes away from this new development. She was ridiculously pleased by all the eyes on her and the shocked whisper she caused as she stepped away and removed her jewelry, effectively disowning Onyx. The battle had been a draw, by rules, that was enough of an opening for her to leave him, even if he was by his previous claim considered the victor. Nuance.

The detail that stuck most in Onyx's mind was the way she removed her amari nodum. The cold expression as she tore off the necklace he had poured all of his affection for her into. Dropping and breaking it instead of handing it to him. Disregarding all the care and work he had put into it. He remembered silver beads and bright red garnets scattering across the stones and sand. He could never forget the carefully carved combs for her hair and bracelets that followed suit. The delicate abalone shell that they had been carved from shattered against a stone, adding their silver and garnet inlays to the bits and baubles spread on the stones.

He had not delved too deeply into the tale of Aislinn's lover because he knew the sting a lover's betrayal could leave. He doubted his tale came close to whatever the horror of her tale was, but he could imagine. That day on the beach, Neha may as well have thrown his heart.

Onyx had fallen to his knees. He remembered holding a comb in his palms, a part of him willing it to be whole, to at least have had it handed to him. To have some sign that everything he had done meant something. Neha laughed as she turned to her chosen victor. She had laughed.

Onyx had a vindictive side, one that did not often surface, but callous treatment and pure exhaustion brought it to the fore. He felt used and abused, and had trained himself for years to know precisely where to strike to inflict the most damage, so in his pain, he did. Not her face, nor her beauty; he doubted that even if that had been her weakest spot to strike at, he could have struck. Somewhere inside, even with his new found clarity, she was still his everything.

Her true weak-spot, with this still being the season, was her prized bull. Seal incisors sank in the back of his knee. Everyone was too shocked to stop Onyx before his jaws connected. Onyx was never sure who stopped him or how he was pried off, but he was. Even with assistance though, the male would not heal quickly. His fights would not be the spectacles Neha hoped for. She attempted some kind of healing to her new bull, but her vanity was as deep as the wound, worsening the situation in ways even Onyx had not foreseen as she refused to let anyone else heal a wound a more skilled healer should have seen.

No bull of good standing attacked that male for the remainder of the season, more of the unspoken rules of courtesy. Only a handful of males with few morals and fewer qualms challenged, drawn by Neha's very pretty face and figure. Eventually, one won. She attempted to attract another male, any male. Even on the sexually charged atmosphere of the beach, few fell for her enticements and none far enough to put their heart into the fight. He found out later that she crept away from the beach one night to his family's home, hoping to coax his return. He was no longer there, he had left the island behind for the remainder of the season.

Since then, he had avoided the season. He traveled to this hidden hideaway or some other place that was away so he could be himself. When home he had used his skills to assist Otarii's and the other bull's healings from afar. The other bull had actually thanked him, Neha's allure had lost its pull once the season was over. As for Neha, she had refused to leave the beach and was finally bonded to a bull who had never wanted to get married and did not want to put effort into his fights. He won Neha towards the very end of the season; his family was not pleased and the pair's union would never be pleasant. From reports, Neha's mate often ignored her, no more fawning adoration for her, and her new mother-in-law kept Neha from flirting with others.

Onyx still felt regret for causing that unpleasant union, that had not been his intention. That his regret was mixed with a feeling of spiteful satisfaction did not help. She did not deserve a miserable life, but he knew he was not the only one who had foolishly fallen to her wiles and lost a friend. Neha had revelled in chaos and loved pitting friends against each other and then feigning ignorance, but her suitors were all at fault for not being smarter. He felt he could make peace with his part in that idiocy but the fact he had never been able to find the words to apologize to his old friend was a deeper shame.

Mer had been kind enough to dunk Onyx's head in a tidepool after he returned and tell him that he was an idiot, but Otarii and Onyx had never patched up their differences.

Onyx wanted to apologize, he truly did, but Otarii preferred to avoid him and he couldn't blame him. Space seemed to be the best gift he could give someone he'd once been close to. Even if he had apologized and somehow regained his friend, he couldn't fix everything. Something other than jewelry and trinkets had been destroyed that day on the beach. He had never realized how much he had hoped to be something beyond Onyx the odd one. He was the boy who could have put the witches of the salt brush to shame with his raw healing talent, but was forced to resort to sneakery and trickery to learn nuances of something that came naturally to him. He was willing to learn to fight and put his whole heart into it; but he wanted to be something more than a protector and provider and wanted someone more than a prize and partner won on the sands. Everything in his life felt skewed. That was a part of why he'd been stupid enough to fall for Neha. She had been desired by so many.

To win the heart of one so desired would have meant there was something right with him.

He wanted to be good enough, but that day had shown him that was not to be, that the normal path was wrong for him. Or he was wrong for it. So even though he missed his homelands as he traveled, he stayed away. He would continue with this until he found something to ease his emptiness or change him to what he should be.

Chapter 17 - Trickery

Laisha turned back to the bustle of the market. Stupid male.

Skin hunters. She scoffed at his words. Silly tales to scare pups into staying on their rock. She'd heard her share of excuses for not being able to perform, but that was the first time she had heard skin hunters used for it.

A man blocked the path to the market. She was wary. She was looking for a mate, not a tussle on the beach.

"Good day, sir."

"Good day. Did I hear you call someone a 'tusk-tangler'?" He was smiling and seemed charming, despite looking a bit rough around the edges.

She laughed, embarrassment covering her surprise that he'd understood her yells. "Ah, yes. He... ah... the gentleman was rude and I was angry."

"I've never heard that phrase before. Where're you from that they use that?" He kept his eyes on her, clearly interested and aware she was not a male. She preened a little on the inside, even as she realized she would need to take more care with her disguise.

"There's a chain of islands, far to the north and west of here. The Wyvern's Spine. Have you heard of them?" She let the lightest trill enter her voice. She did not want to play, but a little admiration would go a long way to soothe the sting of rejection from the bull.

"Yes. I've heard of them. I would love to hear more." He took her arm and led her along a side path. He was charming and she allowed it. "Aren't they the isles of the seal folk though?"

She smiled a seductive smile. "What if I told you a secret?"

"Oh, I like secrets, my lovely."

"You are talking to one of them."

His eyes went wide. "You're joking. Pretty creature like you, half beast?"

"Not a beast." She pouted.

"I don't believe you."

"Come. I'll show you." She took his hand, pulling him down the path they'd been strolling down. She knew it well enough and knew it led to an almost hidden little pool. She paused beside the pool, making a bit of a show of removing her clothes. Most humans were so adorable in their embarrassment. The man was no different, raising his eyebrows and turning his head with a cough.

She dived into the water, swimming in the nude for a moment before turning into a seal.

"I don't believe it." He whistled admiringly. "Are you sure you aren't wearing a fancy suit?" His words were teasing, but she pulled herself out of the water to show him and let him come close.

"A true beauty in either form. Thank you, miss. I hope my cousin does as well."

Laisha did not have enough time to puzzle out his strange declaration before the club cracked her skull.

Chapter 18 - Discovery

Onyx paused in his musings on the past once he neared the final rise before his home. He wandered to the waterside, deciding to have a wash and then deciding on a swim. He had been alone with his thoughts too long and was not sure what he would find at home, best to clear his head before returning.

His guest was intriguing, but her mysteries came tangled with their own problems. But he couldn't stop his curiosity. And not because she was a 'rescued stray', or not only because of that. Aislinn was fascinating, and she did not find any of his skills to be bizarre, even seeming to find his abilities intriguing. In the days since she had arrived, he had uncovered bits and pieces of her life, adding slowly to the tale of her, but he wanted to know more. She did not want to tell him everything, but he could sometimes see in her eyes the feeling of wanting to tell someone everything. He was certain he wore the same expression whenever the beaches were mentioned.

Adding to her mystery were the surprises she came up with. He had never thought to attempt using his voice and healing in tandem. He supposed it had become too much of a hidden skill to risk noise, though he had seen the witches singing back home. This new skill was a bit intense, but he had made strides with it the past few days. He was also intrigued by her skills in other magics, even though she had rarely shown him such, other than lighting the fire a few times and nearly drowning herself to communicate. That one she refused to explain further, simply stating that it was best left to wiser folk to explain. She had tried to teach him to light the fire, but they'd both stopped when he scorched the bedding.

He finally finished his swim and threw himself onto the beach to let the late afternoon sun dry his coat. An errant pebble rattled across the shore and brought his head up. A man held a crossbow, a sturdy bolt notched and ready to fire. He did not quite have the angle for a kill, but would clear the boulder in a moment. He was too far for Onyx to tackle.

Onyx reared up and roared, hoping to either threaten the man off or warn Aislinn. If he backed into the sea, the man would wait. If he searched Onyx's bundles or searched nearby, he could realize Onyx was not alone and find her. If that happened, she was dead. He had witnessed enough hunters drowning humans or smashing their bones to be certain they weren't a selkie in disguise. She was stronger than she had been, but she could not run far enough or fast enough to escape.

He mock charged and roared again, hoping that if the man wouldn't run, he'd at least get close enough for an attack.

The man's eyes darted to the side, glancing down the path, but keeping Onyx in his peripheral vision.

"That's why you left the lovely cow by the market. Never heard a bull let out a sound like that unless he was protecting something."

He seemed to be considering which way to go. Hunters often went for the weaker ones first, it drew in protective parents and partners. Onyx was relieved when the man made the decision to ease around the rock for a clear shot at him. "Silver coat and couple cows in one day. Must be a lucky day for my crew."

"Not really. This 'cow' is something far more dangerous than a selkie." Aislinn appeared and she had Onyx's bow aimed at the man.

"That so?" The man was clearly not used to having a weapon aimed at him, but was still managing to keep an eye on both of them.

"It is. I suggest you lower your bow and step away."

"Aw, miss, I don't think you wanna shoot me. You see, I have your friend in my crosshairs and this bow is special. It has a rare little thing you might not have heard of called-"

"It has a dead man's trigger. I can see that, idiot. Anyone with working eyes can see that. It's the only reason I haven't shot you yet. Or did you think my aim was really that bad?" Her tone was dry and no-nonsense.

The man opened his mouth and then closed it, he couldn't seem to find a retort or fully recover from his surprise. Onyx didn't blame him, he was growing used to Aislinn's surprises and he was startled by this new and interesting store of knowledge.

"Well, then you know-" The man tried to regain his superior air, but Aislinn had thrown him hopelessly off balance and wasn't letting up.

"I know that you're going to die one way or another if you don't turn or lower your weapon. You're choosing to have a stare down with a dragon. I was trained in archery by elves and even if I do somehow miss my first shot, I will have the second in you before you've even thought of reloading the crossbow." She shifted slightly, more steel entering her tone. Onyx realized she was avoiding putting weight on her bad leg and wondered how much longer she could keep up with the bravado. "Either way, it will end badly. Question is: how badly?"

"Well, either way, he dies." The man was now turned far enough towards Aislinn that he couldn't see Onyx. If Onyx moved silently, they had a chance. He rolled quietly out of the line of fire before shifting.

"Then so do you. Loose your arrow, assure your death. Lower your weapon, we might all survive this night." Her eyes were fixed on the hunter, but Onyx somehow felt she saw him and was stalling for him. He edged closer to the man.

"I think you're bluffing, little girl, you'd never kill a man."

"Oh, true." Her tone was chilling, the hunter seemed wary now and was completely focused on her. Fair, for Onyx was reminded that she was the creature that had fought the waves and won when she continued. "Never a man. But I have absolutely no problems with cleaning up a bit of slimy rot, whatever the shape it takes." She slightly lowered her bow and the man took what he thought was an opening to attempt a shot at Aislinn.

Onyx was close enough to strike. The crossbow went off and Onyx heard a second shot whistle by. There was a scream from the hunter and, in the same moment, something metallic clattered on the rocky beach. Onyx locked his limbs around the man like a constrictor. The hunter flailed with his arms, attempting to loosen Onyx's stranglehold, but he only succeeded in drawing blood from Onyx's forearms.

Onyx could hear Aislinn stumbling and sliding down the beach through the blood pounding in his ears. There was a sharp crack as something struck the man's skull and he went limp. Onyx continued holding on.

After a bit, he realized she was talking to him. Her tone was soothing, gentle.

"He's dead, Onyx. You can let go."

Onyx loosened his grip and rolled the corpse off him. Aislinn flipped it onto its back and drove a dagger into the heart. He realized she had used the other end of the dagger against the man's skull.

"I thought you said he was dead."

"If you haven't guessed, I lead a very strange life. Always best to make sure." She pulled the blade out and shook her head. "Rondel. Well used. Guessing this blade fits just perfectly between a selkie's skull and the tip-top of their spine." She reversed her grip, flipping it with ease he would have found unnerving if he hadn't reached his limit for being surprised this night. "Weighted and reinforced hilt. Slight point to the top. Perfect for... well, what I just did."

She glanced down at the body.

"Perhaps too nice and poetic of an ending for you to be killed by your own weapon. But an end is an end." She tucked the knife in her belt and scooted around the body. "I need oil. And ginkgo... ah... maidenhair is another name for it... if you have it. Otherwise his friends will be looking for him before we have a chance to scatter."

It took him a moment to realize that she was asking him for these items. He nodded and sprinted to the house. The flask of oil was easy, the ginkgo took a bit longer and he was only able to find a few leaves of it. She was folded over by the path to the market when he returned. He had no idea how she'd reached it so quickly. He spied a small dust devil twirling off into the distance.

"What did you do?"

"I'm buying us time. It won't erase his steps, but it will blur them enough that maybe by the time they think to come and look for him, they'll be gone. Help me over to his body."

Onyx did as she asked, noting it was now closer to the water and in between the tide lines. He handed her the oil and leaves.

"I had few leaves."

"It's enough," she said. He watched as she crushed the leaves and mixed it into the oil. She brushed it in a line down the corpse. Her head was nearly brushing its toes when she reached them. She tore a strip off the bottom of her shirt, apologizing as she did so. "Sorry, I'll find you a new one. I just don't have the energy to wait for rags and I forgot to ask."

She slicked the fabric with the remainder of the oil mixture and wrapped it loosely around her forearm.

"You may want to back away."

He took it as a command instead of a suggestion, but stayed close enough to help her if things went wrong. Every part of him wanted to help more, but he knew whatever she was doing was outside of his expertise. She stared off into the sky, but he swore she was focusing inwards. The rag smoldered for a second, a thin trail of smoke running down it for a moment before it was a line of pure fire. She loosened it from her arm and tossed it, roughly draping it across the corpse. The tiny crescents of oil caught fire, even those nowhere near the burning rag. He pulled her back as the flames became white hot and she leaned into him.

"I'm so sorry. I... don't think I can walk back to the hut," she said.

He half dragged, half carried her back to the hut. He only returned for the supplies once he had her in bed. When he returned he saw that the corpse fire was tightly contained and although it was hard to be sure in the bright light of the fire, he swore a good portion of the body had disappeared in the small time it had taken to get Aislinn to the hut. He tossed the remains of the man's crossbow on top. The thing had been smashed beyond repair in the scuffle.

Aislinn was sitting up when he entered.

"Your arms." She pointed as she spoke.

He felt the burn and sting and looked down to see scratches from the hunter's fingers. His back stung as well, likely from being shoved across the rocks and sand as the man tried to escape him.

"Easy to heal," he said and followed up his words by doing so.

Onyx continued focusing on simple things. Food. There was something roasting in the cooking pot. He reached for the lid and Aislinn advised him it needed a short time more. One thing done. He turned to putting his purchases away, waving off her assistance with these tasks. To delay any further arguments on that, he handed her the clothes and a few trinkets he had purchased for her. She thanked him profusely, but watched him warily. He found himself bemused by her look. She was the one who had burned a corpse, struck the killing blow, and apparently had a whole trove of secret and dangerous talents and she was wary of him.

He pondered this whole situation until he had dished up food for both of them. Rice and bird flesh? Quail or pheasant or something similar? He swallowed and frowned at her.

"Is it not to your liking?" She gave him an innocent look.

"It is delicious. You were supposed to rest."

"I did save you by not resting as you intended. Besides, I'm fair terrible at doing what I'm supposed to do."

"Is that why you can burn a body?"

She half choked on a mouthful of her food and silently fought it before answering, expression laden with chagrin.

"Amusingly enough, no. That's more a function of what I am supposed to do."

"You are supposed to... burn bodies?" He stared at her in confusion. Her homeland was even stranger than he'd heard. He was almost glad he'd never traveled as far as the elven cities she'd spoken of if this was normal.

"Ah... only if we make them and then only sometimes. The spell was an invention of my brother's. He's quite the genius with magic." She winced and leaned forward to refill her bowl.

"More answers, please."

"So direct now. This is awkward."

"Thank you for rescue."

"You're more than welcome, you saved my life." She ate in silence for a few moments before speaking again. "My clan is... we are required to fix things. There were a handful of dragon clans... elected... to such a position. Most have been lost to time. The deAvarics still survive."

"Fix things?"

"Dragons are meant to protect the more fragile ones, whether it be humans or elves or whomever. That is our purpose. But we are strong. Strong in body, in magic, in will. It's almost inevitable that some of us will try to rule or destroy or subjugate instead. When that happens, the elders call on us. While waiting for that call, we find other, similar, work. Don't. Ask. Be glad I'm giving you this much." She pointed her spoon at him to punctuate, then quickly finished her second bowl. She set it down for a moment. "Sometimes we must be covert. That spell? The body should be ash by now. The maidenhair is used in reverse, instead of aiding the memory, it poisons the memory. It's nearly impossible to make someone completely forget, but foggy is far simpler."

"Foggy?" Onyx felt he understood, but wanted slightly more clarification. This was terrifying, but fascinating at the same time.

"His friends may realize he's gone, but when they ask each other, they'll remember the last time they saw him and it will seem like a moment since then. So they won't worry, at least not for a bit. The spell isn't permanent, but it buys us a few days."

"Why would you not use this if you 'fix' someone?"

"Well," she paused and winced apologetically before continuing, "Sometimes a body hung on a pike is a more effective fix."

"Oh." He finished his bowl and set it aside. He was generally talented at catching lies, but she had him questioning himself now. Everything she had said rang true. "So, were you actually visiting your mate?"

"Sadly, yes. And before you ask, I can't kill him. For many reasons. The first being he is actually a good lord to his people. Firm, but he takes care of and protects his folk and his lands. The second being that to do so, I would start a war and… my brothers would be the ones tasked with hunting me. I wouldn't do that to us," she paused for a very long time, "The third being, I can't. These scars on my back… it's a ritual. Once it's complete, you can't hurt each other anymore. At least not directly. Not physically. Magic always has loopholes. I can generally will my way past it enough to slap him, well, it's more like reflexive fury, but even that has repercussions. I slap his face and I feel it on mine. To be honest, killing him might kill me. Though I'm spiteful enough to consider it some days... but pointless either way. And I can't undo it. There's... more, but those are the most relevant ones. So... any further questions?"

"Yes, but not on that. Not right now." He was so curious, but he forced himself to focus. "We have time before we are followed?"

"Most likely a few days. At most. I could reach out to my brothers, but spellwise, I'm drained enough I'm not sure I could reach them tonight and once I did reach them... it would take them at least a day, if not more, to locate us and then to get here... it depends on which method they use to come and we should be on the move by then. I'd rather get some space between us and hunters before calling out to them."

"You can't travel far on that leg." Onyx was healing his arms and back as he listened.

"I can fly."

"But what would you eat when you land? And where would you sleep?"

"You had to distract me with details." She laughed a hollow laugh. "I must try to travel. If I don't, we're dead. Oh, and the girl. He said two cows. We have to try to warn whoever the second one is."

"She was near the market. She is gone. I tried to lead her out of there, but I offended her." Onyx winced.

"How?"

"I pretended interest and once we were out of the market, told her of danger. She did not like rejection."

"Ah. Well. Yes. Of course you offended her. Nobody likes rejection." She paused in thought. "No longer our problem. You tried." She stared at him for a moment, then suddenly laughed. "Oh. That's what the mark on your neck is."

He blinked, winced, and closed his eyes.

"Yeeees."

"I thought you said you rejected her." She smirked and he began to squirm. She refilled her bowl and mercifully switched subjects. "I'm starving, do you like the food? Have I asked you that already?"

"Is your whole family like this?" He wasn't sure where his question came from, but he wasn't certain what else to say.

"To varying degrees. Why?"

"I think maybe insane."

She laughed. "It's been mentioned a few times, and sometimes more of an accusation, but what some people call insanity is merely doing what is not expected and when you aren't where others expect you, doing what they expect you to do... well, it's that much harder for them to kill you."

He blinked. "That made sense. I'm afraid am becoming like you."

She laughed, a low laugh with a sly smile that sent pleasant shivers through him, even though he knew it wasn't meant to.

"I don't know if I should pity you or be complimented, Onyx. Either way, that may get us through this."

The rest of the meal was eaten in silence and all the plates, shells, and utensils cleaned and put away before more discussion took place.

"Do you know of a place to hide nearby?" Aislinn asked, breaking the silence.

"There are a handful of islands near. Any would work, I have small canoe hidden nearby, we could use it and go..." he paused, weighing their options, "South. We should go south. There is an island... one most avoid. Legend says is alive. Magic. Magic makes most hunters afraid."

"Unless they can turn it into coin."

"The island is not like that." He shook his head, trying to think of how to describe it.

"You've been there?"

"Once. It made me..." He searched for words. "It feels strange."

"Ah. One of those places. Well, that could be beneficial or horrifying. We'll try it though. For now, sleep." She slipped between the blankets and laid the hunter's knife within easy reach.

Onyx was removing his clothes so he could switch to seal when she made a sound. He turned to face her, not sure of the meaning.

"Stay in that form for now. I trust you and if we can't sleep, we can plan. You're quite adorable as a seal, but your conversational skills are lacking."

"Maybe you need to learn to speak selkie." He edged under the covers, clothes somehow making him more aware that he was beneath the blankets with someone. "I know how to speak your language."

"My language - well, the one you mean - is Elven, you know how to speak Amarantine, not quite the same. That said, I would love to. In all forms. Right now doesn't seem like the best time for lessons." Her tone was dry, but the slightest smile curled round and warmed the edges of it.

Her back was comforting and warm against his. He would have to see what he could do about her leg in the morning. She was asleep almost before he was completely settled in and he found himself wondering what further surprises would occur.

Chapter 19 - Flight

Aislinn woke first. Her leg was protesting being used and her body was protesting the drain from magic. Her mind was surprisingly sharp, courtesy of her dragon blood preparing for a fight. She sighed, resigned and frustrated that the sleep she needed was no longer a possibility, and eased out from under the furs. Onyx snapped awake at her movement, alert and poised to fight.

"Calm. Just hurt a little and waking up. No hunters." She winced as her movements made her aware of how stiff she was. Build the fire up. She needed to start somewhere and that was an easy task. At least it would be once she crawled there. "Do you always wake up like that?" He mumbled something in response she didn't understand. "Could you repeat that?"

He shook his head and she realized he wasn't quite as awake as he had seemed.

"It means... beach sleep? In season, you sleep lightly and wake ready for a fight. I thought it best to reach that state of sleep for now." His words were slightly slurred.

"Careful. You're the healthy one of us. You can't be wearing yourself out."

He grunted and rolled out of bed, shifting the pot over the fire to reheat last night's supper.

She watched him drowsily move about. Drowsily, but efficiently. At least until he edged up beside her to work on her leg. He lingered for a long moment with the rag above the bowl, seemingly somewhere far off. He blinked suddenly, shaking his head again.

"You have interesting tattoos." He began work on her leg nonchalantly, alternately focused and drifting off into... Aislinn wasn't sure where his mind was, but the tattoo comment led her to believe it was not quite as far as imagined. Her clan tattoo was nestled between her breasts. She had a handful of others corresponding to various ranks and connections and they were scattered about her body. A tattoo of the elven knights rested on her right hip and a mark indicating her rank within the deAvaric clan had been placed along her left inner elbow. None of those should have been visible to him as most of her tattoos remained invisible unless needed to be seen, but the elven was not far above where Onyx was working and he was surprisingly adept at seeing what he shouldn't. The only constantly visible one was a colorful traveling folk tattoo on her left shoulder blade, and he was not at an angle to see that. She kept silent, he didn't seem to expect a response and as much as she trusted him, she couldn't tell him the meanings of all of them. She put his ability aside in her mind, it was useful, but not to them at this time.

He paused in his ministrations after a few moments. His sleep-mussed hair was now falling in his face. He re-tied it and paused again once he finished, staring at the basin dumbly for a moment. He was clearly not awake. He glanced at her and his look lingered; she heard the low hum begin in his throat. Intuition warned he would attempt to kiss her but then the second passed and he was working with the rags and water again. She hoped he would not wake up this way every day. A tiny part of her also hoped he would. Her indecision and the resulting lack of focus on their immediate problems irritated her.

By the time he finished with her leg, he seemed mostly awake and breakfast was ready. While they ate, she watched his eyes scrutinize every item in the hut. Once the meal was finished, he found an extra pouch and a pack that would work for Aislinn and she began packing. She was fairly efficient, as she had almost nothing, so waited on Onyx, knowing she would need to take part of his load.

He started out hesitantly, picking at items and looking torn. This she had expected and she was prepared to help him choose. Then, he became another Onyx; one that was ruthless in his sorting. If it was not to go in one of their packs, it was tossed in the fire. He contemplated the bow and arrow for a moment and then handed them to her. He grabbed a short spear. Trinkets too delicate to pack or not likely to be useful for a quick trade were tossed in the fire, even a few she'd watched him work for hours on. It was agonizing to see all his work burn.

She reflexively snatched one item before it hit the fire - the half-finished bone pendant in the shape of a six pointed star. He had placed white stones corresponding to the elements on the white half of the star, and dark stones on the dark half. It had no back signifying spirit yet. Even so, it reminded her of childhood tales of the elements and how the different peoples were born. It also brought to mind her son, carrying her pendant with pride. She realized if she died at the hunter's hands, it would make it too easy for Kaienar to pretend his lies were truth. That spite gave her a cold focus, while at the same time she was warmed by a nearer memory of watching Onyx create it on that safe day that felt like an age ago. She looked up and met his eyes that were wide with surprise.

"Some things are too nice to waste." She flashed a lop-sided smile at him as she hung the pendant around her neck and continued packing. Any supplies not packed went into the fire. They finished long before daybreak and Onyx led the way to the shore, pausing frequently to scan the horizon for any sign of hunters. A small boat rested on the beach above the tide line. They moved it to the water and Onyx lifted her into the boat, ignoring her protests. She stuck her tongue out at him once she was settled. She was rewarded with a now familiar teasing tilt of his head for a moment before he prepared to shift.

Aislinn took his clothes as he stripped, tucking them in one of the bags and mostly keeping her eyes focused on the land and not the sea where Onyx's physique was swiftly becoming more visible. She sighed inwardly. Exhaustion and his earlier mood was ruining her focus. Pants hit the side of her head and she twisted about to yell at him. She froze and kept her eyes stubbornly locked with his when she realized he was still in his human guise; she was trying not to laugh. Onyx smirked impishly before shifting and grabbing hold of the rope tied to the front of the boat. Silver-coated brat.

The rope ended in a loop tied into a makeshift harness that allowed him to tow the boat along easily. Aislinn stayed low so as not to be seen, frustrated there was not more she could do at this moment.

The second island took almost an hour to reach. Once there, Onyx carefully circled the boat around to the far side before pulling up on shore. She was impressed with his ability to navigate in the dim light and the morning mists and rewarded him by not fighting when he assisted her exit from the boat.

They rested in the dampness beneath the tall trees, letting weary bodies sink into the moss carpet for a few moments. Aislinn kept guard, Onyx allowed it without a fuss, well aware he was their transport and navigator. The morning mists had not yet cleared by the time they set out to the next isle. When they paused on this smaller island, Onyx actually slumbered for a bit.

Aislinn wished she could join him, but even if she hadn't been on lookout, she already felt the presence of the island they were headed towards. It was ancient and wild and sang at the edges of her consciousness in a way that would not let her sleep. She hoped this was the right choice, but events had been set in motion and they risked more by turning back now. She thought of her brothers and could remember Daren teasing her as a child that she had no reverse. It had been followed by Damian's instructions not to hesitate. Better to choose wrong, commit, and adjust. Hesitation was standing still. Rin's archery lessons taught her all she needed to know about standing still.

She fiddled with the dagger she had taken from the skin hunter. She hated using tools of an enemy, but she had checked it for spells - even having Onyx glance at it - and his hut had not been overburdened with weapons. The knife she used around the house was not built for fighting, even though it could be used as such in a pinch. She wanted to call for Damian while she waited; she had accidentally tried in the night, but wandered, unable to find him or home. It had made for poor sleep, and they needed more strength than they had if hunters found them. She was talented enough at a fight that she was almost certain she could compensate for her leg in a battle with a single opponent, but lack of knowledge on the size of the crew following them dampened any confidence.

She flipped the dagger, caught it and watched as the mists cleared. All except in the direction of the isle they were bound for. Ominous, but expected. She knew there were more than a few bastions of old magics in these waters, including some under the water itself. She wished again she knew more about the skin hunters trailing them. Most would avoid a place steeped in magic, but the hunters' proximity... those that did not could be dangerous beyond belief.

She watched Onyx sleep. He looked so sweet and innocent and he had the lips of a sleeping prince in a folktale Daren had once told her. They practically begged to be kissed. She leaned against a tree and sat down, reaching the limits of what her leg could take for a bit. And the limits of her self-restraint. She decided to let her mind wander a wee bit and indulged in the stories for a bit.

She suspected the originals did not go as Daren told them - likely only similar in passing, knowing her brother - but the tales of a useless prince and clever lady of the night were amusing nonetheless. Not really helpful to their survival at this time, unless one counted that re-telling them in her head was a reasonable way to pass the time. Experience had taught her how long each tale took to tell herself. She'd often used her brothers' songs and stories as a way to track time. She had reached the third story of this series and the part where the heroine had seduced the guards when Onyx awoke. The day was cloudy, but she knew a quarter of the daylight had been spent resting, more than enough time to reach the island before nightfall.

"I feel the island." He exhaled slowly and stared off into the distance.

"I know, I can sense it as well. Ready to go there?"

"No, but we will be safer there than here."

There were oars in the boat and this time Aislinn used them while Onyx swam alongside. Both doubted that they would be spotted and neither had the energy left to do more than their share. Once they reached the bank of fog, the previous island refused to get further away no matter how hard Aislinn rowed. Onyx began towing the boat again but was unable to make headway either. They attempted to turn around and the edges of the fog would not let them return to their previous destination.

After hours of fighting to make headway either direction, and nearing exhaustion, the day slid into night. In the moments between, the other island disappeared and fog surged around them. The pair threw every last bit of energy into propelling the boat along, landing on the shore just as night closed in. Aislinn felt the ethers and magics of this place close in as well; to her senses it was as solid as a gate slamming shut against intruders.

"Only in or out at the in-between times," she said as she gasped between breaths.

Onyx glanced at her, he hadn't bothered to change back, and his grey flanks heaved with fatigue.

"We weren't moving until afternoon edged into twilight. The island limits passage." She pulled the boat as far up on the beach as she could, then lifted their supplies out of the boat and knelt beside Onyx, pressing her face into his side. "It means they can't get in at just any time. It also means we can't escape at any time." She inhaled his damp and briny scent and he gently nuzzled her head. Neither one had the energy to leave the beach, but they somehow forced themselves to after several moments and Onyx returned to his bipedal form.

Trees rose above them like ancient sentinels silently watching over the island. An uneven carpet of moss, ferns, and fallen needles spread beneath their branches, and their feet sank silently and somewhat gratefully into the soft green. The air pulsed with power, like the steady heartbeat of a wild creature. There was no taming of this place, and to even think of such felt like sacrilege. It was a dangerous place for the unwary. Despite that air, the island still felt safer than attempting to fight the skin hunters.

They stumbled into a comfortable patch of moss between the trees and collapsed. Onyx somehow found enough energy to dig out a blanket to cover them. Aislinn buried her face in his shoulder and closed her eyes, letting sleep overtake her.

Chapter 20 - Hunters

Aarn frowned at the waves. It had taken him half a day to realize Peli was missing, and when he did, nobody could remember when he'd last been seen. He had finally sent a few of the boys out to see if they could find where he had wandered off to. Vari had managed to track him to this beach.

There were traces of soot on the rocks and a smell in the air that spoke of cremation. Aarn doubted he'd ever see his brother on this side of the veil again, and their confusion made more sense. Bodies did not burn so fast without the help of magic. He would fair love to know what trickery had been used to turn Peli's body and memory into so much ash. He doubted the chance of learning such a useful trick as he scattered the ashes with his boot. His cousins, Dalan and Gamble, called to him from over the rise. They had found the creature's lair.

Aarn limped up the beach. His leg had nearly been torn off by a huge bull years ago, but that limp and a tattered scar were the only remaining traces. Mostly, the limp was minimal, but the wound was acting up with the shift in the seasons. It irritated him to no end when it did that. Other than the leg, he was a sturdy, barrel-chested man; practically a dominant bull on two legs, but the limp slowed him down when he least wanted it.

The hut was small, hidden amongst downed tree roots and seagrass. To his eye, it also had the look of being recently abandoned.

He shoved his way inside to verify his suspicions, eyeing the chaos with a scowl.

"Vindictive bastard." The other men all looked at him. "Tossed everything he wasn't taking in the fire." Aarn noted the things in the fire had not burned as thoroughly as his brother.

"Looks like there's two sets of tracks heading to the beach." Vari had reappeared silently and was leaning against the door frame behind Aarn, if leaning was the word. He was half bent over as his tall rail-thin frame overflowed the top of the door.

"Bull had a missus hiding here. Or maybe another bull." Aarn squinted at a speck on a low shelf and scraped it loose. Grey fur. Seal by the texture. "We got us a silvercoat. At least one, mebbe two."

"That Shay mage I sell to is mad for one of those. Said for years that he'd pay us at least ten times the going rate for a silvercoat male, twenty for a female," Dalan offered.

Aarn nodded appreciatively at the information. The mage Dalan spoke of was a steady client, a guaranteed profit. He prayed the grey belonged to a female, but even if it did not they'd be well set for a while. He knew the odds, and either way, they were in his crew's favor with this hunt. Enough males traveled to other colonies or ran off to lick their wounds that finding them alone or in small groups wasn't that uncommon. Females were so much harder to find outside their colonies, and almost never alone. But they were much more likely to have a full, unabused coat for trade, like the one Dalan had caught yesterday. With males it could be a game of how much skin could be salvaged. He was surprised more of the bastards didn't die with how hard they beat on each other. Some days he wished they would, as any part could be sold, even if skins were worth the most and had the most stable going rates.

"Well, looks like they finished off Peli. My brother never was smart enough to know when to back off and call for a second hand."

He glanced around, the others waiting expectantly. "We'll follow them and finish them off. For vengeance and for profit."

Aarn stepped outside the hut and unsheathed his dagger. The speck of fur would never be enough to trace the seals, but he hadn't seen his brother's dagger anywhere. Not even a big enough lump of metal by the ashes. The blades were twins forged of the same metal on the same day and under the leather wrapping of their hilts were a few strands of each brother's hair. Subtle and very easily missed, even if checking the daggers for trouble. Tracking the other blade was about all that could be done with it, but it had led them to more than a few pickpockets. A good blade for hunting selkies was hard to come by.

"Heading south."

"Not back home then. No colonies left in the south. And he looked to be from the selkie cities if it's the one I saw with the cow in the market," offered Gamble.

"She was from Wyvern's Spine," added Dalan.

"Then what's south that a seal would head for?" Aarn mused on it for a few moments before finding the answer in the vast sea charts stored in his memory. "Muquin."

Vari nodded. "Makes sense, one of them is a magic user."

"We'll head back to the market. Grab Stanen, pack up, and head out with the ship before the next tide has turned." Aarn tucked his dagger back in its scabbard. "Might even have a chance to use one of the dogs on this hunt." The men had varied reactions to that. Gamble was silent, eyebrows raised in surprise, but said nothing. He rarely questioned his captain, at least, not out loud. Dalan smirked as he toyed with his cudgel, the dogs were his specialty.

"Do you think either one is ready, captain? They still seem a mite unpredictable to me." Vari was never much for new ideas. He liked the tried and true methods.

"Longshanks ain't by a longshot, can't even remove that one's muzzle without trouble. Dark should be good to go though." Aarn tossed his keyring to Gamble. "Get him up on deck and ready when we get on the ship." Aarn was far from pleased by the day's turn of events, but perhaps a small win could be pulled from it. He would take what he could.

Chapter 21 - Cover

Aislinn woke first again. She sleepily brushed Onyx's hair out of his face and a very light sound escaped his throat. It was full of seductive selkie overtones.

"Must be a very good dream." She was amused, but spoke softly as she carefully edged away from him. The air was chill. She could almost feel the sunlight at the edge of the blackness; the world was poised in the inbetween hours, waiting for the change to morning. She explored nearby, finding a shallow cave that had potential as an actual shelter for them. No telling how long they would have to wait here, moss beneath the trees was comfy enough for a night, but she'd feel safer with cover. She hoped the hunters would at least stay back until her brothers arrived, but if their backs were against a wall, she preferred a more solid wall. Best case would be the pursuers leaving without even trying, but best case was often the rarest case.

She sniffed the air as she edged into the hollow space and looked about. She wanted complete assurance that she wasn't encroaching on any creature's home. The cavity turned slightly after the entrance and stopped shortly after that. Perfect. She gathered firewood and tinder from nearby and quickly had a fire started. She put it right after the turn in the cave.

She left the cave to gather their things and almost stumbled into Onyx.

"You are too quiet." She tried to keep her annoyance with herself from entering her voice. She should have been paying more attention.

"I woke and you were gone."

"I was looking for a better place to camp." She gestured to the cave "And I found one."

He stepped around her and nosed into the cave. He circled around the fire, examining the floor space before ducking out and returning moments later with some of the packs. He dropped them and ducked out again before Aislinn could protest that she could get her own things. Once he returned with the remainder he began laying bedding out and organizing things from the packs. He noticed her watching and paused mid crouch as he was setting a small pot by the fire. She shook her head.

"You'll run around naked, but the winds and tides might stop if our packs stay packed a moment longer than necessary," she said.

"If you would not worry so much about wearing clothes, we could do more," He pursed his lips, then laughed, covering his laughter with his hand as his cheeks turned red. "Those words were not what I meant." He hung his head in embarrassment.

"Are you certain? Sounds like you were trying to take advantage of our situation." She laughed and assisted with sorting out their packs. She had grown somewhat accustomed to his nudity. Somewhat. He honestly seemed to forget to wear clothes if they weren't needed for something. She wondered if he did the same back in his colony. She then found herself wondering if everyone did the same back at his colony. The thought was distracting and she realized again how little she knew about selkie culture, even though she had tried to learn about it as a child. She wondered if outsiders were required to follow whatever the selkie nudity rules were when visiting.

She looked up once she realized Onyx was now silent. He was still red-faced and smiling nervously at her. She smiled back. He looked towards the entrance.

"Sleep. I will watch," he said.

"You need rest too."

"You are healing, and I only need to watch during the turning hours." He waved towards the bedding. "Sleep."

She laid down. No reason to argue with him for now. She honestly was not certain she could rest, but her body welcomed the feel of bedding like an old friend. She closed her eyes and was asleep almost before he left the cave.

Chapter 22 - Sea Dogs

Once they were a short ways out from shore, Aarn went below decks. The first thing he heard was Gamble cursing.

"What?"

"Longshanks. Kicked his food and slop bucket all over the place."

Aarn sighed. "We may have to process him if this keeps up. And Dark?"

"Take a look. Dalan did well. With that one." Gamble waved him into the hold.

Aarn was pleased to see that Dark - named for the near black color of his seal pelt - was sitting in his cage in human form, head bowed, calm and quiet. His pale skin was scarred and he was missing part of an ear, but that was better than how they found him. His skin wouldn't have fetched a decent price at market, but Dalan had suggested that with training Dark could help them catch more of his kind. Aarn's hopes this would pay off seemed to be looking up, Dark had proved trainable.

Longshanks, well, that one was sitting and glaring at Aarn and Gamble. He had been fairly torn up when they'd found him a few weeks back, mostly in his attempt to escape them, but his skin had healed well, he might be worth more as a skin. They couldn't uncover his mouth for much more than eating. He would try to influence Dark if they did and the cheek he threw at them was beyond belief. Aarn was almost certain they would have to skin that one. What a waste of time. The infuriating creature smirked at him with his eyes as if reading his thoughts and daring them to try.

"Take Dark topside. We'll deal with Longshanks later. Let him sit in his filth."

The selkie's eyes darted to the floor and back to Aarn's face. He could see a grin even behind the gag and muzzle. Gamble grumbled.

"He somehow kicked it clear of hisself."

"Later. Leave the filth about. We have a hunt."

Gamble looped a thin leather strap around Dark's neck. The selkie trembled slightly but did not fight or strain the strap when the cage was opened and his shackles were released. He followed Gamble to the deck quietly and obediently.

Aarn felt something smack against the back of his head as he turned to follow. He touched his hand to the spot reflexively, even though there was no need. He could tell by the smell what it was.

He turned to see Longshanks wiping his foot on the side of his bars. Aarn had no doubt now that he was smiling behind the gag.

"You won't be smiling when you're being flayed alive."

Longshanks raised one eyebrow doubtfully. He had quickly figured out the limits to when and where they would beat him, another issue with him. Aarn stalked away to the top deck, annoyed that they were likely both aware that if Dark was being used, the crew did not have the time to deal with the other selkie. Aarn consoled himself with the fact that at least one of the selkies had been trainable.

The winds and tides were favorable and brought them near Muquin sooner than expected. Unfortunately, that meant little as the timing was not correct to enter the waters around the island. Dalan carved up fish and tossed them to the selkie who was now in seal form. It obeyed his every word. Dalan was an uncompromising trainer, it was surprising he could not make the other one behave. Then again, Dark had taken a few months and he had been more pliable than Longshanks to begin with. It had been a risky gamble, but one did not make coin without taking some clever risks and at least one had paid off. And Longshank's skin would be worth more now than when he had been discovered.

Aarn attempted to locate his brother's dagger again. It felt like it was on the nameless island behind them, but it was there so suddenly after traveling steadily in the direction of Muquin that he suspected a trick of the island. No harm in being certain while they waited though.

"Vari, Gamble! Take the dinghy and check that island." He hooked his thumb in the direction of the visible island. "Knife's tracking strange and I wanna make sure we don't miss our silver coat."

"Skipped back?" Dalan tossed the last strip of fish to Dark.

"Yep. Likely Muquin playing her tricks, but worth a look."

"We can send Dark to Muquin if they aren't back by the turn of the tide." Dalan scratched the seal's chin. "What do you think, Dark? Can you find a bull and bring it back? Bring him back in the condition you brought that last seal back in." Aarn noticed Dark was wincing less at Dalan's touch now. He was almost leaning into the scratching.

"Sounds alright to me." Vari nodded and sheathed a knife he had been sharpening. "But if we lose the dog, ye can't blame me and Gam for being dumb enough to let him go with no supervision."

"Hush. I'll bet you that fine brocade coat you bought at market that Dark can bring back something worthwhile before you," said Dalan.

"Challenge accepted. I'll take that bottle of wine you've been saving if I win." Vari tipped his hat as neared the ladder.

"Done. When you lose, I might even give you a sip while celebrating in my new coat," said Dalan. He roared with laughter as Vari gestured rudely before disappearing over the side.

Everyone went their separate ways and Aarn kept his eyes on Muquin. She was a tricky one. Feast or famine for hunters who touched her shores. No in-between. He was staring her down now as he always did when hunts brought him this way. She had not beaten him yet and he felt certain this time she would give up her treasures as well.

Chapter 23 - Betrayal

As she slept, Aislinn was trying her hardest to reach out to her brothers, but the island kept twisting her back to places in her memories she would rather not revisit.

She had never been good at obedience without a reason. Maybe that was why she couldn't just listen to her brothers the one time it mattered most. Most things were self-explanatory, so she rarely rebelled. Perhaps that was why they had let down their guard with her rebelling. And even though she trusted one of her brothers beyond measure, when Damian had informed her that wedding Kaienar or binding herself in any way to him would be ill-advised, her heart had refused to follow its normal path. And he gave no explanation she could see or grasp, merely told her to ask Kaienar.

In hindsight, Aislinn understood why he had made that choice. She was in love, the explanation would have had more weight coming from the object of her affection. Kaienar was honest and honorable.

At least until he wasn't.

She was watching the waterfalls in the woods. They were rushing torrents, swollen with spring floods instead of their usual lacey curtains of water. Kai landed in the clearing behind her, clearly eager for their union. She was eager as well, even though her brothers' misgivings left worry she couldn't put aside.

"It's different in the spring, wilder." Speaking about their secret clearing in the woods seemed safer than asking questions she might not want the answer to.

"Have you decided?" He was nervous, for him. She could see the slightest hint of panic in his eyes that she might refuse him, even though the rest of his face remained stoic.

"Why are my brothers opposed to our marriage?"

"What do you mean?" He looked confused, she thought it possible he didn't know.

"Damian said to ask you why marrying you would be a bad idea." She waited for an answer. Now she knew that wait for what it was, but at the time, it seemed as if he was carefully weighing her question and not wanting to put words into their mouths.

"Between clan politics and the restrictions of my court, your brothers believe this would be a long slow death for you." His answer wasn't a lie, but it had lacked the most important reason. And his next part had been a lie, in part. "I... I don't think they're wrong, but I swear I will do what I can to make a life for you here."

Her mind ran with this simple explanation, never thinking about the fact Damian had never placed enough importance on status and politics to stop her. He would remind her that their clan had duties and that wedding a member of another clan could look like favoritism, but the deAvaric clan was connected to many clans. If anything, a clan implying that being a deAvaric was not prestigious enough for them would have made him more likely to encourage it. He did not wish to lord over others, but he tolerated no belittling of their status.

Kaienar's court being too restrictive made sense, and she found out later had been one true concern of Damian's. They had a culture that prided itself on self-discipline and harmony. Aislinn could live in it, but had caused more than a few waves in her visits.

She remembered standing there for a few moments after the decision was made, both breathing the other in, deepening the connection dragons gained through scent. He began to nip and lick at her neck and she reciprocated.

Sensuous turned threatening as dragons were made for fight; even their bonding rituals were bloody. She moved first, dancing out of range of his hands, she had her wings out, tail twitching slightly. Then they were fighting and it made any prior sparring matches look tame even though they had no weapons. It went on for nearly an hour and they were both breathing hard by the end. Kaienar tried rushing her in a final attack and she threw him to the ground. They were exhausted, eyes blazing like bonfires after their fierce battle. Males had to be able to best their mate before they could claim them and neither of them could attack again. They were at a draw, a surprise to both of them, so now it was up to her. She held his gaze, head high and proud. She saw another moment of uncertainty as he tried to read her expression. It was her choice now. She gave a half smile, her eyelashes lowered seductively and wings tilted forward as she exposed her neck, signaling her acceptance of him as a mate.

She could almost smell the blood, even in her dreams, and wished it wasn't a memory so she could take back her acquiescence. She could feel their claws digging into each other's backs to leave the marks of ownership. The last time either would be able to hurt the other. In theory. The bond left so much out though. The beings that created dragons hadn't understood pain of the heart.

They were in Kaienar's study, a few days later. The day prior, Aislinn had performed a touch of magic to remove the tattoo that kept her from accidental offspring. It had been painful, but at the time, it seemed worth it. She was now a lady to a lord, it was her duty to produce an heir. The claw marks left on his writing table when they'd mated in the middle of whatever paperwork he'd been trying to get caught up on seemed a positive step in the right direction.

She'd been determined to have everything in order before her brothers could swoop in and attempt to separate them, because there had always been that fear in her of something. She hadn't realized her fear should have been directed at Kaienar.

She wanted to wake and avoid the memories of what came next, but the island was cruel. She would have to relive a bit more misery before escaping.

The garden again. Shortly before a party. One of her first and only as his lady. She hadn't been officially announced as such, not before it ended. She wanted to wait until she told her brothers, but had been coaxed into a small gathering of celebration against her better judgment. She was thinking of her brothers as Kaienar was fiddling with her hair, attempting to cover her ears more. She sighed in exasperation as she had carefully redone it after her ladies had tried the same.

"I'm part elf, love. And I'm not ashamed of it." She brushed her hair back behind her ears.

"Neither am I, but I am not everyone, and I would rather the nobility had less to attack you with than more."

"Let them, I can hold my own."

"I am aware, but again. I would rather they had less to attack you with. Try to remain calm. Your temper is endearing, but not in situations such as this." He shifted her hair again and she let it remain, not able to place exactly why she felt as if he'd stabbed her when he was attempting to protect her; in his own way. His country did have rigid rules and customs after all, at least they felt that way to her. But who was she to question? She traveled from place to place with her clan's business. There were many customs.

Kaienar's room again. The day things irrevocably changed. They had bonded in the late spring and she was pregnant almost immediately. With the distance and Kaienar's parents pushing to make some kind of match with other families in the Dawnlands,

Damian had accepted their extended 'good-byes', at least for a while. He believed her lies, or at least tolerated them.

The first couple of months had passed uneventfully, nothing unexpected for pregnancy at least, Damian later described it as the child establishing a foothold before attacking. And attack it did, with pain that felt like parts of her were being torn to shreds. She collapsed while practicing spear forms in the courtyard, and was taken to her room. Kaienar held her as she shook, but it continued in unending waves. She retched and up came a blood-like substance. Smell entered her memory again. She practically tasted the sharp bile mixed with coppery blood and something more. Aislinn always thought of it as blood-like; she argued when Kaienar called his healers and they believed it was blood from an excess of morning sickness. Something had been off about it, but Kaienar was adamant his healers could fix this issue.

She tolerated their ineffective ministrations for days as the pain slowly grew worse, trusting him, yet... something in her was reading the pauses and his expressions of sorrow for her pain as too nervous. Something in what everyone was telling her was off, just like the 'blood'.

Another day. She had the mirror she used to communicate nearby and was reaching out to her brothers, without consulting Kaienar. It had taken time to find a moment where he was not around and to convince the healers to give her space. Something in her had known.

"Hello, youthling." Damian's face was tight, the burn scar across the side of his face bloodless and pale. He was upset with her. At the very least she had let him down and lied. So many lies to keep them away. She was trying not to cry.

"I did something you told me not to, I'm so sorry. Please, please, help me," she started off by begging, her pride was not worth the life that would be lost. Damian, who could be hard and furious and more dangerous than a sudden storm at sea, had softened before her first sentence was even finished.

"What is wrong, little one?" He paused before adding, "Has something happened since you wed?" She later discovered he had learned of their mating that day from a shopkeeper they paid in Minado. They'd suspected, but leaned towards trusting her. He'd been planning to reach out to her, but the twins had decided to wait one more day before contacting her to calm down.

"How- no. Not important. I'm not sure. It feels like I'm dying. Please, help me." She broke down in tears when she realized she could not even manage to hand him specifics of her case. Incompetent. "If I can't be saved, at least save the child. Please."

"What child?" His voice was now cold, restrained fury. And he was giving her a questioning look.

"I'm carrying Kai's child."

"We are coming."

The glass went dark and Aislinn laid down, hoping their boats would be swift and the wait short. Hoping she could last the few weeks it would take them. She managed to find a spot of rest in the pain. It was soon disrupted by yelling in the courtyards. Her first thought was an attack and she forced herself to a sitting position, trying to find a weapon. Then she felt a familiar and overwhelming presence and knew weapons were useless. They'd used a gate.

Damian snarled at the servants by her door that dared attempt to delay him. Most wisely scattered. She was trembling when he opened the door, fearing the anger she was certain was meant for her.

Instead she felt a gentle hand on her head, and when she could finally meet his eyes, there was only concern.

"Why would you throw your life away, little one?"

"I love him. I don't care about the cursed politics! A difficult match isn't throwing my life away!" Anger gave her a surprising and fierce energy.

"I don't think she knows, Damie." Daren. Low and calming and worried beyond belief.

"You asked Kaienar why I was against this match?" Damian's voice was cold, his suffocating presence was folding in upon itself, barely leaving air to breath.

"Political rigamarole and the restrictive nature of the Dawnlands.." Her words were greeted with silence that lasted forever. Finally Daren broke it.

"Damie, I can hear what you're thinking, we can't kill him."

"Politics makes your marriage complicated, not impossible. The restrictions do worry me, that is true. I will elaborate on that once you are well." He would say no more as he eased her down on her mattress and began examining her. The atmosphere felt heavy as his hands passed through the air above her, sensing the shifts in her aura. Damian exhaled slowly when he was finished, eyes still closed.

"As I feared. The child is killing you, little one. It does not mean to, but it is. It is trying to displace anything that is not dragon blood and since you have only partial dragon blood, it believes you need that correction as well. Daren, have her drink this. Have someone bring you water to brew it, let no one else touch it past that. A well-meant addition could be fatal. I need to discuss some things with our 'host'. Do not worry. I will not kill him." Damian was gone before either one could stop him.

Daren and Aislinn sat in uncomfortable silence for a few moments. Daren could not let it last too long.

"Here I was, rushing in with our brother, ready to beat anyone that hurt my little sister and you have to go and choose someone that politics protects."

She laughed weakly. He sniffed the herbs Damian had left.

"I know you hate this, but smells like he wants you out for awhile." The memory of Daren's hand on her forehead was so very real feeling. It had been a moment of relief she had felt beyond able to get. "Damie's not gonna let anything worse happen to you." Daren meant well with his words, but he was wrong in how bad it was going to be. She supposed it was true that Damian did not 'let' anything worse happen. He fought with everything he had.

As Aislinn felt like bits of her were getting ripped and torn or absorbed and replaced, she did not argue with any of the medicines used. The next months were a haze, but she would never forget the sickly sweet taste of the medicine. Her body was amazing at overcoming poisons, even if the 'poisons' were drugs meant to help her, so she never went under as deeply or as long as hoped, but her brothers kept her heavily dosed so she was rarely awake enough to feel the pain.

After the second afternoon, she did not fight the sleep. She had woken up with enough pain centered in her lungs that speaking, even screaming, felt impossible. She tried to reach out to the voices she could hear outside the door.

"Let me see my wife." Kaienar. She just wanted him to come and hold her, but without air, even reaching out through their bond was difficult.

"Until she is able to ask for you herself, I have no intentions of letting you near her, High Lord." Damian's tone was deadly sharp.

"I did not know-" Kai was cut off before he could offer an explanation.

"You knew. More than enough to know it was a probability - dare I say likelihood - even if you discounted some of the legends. I am not a fool. I may have only assisted with your weaponry training, but I did pay attention to what else was taught you. And your family has always been fairly clear on what happens when taking a half-dragon for a wife." Damian was stirring something as he spoke by the clinking of glass. His voice was mostly calm, but that edge was still present.

"I thought they were merely tales." Kaienar's tone was too even, placating. He was accepting the accusations too easily.

"And did you think it merely a tale that a full-blooded female dragon would be more acceptable and prestigious to your clan than a mixed-blood?" retorted Damian flatly.

Kaienar was silent at this charge.

"You have knowingly placed my sister's life in danger. Say what you will, it was not for love, it was for your pride and your vanity and the glory of your clan. I will not stop her if she decides to stay with you, but I will make clear what has happened. And I will correct my mistake of placing my trust in you. I believed you honorable enough to let her know the risks," said Damian. She heard what sounded like a glass stirring rod hit the table hard enough that she suspected it cracked. "At first I believed that she decided the risk was worth it as I could picture her stubbornness more easily than your duplicity. Now, go. Away. I care not where so long as it is not near us."

"You are in my house, Guardian deAvaric." She heard the threat in Kaienar's voice.

"High Lord Bryndagr, my fear of you and your clan is very limited. Even more limited now that you toyed with my little sister's life. I am attempting to limit this disaster. With good fortune, I may even be able to save your heir. If I am extremely lucky, and the elements smile upon us, I will save my sister as well. But your feelings and pride? They are not on the list of things I care to put effort into preserving, in the present or future. Now, assist me by leaving or I will assist you in leaving. You may be talented, but only one of us has the full capabilities of a weapons master."

Aislinn could feel the stare down occurring outside, and finally managed to make a sound. Kaienar glanced in, but did not force the issue at Damian's growl.

Food, herbal remedies and then the blessed relief of the sedating drink. She could remember being in and out of it and to dream of it was somehow worse. It felt clearer and sharper than the actual moment.

"Damie, I got some stuff from the market... for... you know." Daren. Voices outside the door again. She fervently wished for people to stop talking outside her door. She did not want to hear it, she did not want to know any more.

"Daren." Damian sounded so tired.

"I know it's not ideal, but maybe... get rid of it and-" Daren's meaning was obvious and Aislinn wanted to hide, she could not fight them if they did dose her.

"She wants to save the child. And it is too late for that. The balance has shifted to where she would die from the loss. The child anchors and restrains the change somewhat."

"Damie-" Daren sounded hopeless.

"I know, brother, I know."

She had cried out in pain then, accepting all the care received, but actually only wanting sedation again. The next few months were a continuous blur of pain and misery and half-heard conversations that Aislinn wished she could unhear. At some point, Kai's brother, Eingeir, became a regular fixture in her room. He was able to draw more energy from the surroundings than her brothers and feed it to her weakening body as he, like her, was a conduit. He talked to her while he was working and she realized he assumed she knew of the dangers beforehand. She corrected him automatically, not even meaning to snitch on Kaienar. If Eingeir hadn't been trying to pass magic to her in that moment, she never would have sensed his rage. That anger tipped the scales for her in regards to Kaienar.

She'd saved Eingeir's life on a wyvern hunt once, he had never forgotten it. She was, somehow, one of a very few people he respected, which was a very dubious honor. It was almost certain he was why she did not have to interact with Kaienar after that point in time; though she often felt his concern through their mate bond. She suspected Eingeir was also responsible for the drugs finally sticking in her system. He was like her in that regard: very hard to poison. Damian had a new plant to study when they returned to Seacove, one that extended the effects of medicine for her.

All those little things were kindnesses from someone who was faithful to his brother. But from that rage, she knew Kaienar had never mentioned to Eingeir his failure to tell her. Kai's silence spoke of shame and trying to hide the truth. She had become paranoid after that and begged her brothers to get her away once the baby was born. She couldn't run until then and even in a haze, she knew the ramifications of running off with his heir.

With the drugs and sheer exhaustion as her body was wasting away, she was barely aware of her own son's birth. She knew she changed into a full dragon for the first time during labor and tore up some of the cavern she'd been put in for the birth, they told her that. All she remembered was a feeling of suffocation, her breed birthed in forest clearings and shallow caves and the Bryndagrs' ancestral caves were deep and isolated from the outside. She took care of Enar for a few blurry weeks, enough that his scent was deeply imprinted in her senses, but not enough for any real memories. At some point, he'd been passed to a nursemaid and her brothers had taken her from the Bryndagr castle. She woke on the ship home, clear-headed for the first time in ages. Damian was sitting by her bedside, eyes closed, goblet of something in his hand.

"Damian?"

His eyes slowly opened. She could not even find the words to ask.

"Your son is with High Lord Bryndagr. That, unfortunately, is due to political rigamarole. He is heir to the title and house and to take him would cause friction between dragon clans, and countries. Friction that will not aid your recuperation. High Lord Bryndagr will unquestionably take care of him." He sipped from the goblet. "He is well. Healthy and strong."

She tried to inhale, but her lungs locked up.

"Once you are well, you may return to him, if you wish." Damian paused and the next part was soft, but clear. "And if you wish, we will tear down cities to assist you with retrieving your child."

"Why... why do you blame Kai? What was that sickness?" She knew, mostly, but she wanted to hear it from her brother, so she knew she was not going mad. And she couldn't focus on her son, not right now. Everything hurt too much.

"Because he was well aware of the risks, and chose to go ahead even when those risks were not to him." Damian sighed and drained his glass. "Do you remember the tales of our origins?"

"Yes. When magic was strong and wild, dragons were created of the strongest warriors to protect man from things beyond their fragile strength." Aislinn felt something itching at the back of her mind, a lesson maybe half-heard when she was a child.

"Because it was only a handful of warriors, dragon blood ran true. A child of a dragon was a pure dragon, no matter whom the other parent was, correct?" He asked the question already knowing the answer and she felt him leading her somewhere, but continued in recitation of known facts. Recitation was easy.

"Yes, and it was that way with all clans until the betrayal, when some clans attempted to enslave or destroy the other races. One of the last great feats of magic made the betraying clans' blood no longer breed true, causing them to die out slowly. Five clans were included on that list that had not betrayed our cause, including the deAvarics," she inhaled and spoke quickly and in a flat tone, "Nothing could change us back, but because we held true to the cause during the wars, our clans became the enforcers of the cause. We bring down those dragons or clans who would enslave or destroy those weaker than us. And I understand why that makes it highly awkward for me to wed the lord of one of the more influential clans."

"If you had told me of your plans, you may have been demoted to a lesser rank in our clan to avoid the politics. Also, I should have clarified regarding children. Bryndagr blood breeds true. If you were anything other than half dragon, that would not be an issue."

"I don't understand." She lied, she did not *want* to understand. Part of her hoped Kaienar could be innocent, that what had happened to her was an unfortunate and rare occurrence, not a certainty.

"If something's only part dragon, the magic wants to change it to all dragon, Ais." Daren had entered the cabin quietly.

"For the child, that was less of an issue, it is growing, changing, being created. The mother is more fixed and immutable," said Damian.

"It's tearing half a building down with no regard to what pillar holds the ceiling up," she said, voice dull and wishing she didn't understand so well. "I should have died, shouldn't I? When I chose to have a child with him, I was choosing my death, wasn't I?"

"If you and Damie weren't so stubborn, you would have." Daren handed a bottle to his twin. "And if Kaienar hadn't had a conduit as a brother." His face scrunched up as he gave that credit. Eingeir and Daren had never gotten along.

Aislinn smelled a coppery tang and realized what Damian was drinking. Blood. He had pushed his skills to the darkest of limits, all because she had been a fool.

"I am so stupid. I'm sorry," said Aislinn, "I should have put it together."

"Little one, you were in love. I, above all, realize what that does. I believed Lord Bryndagr to be more honorable than he was and forget that you are," he paused and stared at her, "far more like myself than I want to admit."

Perhaps it was the light, but his fangs and the burn scar on his face seemed especially prominent as he looked at her. Both were mementos of the lengths someone would go to when they cared for someone. Scars he gained protecting his loved ones. She found another prick of blame in her situation: she should have reached out to her brothers sooner. Perhaps more could have been done. Damian continued speaking.

"I should not have expected someone else to clarify the danger in something so important to you. I am certain it was mentioned at some point in your education, probably when you were very young and our dearest brother told you something he should not have," Damian paused as Daren made an offended sound at the accusation, then continued, "but you had so little interest in your dragon half beyond our family, I did not think to stress it until too late. I should have reminded you." The assumption of any responsibility on his part and lack of judgment towards her both soothed and hurt every time she remembered it.

She finally stepped away from her memories before the next part. She had no desire to relive that moment. The memories twisted into nightmares as she came closer to waking. Kaienar was a monster. Her brothers threw her to him. She was drowning and Kai held her under the water. She gave him more children and he took them from her, locking her in a cell after she did, and forcing her to continue until there was nothing left of her. He came to pull her from her cell and she struck his arms as hard as possible.

Chapter 24 - Reality

Onyx curled up next to Aislinn once he was certain that the day was advanced enough the island was closed to others. He dozed in fits and starts, waking the final time to Aislinn twitching in her sleep. He stroked her forehead, trying to smooth the wrinkles and singing softly to her. After a few minutes, he pulled her closer to comfort her and she woke in a panic.

She shoved him away with a growl. "NO!"

Onyx wrapped her in his arms and continued soothing her.

"I am not him. Not him. Please don't kick me."

"Onyx? Oh. Oh no. I'm... I'm sorry. I just..." she shook her head, "I dreamt I had twins and he was taking them away. And locking me away."

"It was only dream."

"Too real of one." She brushed her hair out of her face and took a shaky breath. "I was attempting to reach out to the twins - my brothers, not the ones in my dream - but... the island makes everything convoluted. It twisted me back into my own mind. I could maybe reach them if I went offshore, but it won't work here."

"You would be noticed as a dragon and you can barely walk." He was rubbing gentle circles on her back.

"I can walk but I won't try it again here. I won't go through him taking my child again. Even if this time the children were only a dream." She sat forward and rubbed her eyes.

Onyx continued rubbing her back in silence for a bit, not certain he had understood her correctly. He lowered his eyes when she turned to look at him.

"What now, Sea-cat?"

"Hmm?"

"Your face. You get that look when you don't want to ask something that you want to ask." Aislinn sounded exhausted.

"Why can't you try here?"

"My natural magic and the island's... align too closely. I'm horrible at dreams and astral projections. They aren't solid and tangible. This place... there's something raw and elemental and... well, that's more my thing. This magic wants to run through me as soon as I try something, but it's near impossible to control. Especially with something as delicate as reaching out via dreams." She smiled. "You still have that look though, and you looked far too innocent when you asked, so... what's really on your mind?"

He paused for a long time, not certain he wanted to pry.

"Onyx, we're going to have to continue depending on each other, at least for a bit, and I consider you a friend. What's bothering you?" Her words and her recent dream gave him an idea mostly unrelated to his question.

"You said... you said he was not evil. Maybe you could call him? I'm healthy and can outrun them." He did not like the idea of her having to go back to him, but it seemed she could leave him, and at least she'd be alive. He cringed in preparation for an imminent explosion. He was surprised when the only response was a sigh.

"I thought of that. More than once. But... honestly I'd rather die than owe him my life and your scent is all over me. He might hunt you down to rip you to shreds just due to that. Believe me, if it would actually save you, I would," she paused for a breath but cut him off before he could interject, "And, knowing the hunters are around and that you're a prime target to them, I don't consider leaving you to make a run for it protecting you. You've saved my life, I'm not leaving yours to chance. And if you need another reason, think of how long it took for him to reach out to me. He is a lordling with lordly things to do. I do not follow his bidding, so I am not a priority." She nearly sing-songed the last part.

"Why do you hate him?" He paused, remembering an earlier mention. "Is there more than the elfsong?"

"I believe I've said: I loved him so much and he hurt me so much more."

"I understand betrayal." Onyx rested his forehead against hers briefly, not sure when these little gestures had become common between them.

"Not to compete, but he nearly killed me, cut me off from elfsong, pulls me about like a puppet on strings, and tries to use our child for bargaining." She sniffled slightly and laughed a rueful laugh. "I think I win."

Onyx straightened up, certain that this time, he had heard her correctly.

"You have a child?"

"No, he has our child. Because I'm foolish and selfish." She was near crying now.

"You promised. No tears unless someone died." The words spilled out before Onyx could stop them. She laughed.

"I did, didn't I? Sorry." She attempted to sniffle back the tears.

"You are not."

"Not what? Sorry?"

"Foolish. Selfish." He shook his head. "You may be frightening and dangerous, but you are not foolish. I have learned your madness contains sense. And if you were selfish, you would not worry about me." He stroked her hair.

She was leaning against him now, limp and out of fight. He wondered again exactly what had happened to make her this way. He had the pieces, but it felt like something was missing.

"We have some time. I know you're curious. Do you really want to hear?" Her voice was hollow.

"Yes."

"Even if you end up thinking I'm foolish, vain, and selfish?"

"Friends say I see the world as I wish it, not as is, so it should not change my ideas."

She laughed weakly and began to tell him.

Chapter 25 - Loss

Aislinn paused when she reached the part that woke her. She was tired, feeling as if she had run a marathon, even though they had paused in the telling for food and while Onyx had patrolled the area during the day. She suspected the patrols were Onyx's way to give her a break from her tale with all its attendant emotions.

She stared long and hard into a cup of hot water she was now holding, watching the ripples from the shake of her hands and the way the steam rose and curled. Then she took a sip, then a deep breath and continued.

Why did this - out of all moments of pain - always hurt so bad? She could never pinpoint it. Perhaps because it was such a clear moment in a time that was shrouded with a haze like that slowly rising above her cup. She could see the ship in her mind, particularly an almost triangular knot in the planks she had stared at while thinking over her brothers' words. She could almost feel the waves rocking the boat because every sense in this memory was so clear.

Or perhaps it hurt so much because it was when she first realized another part of what was lost and almost broke. Until *that* moment, she had felt hurt, but surprisingly calm.

It was so simple a thing. She was tucking her hair behind her ears, and something felt very off. She was, or she had been, part elven. Damian and Daren weren't her only siblings. There was Edorian and his books and studies. She'd been adopted into the twins' family, but he was blood. Elven blood. There should have been a delicate point to the tip of her ear. That was gone, a rounded humanesque ear in its place. The tiny change in her appearance made her feel cut off from her brother, her home, so many things. But maybe...

She tucked her hair back again, this time trying the other ear, as if somehow the tips would return. Or having one tip would mean she had both. She regretted the attempt.

She hit a dried bit of skin and she felt the remnant detach, like a scab popping off a healed wound. Gone. Both gone. And then she realized something else: the ship was quiet.

There were creaks of wood and ropes, the splashing of the water, a deckhand yelling something up above, all those sounds had hidden the lack: there was no elfsong. The song had never been loud for her, but it had been constant.

And now it was gone.

Damian looked at her sadly. Daren was edging towards the door.

"No. Nonononono." She tried not to cry, she tried so hard not to cry, they had done so much it was not fair to subject them to more of her misery. The tears came anyway and Damian wrapped his arms and wings around her the same way he did when she was a child with a nightmare. They could not make this nightmare go away. Or stop the tears.

No matter how hard she tried in the next weeks they came out at different moments. She fell to her knees when she arrived in Elvenhome and the silence continued. She'd hoped that her sense of the song had dulled, not died completely. Seeing Rin, knowing he could hear what she no longer could, had been remarkably painful for the first year or so. But she refused to let Kai take more from her, and she'd fought to find some center, some balance.

She cut off her hair so she would not have to accidentally feel her ears when pushing it back. Those close to her gave no comment beyond that she looked lovely and that hair would grow back. The silent acknowledgement made her smile and weep at the same time. They understood enough to know that they could not understand and the kindness almost made it worse.

When Kaienar arrived a few months later, she did not cry. By that time, her fire had begun to return and it was smoldering with held-back anger.

"Come back with me. Come back home." His voice was soft and cajoling. "I miss you. Your son needs you."

"Why?"

"He is but a child, all children need their mother."

"Not that. Why did you do it?"

"I did not believe… that you would be in danger." It wasn't his words that made her realize that he truly had avoided telling her the complete truth and why. It was the silences and the moments where his grey eyes could not meet hers. She considered returning, even then. There was a child and she loved him even without having a chance to know him. She did not want to ask the next simple question. She wanted so much to let it lay. But she knew she would never be comfortable with not having the answer.

"Did my mixed heritage bother you?"

"No," he wrapped his arms around her, "I love you, all of you. This has not changed anything about who you are. To the court, it is clearer and simpler, but to me, you are the same."

"The court?" She pushed him back slightly. Her hair wasn't yet long enough to brush back, but she went through the motions anyways, disquiet in her soul as she ran her fingers along the faint scar for the first time. For some reason, her ear tips were the only spots that resisted enough to show a scar.

"You have had my heir, you are a full blooded dragon now, they have nothing to hold against you. Come back. We'll build the family we dreamt of." He was clearly only seeing the good in her being a full dragon. Another child probably wouldn't kill her.

"They have almost nothing." She laughed. "Something will always matter, won't it? And with you, it doesn't make a difference... until it does. In the shadows, it's fine. Until you realize it's a 'weakness' someone can slight you or your court with."

He stepped away, he knew her well enough to know that the laugh he heard from her was not a pleasant one.

"No. I will not return. Our child may stay with you for the time being," Everything hurt again as she spoke. Parts of her were still being torn off and replaced with something else. "He is an heir to your clan and I will not subject my brothers to the battles that would happen if we took him. We've all suffered enough. There were magics and skills I had as a child, and they've disappeared, like the tips of my ears. But you don't seem to care." Aislinn continued fingering the top edge of her ear as she spoke, it was almost a compulsion. Short hair had actually caused her to fiddle with her ear tips more.

"Aislinn-" His eyes were full of sorrow, but his voice... it felt more pleading than apologetic. His logic could not make her trust him again. Logic was what had dictated that his course of action was the correct course for all involved. Logic said that she was not quite good enough, but could be. Given time and corrections.

"If I return... what will you take from me next, Kaienar?"

"That is not fair. I can't undo what has been done." He was angry now. Good.

"No. It's not fair. And you have no intention of making it fairer. But you do not own me!" She was being childish. She did not care.

"You are my mate!"

"I would undo that if I could in a heartbeat!"

The silence after that statement crackled with tension, but deep inside she knew the truth of her words. She truly would. It wasn't that she didn't love him anymore; she did. So very much. She was furious with herself for still loving him. It did not matter how she felt about him, she could not be as he wanted her to be and could not trust him not to hurt her for the facade that was Highlord Bryndagr. From her words, it had devolved into a fierce argument, but Aislinn held firm. She was clutching at that one truth. She wept in her room for days after he left, but she held firm.

Then the first summons came and she fought a compulsion that seeped through their bond until she couldn't. And the next. And the next. Every time she went, she felt another piece of her crack.

The knowledge that the bond would not have taken if there hadn't been some kind of match in their spirits didn't help. It was another voice whispering she should let the past go. There weren't many voices like that around her, especially not in her inner circle, but there were enough. But every time she came near to fully giving in, he would do something to incite her ire. He attempted to use their son against her, not allowing her to spend time with the boy after her first visit. Not unless she decided to stay. That decision was one of his worst. He gave reasons, but all it was to her was a visible power play. If she behaved exactly as he asked and did as he wanted, he would deign to allow her to interact with the child she nearly died for, but it would be on his terms. She thought of giving in and returning, but something inside always rebelled harder, knowing she would become less than a shadow if she did. She wasn't foolish enough to believe that he would stop using a good bargaining chip just because she returned.

When she finished her tale, she took Onyx's hand and brought it up to trace her eartips. He tried to withdraw when she flinched, but she stopped him.

"It's okay. Damian thinks a part of me was stubbornly trying to hold on, but I was fighting for our lives and there wasn't enough left over to hold on to that part of me. So it scarred. Only thing that did," she paused, "I was never strong in my elven side, but not having it... some days I want to scream it out just so it's known."

He ran his fingers along it. She knew there was the barest hint of a ridged scar, she couldn't see it in a mirror, but she could always feel it. She found herself waiting for him to try to heal it or hum to calm her. Something.

Onyx surprised them both by leaning forward and gently kissing the tips of her ears. He froze for a moment before scooting back and looking away.

"I understand how you were on the beach now. You are strong, Sky-cat." Onyx looked to the fire and made an impatient hiss. The kind he made when he was late to doing something. She let him be distracted. She needed distraction as well.

Chapter 26 - Complications

The day was ending by the time Aislinn's tale was finished. Onyx tended the fire, banking the coals and smothering a few brightly burning logs so the hunters would not see flames if they came ashore. He tried to ignore his misstep a few moments earlier. It was difficult, as the evening was bringing in the chill and the two huddled together for warmth in the glow of the coals. He was also pondering what he had learned, which didn't help. He wanted to be closer to help her heal and a thousand leagues away so there was no danger he would encroach upon her wounds.

"If he had loved you..." he trailed off, not certain where his thoughts were going.

"He did once. Not certain when it became something else," her correction was gentle.

"We... he... with selkies someone else could have fathered the baby. Or he could have had another cow carry his heir. There were ways," Onyx knew that was not the entire point, but the whole thing felt wrong. It was twisted. It was like taking a silvercoat and flaying them alive in hopes they would have a normal coat underneath.

"Yes, there were, but he neither chose to take them nor to let me know the price to be paid," replied Aislinn. Her voice was still, like stagnant water. She leaned into him, huddling into her thoughts under the blanket. He'd seen this mood from her before and hated it.

He touched the side of her face and gently stroked her cheek. Her eyes widened at his surprise contact. He tried to draw his hand back.

"Please, smile. I mean…" he looked off in the distance, "Be happy again." The words caught in his throat, he was not saying the right things.

She laid her hand over his and smiled as she leaned her cheek into his palm.

"Thank you. I will, and I do. I just have to make him understand that what we had is done. And find a way to do so without making my child suffer."

"He does not own you. You are right. He can't own you," said Onyx. He did not know why her tale distressed him so that it was hard to find words. It was familiar and so different. Not right. They were not enough. Beads scattered in the sand and stone.

He found himself sharing his reasons for his separation from the clans during the season. He stumbled in shame over the parts where he had hurt a friend and attacked the other male, but refused to leave them out, even knowing she would think less of him for this. He hoped she would understand the desperation and pain that had fueled his idiocy - not forgive him, his choices had been wrong, but understand the foundation of the true pain. It was not the loss of his potential mate, that part had healed, but the knowledge that everything he had done was not… right. Not enough. Even though his foolish moves had been waved away as resulting from youth and tempers, it did not mean elders saw him as more than an odd one out. And they never would. Gentle fingers traced the path of his tears when he was done. Their faces were a breath apart now.

"We are quite the pair of painful pasts, aren't we?" asked Aislinn.

"Yours is worse."

"Not a competition, even if I claimed the win earlier." She half-smiled and leaned her head against his. She held up the elemental star pendant, half laughing. "This isn't amaru noda, is it?"

He smiled as he shook his head no.

"We make jewelry and trinkets other than amari nodum," said Onyx.

"Good, you are very sweet, but I do not wish to deal with an accidental betrothal. Intentional ones have given me enough troubles."

He held the pendant, examining it as if seeing it for the first time.

"I would not trick you into wearing them. I do like seeing you wear my work though," Onyx gently released the pendant and without thought, placed his hands on Aislinn's face, turning it slightly so their lips could meet. Aislinn responded after a hesitant moment by leaning into the kiss. Lips parted slightly, tongues explored cautiously for a few heartbeats and then they broke apart for air.

"Onyx, I-" Aislinn began but Onyx placed his finger on her lips.

"I apologize. I should not have done that." He looked away, not wanting to admit to things he had only fully realized in that moment.

"It's fine. It's the season and after all, I did mistakenly attack you awhile back, so it's understandable." Aislinn remained under the blanket, but he felt a chasm between them.

"It is not." He stared at the floor as he attempted to clarify. "It is not fine. And it was not just because of the season."

"You've healed me and helped me. It's natural that you have some feelings towards me, but they're just passing and… even if they weren't, I'm not free." Aislinn's voice was unnaturally high-pitched. She was nervous, scared. He understood why, but hated her attempts to re-define his feelings.

"Please don't confuse my feelings." He looked into her eyes, she did not look away.

"I'm sorry. I didn't mean to confuse you."

"I mean... you didn't..." He paused, realizing he'd spoken wrong. They'd been pushing the language to its limits. "Don't say it's passing."

"I know." Her voice grew husky. "I could hope though. The alternative is more of a mess than we can deal with right now."

"I apologies for being a mess." That wasn't right, he knew it wasn't. And it wasn't what he meant to say, but his frustration was making his language skills fail and after telling her his tale, this messy not quite-a-rejection hit an exposed nerve.

"Onyx, that's not what I said. I'm not free, likely never will be. We have men hunting us and injuries and..." she exhaled, "I just can't."

"He does not own you." Onyx was annoyed at his stubbornness, his temper, and the part of him that felt hopeful that she was not denying feelings.

"Kai is not the only problem I listed." She half-laughed.

"Skin hunters always chase me. I carry a silvercoat. My colony did not disown me, but everything I did..." Onyx was distressed. He wanted away from this place. Now. But at the same time, he did not want to leave her alone with her hurt. But he didn't want to add to that hurt either.

"Nothing you could do could overcome what you were." Aislinn's voice was sad and full of pity. He did not want pity, he wanted something else. Something she had made clear she was not willing to give. Or not willing to give now. Which amounted to the same thing.

"We need more wood. It should be safe to gather. You get the fire restarted." Onyx fled the cave then. Exactly like he fled the beaches.

He hurt, and at this moment, it felt that particular hurt would never heal.

Chapter 27 - The Hunt

Dark edged up on the shore, trying not to think. He did not want to think of anything other than his mission, not his name, not the home he left behind, nothing. He knew he should not follow the skin hunter's instructions, but following instructions was better than having the strap he couldn't remove tighten around his neck until no air could be breathed. It was better than having strips of his skin peeled off while tied down and unable to shift or fight. It was better than anything he could imagine them doing. Survival, plentiful food, maybe even a mate. They had discussed breeding their 'dogs'. He could stand being called a dog if it meant he was able to keep all his parts. They had also discussed the alternative, apparently castration made livestock more docile. The foolish newcomer had made that discussion more common. He would learn. Dark had learned.

He raised his head high and scented the air. A fire had been smothered recently, the hunters would not be able to smell it, but he could and he took perverse amounts of pride in outdoing them in at least one aspect. He shifted to human form and moved carefully towards the scent. He edged over the needles and bracken that covered the forest floor, nudging aside the spring's new ferns. The scent was definitely getting stronger. He could hear voices. He flattened to the ground, definitely two, speaking... something from the continents. At least that was what he guessed it was. Languages were not his specialty. He felt uneasy and disappointed that the language wasn't selkie. What if one of the two was not a selkie, would that be blamed on him?

It took Dark several minutes to pinpoint the source of the sound. It was echoing slightly, and muffled. He finally found the entrance to a small cave and wondered what he should do next. He knew one was selkie, but the other… if he did not report correctly and completely, there would be consequences. That was certain. However, they were in the cave and had the advantage in numbers and knowledge.

Someone stormed out of the cave and Dark edged back. It was a male. He did not need smell or sound, bulls always knew bulls once winter broke. There was a sense of challenge they gave off. Even that irritating dog angling to die on the boat gave that feeling off. He was relieved that whatever had been discussed had upset the male enough he did not sense Dark's presence. He had sized him up instinctively and was certain he could win against him, but the second person was an unknown. Fire flared in the cave and he debated for several moments what he should do. The male's presence was receding into the distance and soon was out of range. It was possible he could take the other one while he was gone.

He was still considering his options when the other stepped out of the cave. By the silhouette against the firelight, this one was female. He relaxed. He scented the air, trying to catch a hint of what she was. No luck, the fire and smoke covered whatever her scent might be. For all he knew, she could be selkie. Not likely, but a few of the more distant ones were known to prefer continental tongues to the speech of the selkie. Strange clans that actually lived in small tribes along the northern edge of a continent as opposed to the islands. He needed to make sure before risking return to the ship. And maybe, if she was a female selkie, he could get an extra reward when he returned.

He held his position for a moment. He would do anything for whatever scraps they would throw his way. He knew it. The sting of it was almost gone by now and he waited for the right moment.

Chapter 28 - Attack of Conscience

Aislinn fell back against the wall when Onyx left, not even sure what she could have done differently. Onyx was like the waters he swam in, constantly moving and changing, not solid like earth, but not as ephemeral as the shifting winds. He was unmistakably tangible - like tides cycling and rivers relentlessly traveling until they carved a new path. Impulsive, romantic, foolish, so much on the surface, but - she paused, rubbing the back of her neck and working out the tension that had appeared – he also held depths, and secrets. Some were easier to find, others not so much. She felt he had a thousand tales, most people did, but his would be trickier to discover. She was not certain he knew some of them himself yet.

She rekindled the fire. He fascinated her, and she wanted to draw forth those tales. It was not a feeling that pleased her. He hadn't been wrong in pointing out the weakness of her excuses, even though he hadn't called them weak. Even calling out Kaienar's string pulling was...

She spent so long feeling broken and trapped, even with her protests to Kaienar. Hearing Onyx say that she was free made her breath catch for a second.

As for his feelings, she wanted to say he was only feeling infatuation, but she had a sense that in some regards, those feelings already ran deeper. Attempting to downplay them would result in, well, there was a reason she was now alone in the cave. And they didn't need to be fighting when there was enough trouble headed their way. What bothered her most was if she told him that she had no feelings, she was certain he would be hurt, but accept it and all would be cleared up. So why hadn't she said that?

She focused on her leg for a bit, stubbornly ignoring the part of her that was admiring his handiwork while teasingly mentioning the possibility of Damian taking him on as an apprentice. She knew what that part was hinting at, Onyx wasn't the only one with feelings, but she refused to try and sort out what hers were right now. She used her own skills to strengthen her limb. The island was rich with power that she could use to boost this, Onyx had taken care of the more delicate parts of the healing, now it was finishing the job. It was hard to have too much raw power for that. She sighed and tried to control it anyways, aware she needed the practice. Especially if she wanted to be able to attempt anything as delicate as reaching out in dreams without going offshore. Although Onyx might be more supportive of that now. She leaned her head on her knee when the attempt at healing finally exhausted her.

He wouldn't. She knew that, deep in her being. Whether she cared for him or not, he still would for her. Waves and tides; shifting, yet constant. Once his spike of anger - and she was certain it was just a spike- washed away, he would want her safe from harm. That meant keeping her on the island until the leg was healed and the hunters gone if at all possible. Even if she found him in his current state of confusion and frustration, he'd worry for her.

Part of her wanted to shift and fly away, but even though she had offered, she remembered tales of the dangers of shifting with something as unhealed as her leg. That was part of why she had not pushed it. It wasn't a certain outcome, her brothers even said it was rare, but any half-warning tale left her cautious since nearly dying. And shifting beyond half was still difficult. And she was stubborn to a fault. She would see this out. The only way she was flying off this island was to tear the hunters' ship to the waterline.

If she was honest, it was that same part that faced Kaienar time after time. Her brothers had offered to help her avoid it with sedatives or sending her on trips to exotic locals. Unfortunately, Kaienar's stubbornness matched her own. Oddly, it had been part of the attraction. Was likely also part of her attraction for the sea-cat.

That similarity with Kaienar also led to the knowledge that if she kept away, he would persist and eventually come to her. She preferred to keep him in his lands, away from her home. She could slightly limit the things he ruined for her and steal a moment's glance at her son.

She stood and limped about a little, testing the limb. With luck, she would soon be fine. What happened then would be anyone's guess. She had to crouch a little in the cave to avoid hitting her head, so she headed towards the entrance for fresh air and a better stretch for her leg.

She stared at the sky and breathed in slowly through her nose and then through slightly parted lips, trying to locate Onyx. She could still taste his scent in the air, along with other scents she was trying to place, but she could not hear him. Either he was silently sulking nearby or too far away to hear. Neither one was worth the possibility of damaging the nearly healed leg. He would return once he calmed down and then they'd figure this out. Somehow.

A fern rustled slightly in the dead air. Aislinn pivoted, claws out. A man was well hidden in the darkness, but Aislinn's breed of dragon was meant to hurtle up and down mountain crags in the dark of the night. He wasn't hidden near well enough to escape her notice now that she was alert. She cursed herself inwardly for not noticing him earlier.

"I see you. Are you one of the hunters?"

He stood in response to her question; not speaking, but his eyes were fixed on her.

Dark watched as the cow stepped closer. He roughly understood her words, but he had not been given permission to talk, and even if he had, he was not certain if he would. Talking was not what was needed for this, at least not much. And no words.

He began to hum softly, if she was selkie, she would react quickly. If she was not selkie, she would at least be lulled. Her eyes lowered, relaxed, she stepped back slightly and shook her head, but she did not respond vocally. Not a selkie then.

Dark moved forward, continuing the hum. He came close enough to reach out and brush against her. Her scent was strange, he could not place it. Not human, not selkie was the best conclusion he could come to. He wasn't sure what to do next. Selkies they had an easy enough response for, this female may or may not be valuable to them.

He nuzzled into her neck and inhaled deeply, trying to fathom what she was. He did not notice the knife until after it hit.

Aislinn knew her aim was off the moment the blade connected. Or to be more precise, the moment the blade ricocheted off his rib bone and nearly stabbed her. She pushed hard, untangling the two of them and gaining space. She had wasted her one good chance. It had been hard to ignore the humming while acting as if it had relaxed her, but she had been living with someone much more talented than this selkie and once she honed in on his scent, he stank. His unwashed scent had an almost sickly tang to it that helped her ignore the song.

He bellowed and reared back. She felt her leg hitch in pain, but braced her dagger for another blow. The selkie rushed her, smashing her to the ground. She was certain a rib cracked with the impact, moss did little to cushion the stones at the speed she hit, and she did not have the air to scream when he shifted into an oversized wall of muscle. He was going to smother her and he was too big for her to get the dagger around. Her best chance now was to shift, but the rib left her breathless and silently screaming in pain when she tried the first time. The world was going dark and sparking red. She would have to try again or perish.

Before she could, a silver blur hit the bull with full force.

Onyx's weight threw the bull off balance and rolled him off of Aislinn. His sleek, grey body was smaller, but vocally, even the larger male was intimidated. They both changed back to their human forms, staring each other down. Aislinn edged away and drew power from the area around her to set the rib. It was rough and rushed and might give her problems later, but for now it would work.

The two males circled each other. Aislinn crawled back towards the cave. Her best chance to help this mess was with the bow, and she could not trust her leg enough to stand again, nor her magic to not make the leg worse.

There was a test scuffle and the selkies parted, circling again, both sporting fresh claw marks but nothing beyond that for injuries. Onyx's lips were pulled back in a snarl, the intruder seemed calmer, more confident. He darted at Onyx, but was easily sidestepped. He was confused that his target was not where he should be but was not given the chance to recover. Quick as a minnow Onyx was on him, catching his leg and throwing him to the ground. The strength in his arms became evident as he pinned down and pummeled the other male. It was over when the intruder almost immediately whimpered submission. Onyx rose from him, gaze fixed on Aislinn.

His hum was more sensed than heard as it vibrated through her bones. The look in his eyes was unmistakable. Aislinn stilled, not sure what she should do as he stalked towards her. The moment ended when the interloper decided he was not finished. He rushed Onyx, once again a solid, sleek brown wall of muscle and fury. Onyx dove to the side, seal before his roll had even finished and latched on to the other bull's throat.

The thick layer of blubber and muscle that should have protected the selkie's throat was shredded by rapid and relentless attacks from Onyx. Despite the clear danger, the other male refused to back down. Onyx moved back from him and bellowed a last warning, the bellowing releasing a fine spray of spittle mixed with his enemy's blood.

The larger male disregarded it.

He rushed in again, attempting to throw his weight on Onyx to crush him. He failed and Onyx clamped down on his throat a final time, twisting and tearing into his windpipe and blood vessels. From there it was only a waiting game, and a fairly short one at that. Onyx kept between the huge bull and Aislinn, but did not attack anymore. He cried out his victory to the night once the other selkie stopped thrashing.

A heartbeat later, he was human again and making his way towards Aislinn. The hum deepened to a growl that Aislinn was almost certain was causing the foundations of the isle to tremble. Onyx wiped the blood off his face with his arm, locking eyes with her as he did so. A moment later, he was over her, one knee edging up between her legs to part her thighs. He kissed her deeply and pressed against her. Her hips shifted slightly towards him, even as her mind was trying to untangle itself from his seductive tones.

Claws grazed her skin and cloth tore. The time of year. Selkie instincts. Even her dragon blood was running hot after watching the recent battle. Aislinn was half resigned and half anticipating what was about to happen. She didn't know a way to break through to his logical side without physically hurting him because she didn't trust her voice. He shifted his weight and his hand came down too close to her still-damaged rib and she let out a sharp gasp, tears welling in her eyes as she attempted to catch her breath.

Onyx froze, limbs trembling, silent.

"Onyx?" She was worried, had the bull poisoned him somehow? She hadn't seen a knife or needle, but it didn't mean he hadn't had one.

Onyx mumbled something.

"I'm sorry, I couldn't hear you-" replied Aislinn.

"Get. Away." He bit off the words.

Aislinn edged out from under him, recognizing a battle of instincts and higher thought. It was something nearly every shifter fought with. She scrambled back into the cave and collapsed on the pile of blankets. The brief and bad healing had drained her and without the adrenaline rush of fear, she had nothing left to carry her through. That lack of vigor was irritatingly common lately. She resolved to take an impossibly long nap once this was done.

She stared at the crackling logs and slowly worked up the strength to sit upright. Leg or rib, that was her most pressing question. She decided on the rib as she was becoming one big bruise from the bull landing on her; she was trembling as she attempted healing. She had been lucky, the rib was mostly correct and in line, but it would now have a slight dip it should not have had. Raw magic was in the air on the island so she had plenty to draw from, but she could not finesse it to the delicate healing she needed to avoid further damage. She gave up after a few moments, her attempts only causing her more pain and drain.

She half drifted off to sleep, her body desperate to avoid this new discomfort. She was not certain how much time had passed in that half-awake state before Onyx entered the cave. He was clearly back to his normal self.

"You are hurt?" He crouched by her side, forehead crinkled and lips pursed in worry.

"He landed on me. Hard. I don't have selkie bones. Something cracked," Aislinn replied.

"I'm sorry. He would not have come after us if it had not been for me."

"You don't know that. He could have washed up on shore."

"And I suppose what I almost did out there was not my fault either? Even if I'd claimed you like a bull in season?" his voice was full of self-loathing.

"You attacked him instead of leaving me to fend for myself and you didn't give in to your instincts. Which is pretty impressive when everything has triggered them and you have something you want right there. I wasn't fighting it. You could have just blamed your selkie side once it was done." She shrugged nonchalantly, coldly following facts. She doubted he'd listen to kindness currently and she needed to break through this self-loathing. They couldn't afford him being frightened of his wilder side right now, she had enough problems for the both of them on that count. "Worse has been blamed on instincts with less cause."

"It would have been wrong." His tone was flat, his expression confused. She could tell he had not been expecting her to defend him.

"Yes, it would have. Never said it wouldn't have. But you didn't. The instant I gave the slightest indication something was wrong, you fought yourself and backed off. Plus, you saved my life while I was crawling for a cursed bow because I don't even have the capacity to aim my knife correctly." She rolled her eyes at the ceiling, still frustrated she hadn't ended it with one cut. She was badly out of practice. Onyx was still watching her, clearly confused by her defending him.

"Onyx, I am not angry, I am grateful. We are shifters. To be that is to be half wild. One side pulled by higher thought, the other by instinct. We both know this!" She felt an old anger. She was fine with a shifter's heritage being messy. It was a beautiful kind of messy, when people didn't attempt to pretend they had no wild side or blame every lapse on instincts.

"I should never return to the beaches. I have made bad choices and don't trust me to make good." He laid his hand on her side as he spoke, over her rib. She felt a more powerful surge of healing energy than he had used before, he was drawing slightly from the island. It was over quickly and when he pulled his hand back, she could see whiteness in the tips of his fingers.

"Then don't. Not until you're ready. I know you feel guilty, but I know you love your homelands, I can hear it in your voice every time you speak of them, but maybe it's not where you're meant to be. I mean, you told me I was lucky that you found me. Maybe you're meant to be... elsewhere." She considered him for a moment, she couldn't quite bring herself to invite him to train with her brothers. "At least for now."

He lowered his eyes and was silent for a moment. He seemed to be considering her words.

"You've made mistakes. And you've tried to fix them. I've seen the difference between trying to fix mistakes and trying to ignore them." She sat up, and moved her head slightly until he looked at her. She saw his discomfort. Trying to move forward on a new path was alway so much harder than wallowing in guilt and shame. Like she had been. Oh, she would not pause for that thought. Not right now.

"You should not have healed it yourself, the bone is off," he said, pretending he hadn't heard her words.

"Not horribly so. And I needed to move, I needed my bow." She lay back. Also, if it was too bad, she knew her brother could break it and reset it to heal correctly. Not his favorite thing to do, but possible. Not her favorite either. She kept that to herself though.

"You believed I would fail." Onyx looked dejected as he shook the sensation back into his hands.

"No, I knew you would win. Just didn't like the possible cost. I was going to shoot him before you both killed yourselves. I lost the dagger somewhere. And... I wasn't able to shift in time. Maybe soon."

"Why haven't you shifted?" Onyx's mood passed to curiosity. Waves and tides, shifting and changing. With his brightening, she was almost certain he was beginning to believe in the truth she had spoken.

"Mixed bloods have difficulties that full bloods don't. I'm still not used to full dragon even being possible. If I'm absolutely terrified in the middle of the sea and pain isn't the factor it seems to be lately... well, it works. If I think too hard about it..."

"Is not the higher thought side, is side pulled by instinct." He had a glorious teasing half smirk on his face as he paraphrased her earlier words.

"I'm aware, unfortunately, it wasn't something I gained through a pleasant experience. And I'm not a master quick-changer like present company." She was sore beyond belief, it was time to sleep, at least for awhile.

"Come here." She patted the bedding beside her, surprising even herself with the speed and extent of her forgiveness for a moment before she realized that she held no fear of Onyx. He looked at the space hesitantly.

"Are you certain?"

"We're even now on the awkward things we've done to each other, so, yes, I am certain." She laughed and then stretched out on the blankets. "You stopped that first night when I was weak and couldn't fight back. You had every reason to think I'd asked for your touch. And you've stopped when in full grip of instincts. If I can't trust you, then there is little I can trust."

"I barely stopped myself," he spoke and Aislinn snorted and rolled her eyes.

"But you did. You realized something was off and you *chose* not to continue and fought yourself the instant you realized." She propped her head up on her hand. "And did you want to continue?"

"I've wanted you since before the hunter attacked." His tone was bitter, he was annoyed with himself, and he sighed heavily as his face flushed red in embarrassment. "You're right, I become too fond of you in very short time."

"There you go, you have more willpower than you give yourself credit for. And you're honest. You should see dragons on a hunt, more than a few have blamed their instincts for not holding back from a kill. Sometimes they tell the truth, sometimes the truth is they didn't want to." Aislinn watched the expressions flit across his face. From shy and hopeful adoration to a fearful and empty sadness. She decided to give in to her own curiosity. "What do you want? Do you plan to hide out on your little island mostly alone forever, punishing yourself?"

"No. I... don't know... I don't want to be alone forever," Onyx replied sadly. He gingerly crawled in next to her and turned his back to her as was their habit. He nearly jumped when Aislinn impulsively draped an arm over him. He stared back over his shoulder, eyes wide.

"I can move if it bothers you." She was trying not to laugh at his expression, she hadn't meant to surprise him. She'd thought he might welcome the gesture.

He turned his back to her again, silent. Aislinn hesitated; then began to withdraw. Onyx's fingers tangled in hers and he pulled her arm back as he curled up against her.

"Stay." And then, so soft she could barely hear, "You make me feel not alone."

Aislinn tucked her head into the nape of his neck and relaxed, glad he hadn't asked her how she felt about him. That was too complicated for her right now, but she could agree that it was nice to not feel lonely.

Chapter 29 - Bait

Dalan woke Aarn early in the morning.

"Dark got in a fight."

"Patch him up. Did he find anything?" Aarn did not open his eyes. He was waiting for the reason Dalan woke him.

"He found the other male. I don't think he's coming back to patch up. The collar feels cold and I heard a victory bell last night. It weren't Dark." Dalan was more irritated than Aarn would have thought. Likely they had truly lost the dog then. Dalan had put in a lot of work, it was enough to make anyone sour.

"Lost a fight for a cow. Hope he didn't rip up the other male too bad." Win some, lose some. Aarn rolled over.

"We're down a dog and Longshanks isn't working." Dalan stood there, waiting for orders.

"We'll take the cage and toss him in near the shore at low tide. Worst case, he drowns and we process him. Best case we lure the others out and we can get a look at what we got." Aarn rolled out of his hammock. "Best get ready to do it now. Gamble and Vari are back with the dinghy, yeah?"

"Been back for hours. I'll get him ready to move."

Aarn yawned and took a swig of a bottle tucked near his hammock. Spirits, this hunt was complicated. The rewards would be more than worth it if they could bag a silvercoat. Or two. He heard Dalan swearing in the hold, it was a testament to the sheer annoyance of Longshanks that Aarn did not even want to know what had happened now. He was ready to tip the cursed thing into the ocean right here and now. He moved along to the hold as quickly as he could though. No use having Dalan kill him before his time.

"What now?" asked Aarn. When he entered, Longshanks' eyes had that familiar smirk and Aarn could see immediately what the issue was: the cage in which he was bound had been slid up against a chest of merchandise hard enough to knock the chest over. Not one to shy from spiteful messes, the creature had bescumbered the contents. Aarn had his doubts that it could be made good as new, but there was always someone willing to pay a cut rate price and ignore issues like smell. But it was one more issue on this hunt. "Get him on the dinghy, we'll clean this up later."

They grabbed the cage and manhandled it to the boat. Aarn was glad he was with Dalan. Despite his current anger, he was the least likely to rise to the thing's bait once the gag was removed.

"Spirits - the stench! Why didn't we throw this thing overboard earlier?"

"You told me you could train him." Aarn put his back into rowing.

"Everybody gets to be wrong."

Aarn grunted and pulled at the oars. He could feel the night air shifting into the hours that were neither night nor day, and he could feel the currents working against him, best time to do this. Longshanks attempted to throw his weight against the cage and tip the boat.

"You go over here, you drown, stupid thing." Dalan smacked the cage. "You drown, we pull up your cursed carcass and I will make myself a coat of your rotten skin because we will row away without you until we're sure you've drank the ocean."

The selkie was still, only glaring at them both. No matter what Dalan said, this one weren't stupid. Probably why he was untrainable. Dark hadn't been particularly bright. Not feeble-minded, but far from clever. He continued glaring at the pair of them all the way to the shore. Aarn smiled. He wished he could stay close enough to see all the fear this one would have before he died, but he wanted a good look at their other merchandise and that meant space. Muquin was the last island for leagues in this direction, there was nowhere else for them to escape to. He had no desire to scour the island without knowing what he was up against.

Their quarry could possibly skirt the boat, but Aarn had the ship holding steady near the safest currents to enter or leave the island. To battle the sea other ways was tricky and deadly, he doubted any creature would risk that. Gamble and Dalan had also set a 'net' of sorts in a wide range around the boat. It wouldn't stop a selkie, but once they hit it, they would be tagged and easy to track for several days. It was an old trick, one many skin hunters had long forgotten in a nearly devout avoidance of the magical arts. But Aarn and his cousins were old line skin hunters, their family had been at it since the days when there were things other than sea dogs and diseased wolves to hunt. Besides, avoiding use of magic when their biggest patrons were those most steeped in the arts made little sense to Aarn. They reached the sandbar and Aarn rammed them hard into the side of it.

"Ungag the thing, Dalan." Aarn did not mention how much he wanted to hear this selkie scream, the cursed thing would drown without a peep if he did that. Spiteful seal.

The first thing the vindictive creature did was bite Dalan hard. Aarn smacked it in the skull with the backside of his dagger.

"Shackles off."

Dalan obeyed, much more cautious this time. Longshanks was cautious as well. The shackles weren't even pulled through the cage bars before he was a bull seal though, his bulk barely fit in the cage, but he managed to turn about amazingly well.

"Push it over, make sure we land it upright on the door, and then we anchor it," ordered Aarn.

It took several tries and almost overturned the boat at one point before they got it onto the sandbar how they wanted. Dalan mumbled over the anchors that would hold it in place before dropping them on the ground. There was a trough of deeper water between this spit of land and the actual shore. Their quarry would be forced to come clear out and shift before they could reach their brethren. And once the tides came in, this sandbar would be gone, the spot they'd dropped him was still covered to a depth of about two handspans and the tide was nearly at its lowest. Rocks funneled the waters high when the tides came in and the cage would be covered completely long enough to drown almost any selkie.

Aarn and Dalan both took the oars on the way back out, the tides were in their favor now and their time was limited. They ignored the words the creature threw at them and were soon enough in the space at the edge of the mists. At this distance, the dinghy would look like a bit of mist itself.

Aarn reached in his coat and rummaged about a bit before pulling out a spyglass that could cut through the mists surrounding the island. He laid low in the boat and trained it on the cage.

Now it was down to waiting.

Chapter 30 - Chokehold

Onyx felt Aislinn rustling around in the bedding after a few hours. He was sleeping lightly and she had seemed unable to find deep sleep. He rolled over to face her and she stilled. They both relaxed as her fingers traced his face. Lips touched his, hesitantly at first, and then more insistent. He breathed her name when they parted for a moment. He opened his eyes a slit, staying still and soaking in this bliss, hoping that this was not a mistake.

The moment was destroyed when they heard the cry of a selkie in distress. Onyx's first reaction was defensive, he recognized the voice as another bull. His defensiveness quickly gave way to confusion when he realized the voice was familiar. Aislinn was fully alert as well.

"The sound - is it another selkie?"

"It's Mer." Onyx was outside in a moment. His hut had been left smoldering, Mer would have known to be cautious seeing the smoke, it was an agreed upon signal if Onyx had ever had to abandon his home. He could hear his friend's bellows more clearly in the morning air. The sound changed after a few moments from seal to human voice and Onyx was now absolutely certain he was hearing Mer. He wasn't entirely sure who Mer wished to flay alive if he reached them, but the in-depth description including exactly where he was going to start left Onyx had no doubt he was serious.

Onyx reached the shoreline and saw a cage in the water several yards from shore. His friend was inside it, switching between forms and throwing himself at the bars. The water was up to his waist.

"It has to be a trap." Aislinn had come up behind him, carrying the bow.

"It does not matter. He is my friend!"

"I am not arguing, just warning." She had an arrow at ready.

He dove into water, becoming a seal as he cut through the tides. He was soon by Mer's cage.

"Why am I not surprised to find you here?" Mer was shaking his head, half amused even in his terror.

"I'm surprised to find you here. What happened?" asked Onyx.

"Can I explain after I'm out?" The water was lapping up his torso steadily. Tides were coming in.

Onyx searched for the door.

"It's on the bottom. We need to flip the cage and-" Mer stumbled as Onyx hit the cage with his full weight. He continued through gritted teeth once he regained his balance. "I've been trying to flip it, but I think they enchanted the anchors holding it down."

"Then how..." Onyx ran his hands around the bars.

"I was hoping you would know. Strange escapes and wins are your specialty."

"You're confused – Moni has the dumb luck." Onyx glanced back at the shore as he mentioned their sweet, but not bright, friend. They could really use a spot of his fool's luck, he'd probably fall onto the cage and knock the latch open and anchors loose without trying. He saw Aislinn waist deep in the water, searching the horizon for enemies, not that any of them could see far with the fog. "But we might have a bit of other luck today. I'll be right back."

"No hurry, I'll be taking a relaxing stroll on the sea bottom," Mer snapped as Onyx left.

Onyx surfaced next to Aislinn and changed, explaining the situation as briefly as he could.

"I might be able to do something. Did the cage even move when you hit it?"

"It rocked."

Aislinn waded in and stood chest deep, hesitating.

"Sky-cat?"

"Trying to shift."

He came up behind her and placed his head on her shoulder. "Reach for that wild place inside. Don't think."

"Excuse me! If it's not too much trouble, could I get some help before you two get cozy?"

"Or don't. Mer can hold his breath really long time." Onyx watched closely once she stopped giggling. He could tell she was focusing, he could sense it almost working. He guessed the instant she was on the verge of thinking too much and bit her shoulder.

The distraction and surprise of a near threat was enough; the force of her wings snapping out knocked him far away and beneath the water. When he surfaced, she was already swimming out towards Mer, likely eschewing the sky in an attempt to provide less of a target for any foes. Mer was looking at her and back to Onyx. Onyx wasn't certain if his expression was asking what the dragon was going to do to him or what Onyx was doing with a dragon. It was clams to oysters which question it was. The water was high on Mer's chest now.

She reached the side of the cage, reared up, and slammed against the box. Once, twice, three times. The first hit rocked the cage, the second tilted it further, the third – Onyx hoped that Mer had caught his breath before it tipped beneath the waves.

Aislinn was tearing at the door to the cage, not bothering to change back to pick the lock. Or she couldn't pick locks, but that would have been more surprising to Onyx at this point. As Onyx swam towards them to help, he heard a screech and a pop echo underwater. She had torn the door off its hinges; he was absolutely in awe of her strength.

She jumped on top of the cage to get out of the way and Mer was out the moment she gave him that space. A chocolate-colored blur of a bull seal with the whites of his eyes very visible and completely disoriented with terror. Onyx bumped up against him and Mer nearly shot out of the water. Aislinn stood atop the cage, tail twitching slightly as she slowly searched the mists for a few moments before taking to the air, seemingly satisfied that if there was anyone nearby they were not in a position to attack. She circled once overhead before landing back on shore.

Onyx called to her as she took off and kept his eyes locked on her as he guided Mer to shore. Mer went ashore down the beach further away from her than Onyx's directives. Onyx grudgingly turned away from his dragoness to check on his friend.

"Is that thing safe?" Mer was in his human form, eyes still wide in terror.

"She wouldn't hurt us." Onyx was slightly offended at the thought he'd send something dangerous after his friend.

Mer gave him a withering look. "You don't have the best taste in cows. I may not have liked Neha, but she couldn't eat us."

"She did save you."

"I'm grateful, but I would like to avoid becoming food."

Dalan and Aarn were initially disappointed by the female's reaction. Her reluctance to go in the water proved she wasn't selkie. The beauty of the greycoat's pelt went a long way to soothe that. This hunt would be well worth the trouble.

Aarn nearly dropped his glass when she did change. He handed it wordlessly to Dalan.

"Can't be." Dalan whistled appreciatively and spoke without lowering the glass. "Back leg's got some roughness to it, but she's a beauty. A few little bundles of that mane could get us rations for weeks. One of those wings, just one, that'd fetch more than the silvercoat's entire carcass. Not to mention the coin for each and every scale. Never thought I'd see one of those in my lifetime."

"Shouldn't it be bigger?" Aarn was curious, a trait he didn't often possess unless it led to profit, but this was a very strange bit of luck.

"Take away the wings and the body's about the size of a draught horse. By the book, that's a fair standard for most breeds." Dalan finally handed the glass back to Aarn. "I doubt drowning will work quite as well for her as our seal-skinned friends. Gamble and I have been working on a spell for a while, trying to adapt it to the selkies, but it was meant for her kind. Forces them right into the shape we need 'em in."

"Can you work it?"

"Not elsewhere, not yet, but I got Muquin to draw on. Gimme that and have someone grab a few things from the market, and we got a fair shot." He nodded and considered for a moment. "Might need to adjust some of our equipment. Probably need to dress the carcass on the beach instead of on the boat. But I think we got a shot. I'll take the dog out now, one less problem when we go for her and the silvercoat." He nodded several more times. "This is gonna be a good hunt, cousin. Likes of which have not been seen for ages."

Onyx understood his friend's reluctance, to a point. He wished he knew how to get across that Aislinn was no threat to him.

"If she wanted to eat you, she could have pried you out of the cage like a clam." Onyx paused for a moment, impressed by the memory of her prying open the cage. Aislinn was magnificent. Mer clearing his throat with an undertone of disdain brought him back.

"You've known her how long?" Mer looked increasingly skeptical.

"A cycle of the moon. Give or take."

"I think I'll pass on my thanks and be on my way," said Mer.

"I swear, I eat neither seal nor man. Besides, you look far too skinny to be anything other than tough and gamey." Aislinn came up behind the pair of them, now appearing mostly human, but with wings still out and tail flicking playfully. She was also smiling in a slightly unnerving manner.

"Aislinn of the clan deAvaric, I present to you Selomer of the Crescent Moon clans," said Onyx, nudging Mer slightly forward and hoping his friend would take the hint to politely finish introductions. Aislinn ruined that chance though.

"Charmed, but we should move off the beach before making introductions." Aislinn was watching the sea again. She then turned and melted into the woods. Onyx had a moment of wonderment at how smoothly she disappeared before realizing it was skill and not a bit of magic, then he was even more impressed. Mer elbowed him out of his fascination.

"Well, I haven't been eaten and she's rude, but she seems better than Neha. I will follow you, my honorable brother."

"Next time, you drown." Onyx moved into the woods, not bothering to check if Mer followed.

He heard a choking sound behind him.

"Really? You don't have to come with us if you don't want to, but she's not going to hurt us." Onyx pivoted to see Mer grasping his neck. He noticed for the first time a strip of leather round Mer's neck that he was trying to claw off. Mer shifted to seal and started shaking his head. Onyx was horrified to see the strap change with him. Mer tried to catch it on a branch to tear it off. It refused to slip over his head. Onyx grabbed it looking for a clasp and found none.

He then realized that it held the same sickening sheen he had seen in the marketplace.

"Use the dagger!"

His knife thudded in the sand near his feet. Aislinn had returned once she heard the commotion of Mer's thrashing.

Mer stilled as Onyx tried to cut the band. The leather would not cut. Mer panicked, something Onyx had seldom seen in the years he had known his friend, and switched back to human again, trying to slip out of it. Onyx felt lost, unsure how to help his friend. Aislinn was now on her knees next to them, examining the band. She was the only one who looked near calm.

"Unheal it." Aislinn looked at Onyx. "Onyx, unheal it."

"How?" He had never heard of such a thing. She grabbed his hand and laid his fingers on the band.

"Whatever you do to heal, reverse it. If you push energy into the wound, pull the energy from the band to you. It's made of shifter skin, it's the only thing that they could make follow his form like this. For skins to work like that the spell has to make them function like they are living." Her voice was low and much calmer than Onyx felt. "I can't do this. It's precise. My only other choice is burning the strap, and I'll burn him too. And if it won't cut, I can't guarantee burning it will work."

Onyx shifted his grip, finding a spot where he would damage Mer the least if he was not accurate. Aislinn was talking to Mer, trying to still him.

Nothing happened. The strap did not have the exact feel as a living being, but she was right that there was something similar to it. After several agonizing seconds, Onyx managed to shift something through the strap. The results were not what was wanted. Onyx jerked back in terror as the strip grew embedded in his friend's neck and looked to Aislinn for assistance. Mer's lack of even a frustrated glance unnerved him further.

"Just try again," said Aislinn, voice still calm. She placed his fingers back on the bit of leather. "Remove the strap from his skin, it'll be like pushing out a sliver, and let that movement flow into the strap."

Mer's eyes were becoming bloodshot. Onyx let out a shaky breath and searched the edges of the strap again. He focused on the idea of a sliver and removing it became easy enough. He ignored the oozing wound it left as that was superficial and he needed to continue with the strap. He edged the skin of the strap apart as he had Mer's flesh. It fought him for what felt like forever as Onyx focused, determined not to let his friend die. He was singing softly under his breath as he did.

The band suddenly snapped open and fell to the ground, withering as it did so. Aislinn dragged Mer into the treeline the instant it did and Onyx was close behind.

"How did you know that would work?" Onyx asked.

"I didn't. Magic has loopholes and from what I know of such things, that seemed a likely one."

"You let him try that not knowing?" Mer's voice was barely audible, a whisper of a whisper.

"Other options were let you die or burn you, possibly fatally, while attempting to remove it myself. Let us know later which one you prefer. Now shut up until Onyx has a moment to heal you." Aislinn gathered the rest of their things and nocked an arrow. Onyx could tell she was trying to ignore her leg.

Mer's eyes narrowed, but he remained silent on the way back to the cave. None of them felt safe in the open right now.

Chapter 31 - Inheritance

Aarn and Dalan waited in the mists until twilight and then returned to the boat with their news. Longshanks had unfortunately fallen out of sight of them, so Aarn hadn't been able to enjoy the sight of his death.

His crew was inclined to argue with the change in plans until Gamble brought out the book. Dalan thumbed through the pages filled with fantastical creatures. Aarn watched closely, only the slightest bit jealous.

The book was a precious relic of their family line, handed down from father to son. His cousins' father had been the elder son, while Aarn's had been the younger. So, despite Aarn being the eldest of the three and captain of this crew, Dalan had charge of the book and had his younger brother Gamble store and protect it. Aarn was aware that he could, at any time, claim his right to look at it, but the very idea of having to ask for something that was part of his birthright galled him.

Dalan finally stopped on a page, smoothing it out and nodding decisively before displaying it to the others.

"There she be, lads," he said. "And according to this, she's a rare one."

Aarn stared at the page appreciatively. The long neck, the mane that ran down the spine, the scales, the tan and grey striping, all of it was all there. The red and brown underside of the wing further confirmed she was a female, the males had a mottled blue and brown.

"The island's strange, are you sure that's what you saw?" Stanen was still skeptical. He was the youngest and newest of the crew, having joined only at the end of last year's harvest.

"Sure as I am of anything." Dalan was skimming the pages on their latest target, fingers running down the rows of letters with an ease that never failed to impress the other crew. Reading the waves was more useful than reading letters, so few bothered to learn beyond basics.

"Well, if you're certain, maybe we ought hire a few more boys when we're at market. If it'll make as much money as you say, no harm in spending a bit to make certain we find and capture it," said Stanen. Aarn wasn't certain if Stanen fully believed there was a dragon, but he believed enough that there was something odd and he did not want to go up against the beast without proper back-up. His talents at guiding the ship sometimes barely outweighed his cowardice, but in this case, Stanen was not wrong.

"Once the ship is anchored, you and Vari can see about finding a few new recruits. No more or less than needed."

Vari nodded. He had a good eye for how useful someone would be, he could come back with two men that would do the work of twenty if circumstances were favorable. Aarn had no doubt he'd interrogate Dalan about the beast they were up against and calculate the exact number needed.

Dalan closed the book and went off with Gamble; no doubt they were setting up illusions to keep the beasts unaware of their departure and tracers in case they ran. They left the book on the table and Aarn flipped it open again to the dragon, touching the drawings reverently. Soon, they would get a chance to live up to his family's legacy. This was a rare hunt indeed. It was one he intended on keeping a trophy from.

Chapter 32 - Company

Aislinn was trying not to be abrasive to Onyx's friend. She had nothing against him personally and actually found his obvious wariness of her amusing, but his appearance was suspect. As was the sour smell that was reminiscent of the other selkie.

Onyx led him off briefly to bathe, then returned to the cave to cook. The other selkie returned shortly. As soon as he was offered food, Selomer inhaled it. With every swallow Aislinn caught the slightest of winces, evidence of lingering discomfort. All the while he kept a cautious eye on her, occasionally sending questioning glances Onyx's way. Onyx was silent, seemingly determined to let Selomer rest his throat as much as possible. Onyx's determination spoke to the severity of the wounds, so Aislinn resigned herself to being patient.

She ate quickly, then dug out the dress Onyx had brought back from the market. That day felt like months ago, even though it was... she wasn't even certain how few days had passed. She tossed the dress on while waiting for Selomer to finish. Onyx's knife made quick work of removing the bottom of the skirt. With how the situation was shaping up, anything longer than her knees would only get in her way.

Onyx cozied up to her side when she returned, watching her closely when he thought she was not looking. By his actions, the kisses shared in the morning had not been forgotten - a complication they would have to deal with once other things were sorted out.

She felt she should have been more worried about the possible complications, but instead found herself trying not to laugh. He was covertly glancing between her and his friend; well, attempting to be covert. It was obvious he was gauging her interest in the newcomer and she doubted he was even aware he was doing it.

She supposed it would be understandable if she was attracted to the newcomer. Selomer was tall, thin, and the defined musculature of his stomach would make a sculptor weep at the sheer beauty. Everything else from his dark hair to his lovely jawline to the tips of his feet looked well-made as well. The only obvious flaw was the wound on his neck, and that would heal soon enough. Despite being slender, he looked solid. He reminded her of stone and sea. It felt like his disposition might follow that as well. Onyx, despite his stony name, was wind and waves. Ever changing and with something ethereal in his looks. Even the way he flowed from one form to the other dovetailed neatly with that impression - it was impossibly fluid and quick, she'd never seen the like.

However, no matter how either looked, Aislinn held that seducing anyone shortly after a near death experience was in poor taste. Seducing a friend's friend in such a situation was in even worse taste. Ogling both of them while waiting for more information was probably also in poor taste, but by far the least poor taste and could be an amusing response to Onyx's silliness. She considered allowing herself to do so for the amusement of it, but between her disinterest, the other selkie not being in on the joke, and there being enough problems without her adding to them, she decided to focus on keeping her hands busy shaping spikes from sticks.

On Selomer's third bowl, she decided politeness was satisfied and his throat seemed healthy enough to answer questions.

"Onyx mentioned friends, but didn't mention they would be joining him. What brings you this way?" She leaned against Onyx as she spoke, brushing the back of her hand against his. Too much had been happening of late to start arguing about his lack of calm or lack of a real claim. Whatever they had begun this morning would have to be figured out on the wing. She was certain of Onyx and knew if she was in danger, he would fight beside her.

His friend was another matter.

"The season holds no appeal to me. I thought I'd bother him. What brought you to him?" Selomer's voice rasped only lightly and he was watching her closely. His trust of her looked to equal hers. Aislinn couldn't resist flashing her fangs and was pleased to see she rattled him enough to make him flinch.

"Shipwreck. Well, to be precise, washed overboard during a storm along with poorly secured cargo. I've heard reports that the ship is fine. Onyx found me in the flotsam on the beach."

"You survived the ocean during a storm?" His dubious expression told her how much he didn't believe that tale.

"Did you miss what I was when I opened the cage door?" She countered his flat tone with a quizzical and overly sweet one.

He nodded, obviously understanding the connection, and emptied the bowl of rice porridge before speaking again.

"Are you going to eat us, attack us in our sleep, maim, mangle, anything else that your kind is known for?" He was direct, she liked that.

"Oh no, you'd be awake if I attacked you," Aislinn paused to let that sink in before letting winter settle into her sweet tone, "Also, while we're on this path, do you need a spot to store your skin, or have you lost it? Selkies are well known for taking those off to change to human form, exactly like dragons are known for destruction."

She let the words hang in the air. Both were tales seized on and spread by humans; it gave them justification for hunting things that wore a human face part of the time. Dragons were dangerous possessed humans bent on destruction, killing one was the only way to save the one afflicted. Mercy and defense all in one. As for selkies, it was easier to sell skins if one could convince casual buyers that the owner of said skin was still wandering around alive in human form. More educated buyers generally did not care where the items came from, so long as they were genuine.

Selomer nearly choked on his first bite of his new bowl of porridge, stared at Aislinn for a moment and then looked to Onyx. He spoke in rapid-fire selkie to Onyx, who responded with a red-faced grin. Selomer laughed and Aislinn schooled her expression to calmness she did not feel. The banter did not bother her, it felt relatively harmless, however Selomer's appearance was suspect until it was fully explained. She did not dislike old friends in principle, only when they came from a place where the friend they sought was not always popular and arrived with skin hunters, but with skin still intact.

"If you two are done discussing what Onyx and I have or haven't done, could we continue? Besides, it's an awfully short discussion." Aislinn was pleased to see both males turn red.

"That… it was… that was not how I meant, I meant you would be hard to woo to the beach. I - He- " Onyx's friend looked thoroughly embarrassed and glanced between her and Onyx, mouth moving without words.

Onyx looked away in embarrassment. His head snapped back suddenly, blush fading from his face, and he lifted an eyebrow calculatingly.

"You guessed. You do not know selkie," said Onyx after a long moment, tone thoughtfully accusing. She smiled at him.

"Males are males. Wing, foot, or fin. I guessed correctly though, or close enough to, so remember that in the future. Now, to the problem at hand: how did he get to be in the cage?"

"You *are* scary, even if you aren't going to eat us." Selomer's tone was actually admiring. He ate a little more, blinked in surprise at the unwavering gaze now fixed on him, and finally remembered to respond to her question. "They caught me. Near the market of the Dark Moon clans, I picked up a few bottles of wine. I was going to bring most of them as gifts, but drank one. All of one. At once. In the future, I will not be doing that."

"You are fine until you are not with Dark Moon wine," said Onyx knowingly. By his eyes, he had wandered off into some fond memory. Aislinn would have to ask about that later.

"So, Selomer, if I understand right, the hunters found you passed out drunk?"

"Yeees, or close to. I was injured on rocks instead of escaping." He forced the admission out through his teeth, then added in a lighter tone, "You can call me 'Mer.'"

He looked thoroughly frustrated with himself for the slip up, Aislinn judged his frustration to be at proper level to avoid the same mistake. That was good, but she wasn't done with questions.

"Why are you still alive?" Aislinn's gaze did not let up. He met it with surprising calm.

"They had grand plans and I tore my skin. They want us to help them hunt. They thought I might be afraid when I saw what they did to the other," Selomer paused and shuddered. He closed his eyes, then opened them, but could not quite seem to escape the memory. A haunted look in his dark eyes spoke to the truth of the horror. "As painful as it looked, I don't hunt my kind. One of the hunters – Gam-bell, I think – was in love with the idea of 'dogs', so he convinced them to keep me."

"We have to rescue the other selkie." Onyx was on his feet. His trip down memory lane was very short if he had kept up with the conversation as well as it seemed.

"I heard you met him. Large, missing part of an ear. Scars. Probably skipped conversation because they discouraged speaking."

"Oh." He sat back down again. "I thought he was attacking us because there was a female." Onyx's eyes widened. "I am idiot."

"I'm not questioning, but why now?" Mer responded flippantly. Onyx glared at him before answering.

"If he was wanting a female, he wouldn't have tried to crush Aislinn."

"Happy to hear that's not common in your culture. Even after healing, my body hurts. Can't imagine that as part of courtship." Aislinn closed her eyes and sighed. She could not seem to avoid trouble even if she washed up on a nearly deserted island. Especially with males. She considered avoiding all males, but she had brothers. And a son. Part of her weighed if they really counted. Another, more sensible, part of her mind was focusing on the actual issue and stepping ahead to plan for whatever it was that would be coming. Hunters versatile enough to think to use other selkies would not stop after a simple setback. Not with a solid payoff at stake. Mer confirmed those thoughts when he went on.

"They're hunting for you now. Your coat is valuable. Biggest catch in years. They want her too if she's worth anything. They have a trap across the outbound currents. Not sure what, but it's magic."

"So we're trapped unless we trick or destroy them," said Aislinn. Both males stared at her, open-mouthed. They understood what she was saying, but she could tell they were not as certain of the necessity of the second as she was. Mer turned back to his food, pondering this development. Onyx was the next one to speak.

"You could run, they want me the most."

"I'm not fond of sacrifice in cases like this. They won't stop at your skin. Maybe we'll be safe, but sooner or later they'll hunt others. Besides, I much prefer your skin where it is." Aislinn smiled at him, then closed her eyes to think. "Help won't come before they can attack, but I need to get outside the influence of the island to reach out to my brothers. And I'll also need every bit of information you have on them."

Aislinn was relieved that neither one argued with her taking charge for the moment. She spent the rest of the day gathering information from Mer, cataloging what was available to them, and finding out more about the selkie methods of fighting.

Chapter 33 - Failure

As evening began to fall, Onyx carried Aislinn out beyond the mists. He was reluctant, but she needed the space from the island and she said water amplified her abilities for this type of magic. She was lightly shivering by the time they passed the mists and unsuccessfully trying to hide it by pressing into his fur. Onyx was glad of the makeshift harness that kept her strapped to him. He knew she would pass out before she would admit to her exhaustion.

"I can feel a barrier set by them. I just can't tell how far it stretches," as she spoke, her teeth chattered the tiniest bit.

Onyx nuzzled her and tried to nudge her back towards the shore. She shook her head.

"I have to, Sea-cat. The ship has five trained hunters, plus five other crew members, that's a few more than us. We need more help, especially if they have someone that can put up a barrier like that."

Onyx huffed, but held them steady in the gentle waves, hoping she would find the state she needed quickly. Her shivers were becoming harder to hide and he doubted she'd fare well if the mists closed them out for hours.

Aislinn reached the level of dreaming she needed surprisingly easily, but that was where her luck ended. She did not recognize where she was and found herself wandering through an unfamiliar house wondering what place she had been drawn into. Another corner, yet another unfamiliar room. Frustration turned into hopelessness, then she spied a familiar figure standing near a fireplace. Damian. She would recognize her brother anywhere, even though his back was turned to her.

"Damian, I-" She backed off when he snapped around suddenly. She knew that movement and her mistake the instant she saw it. He was not greeting family, he was greeting danger. He didn't know her yet, she cursed the wildly uneven time flow. She hoped she could convince him that she was not a threat.

"Who sent you? How did you get here?" His voice was low and dangerous. She tried not to flinch as she looked at him. He was both at the fire and next to her with his blade at the same moment. She felt the edge pressing on her throat and knew this was not an idle threat. He could kill her even though this was a dream.

"Nobody sent me, brother. I came to you because I need your help, but I... I failed. I'm decades too early and you don't even recognize me." A tear rolled down her cheek. She could tell he did not believe her; and she knew without a doubt that he had trapped her here. Waking would be no help.

"Let us begin with the simplest of questions. If you are my sister from the future, who are your parents?"

"I am not blood, but you taught me the entire lineage. I'll recite it if you like, but I'm short on time. My lineage is that by long line of disastrous events, I am a sister to Edorian Silverthorne," as she spoke Rin's name, Damian's eyes narrowed in calculation, but he let her continue.

"As I am part dragon, you and Daren adopted me because I needed someone of dragon influence to raise me." She stared into his cold blue eyes, willing something to connect. "My very first memory, I was practically a baby, but I was surrounded by wings and warmth. You told me I'd had a nightmare and woke up screaming, you and Daren coddled me and soothed me back to calm. Daren-" she paused and rolled her eyes as Daren had that effect, "he did a blood pact without asking to mend a feud between you and Rin. Which was very stupid of him, but you know him. If it's an ill-advised path, he will take it."

His face was softening, and in a moment of inspiration, she softly sang a few words of an old Geltanian lullaby. They didn't use the language much, only at home, but it was the twins' native tongue and a song their older sister had sung to them when they were tiny and they had, in turn, sung to her when she was tiny and they all sung to Caeda now.

After a moment, he lowered the dagger, but did not release the barrier. He pushed to search memories from her mind and she gave no resistance. She realized that even now, she did not fear her brother. He could kill her, but she couldn't find it in her to fear him. Whenever she feared his anger, she had actually been ashamed. Whether it was her memories or these emotions, the dagger disappeared and his forehead touched hers.

"Your memories explain the peculiarities of your aura satisfactorily. I am sorry, little one. Why do you need my assistance?" At his words, Aislinn gave a delighted gasp and threw her arms around him. She backed off quickly when he tensed and she realized that 'knowing' and 'being' were separate things. This was not quite her brother, even if he had picked up on one of his names for her.

"I'm trapped on an island with two selkies. We've been cornered by skin hunters because one of them is a silver pelt. They may've also seen that I'm part, well, full dragon, so I'm a target as well. I'm injured, one of them is injured as well. I can barely do anything magic wise because we are in a place of the ancients. I'm a conduit and there's too much raw magic for me to channel."

"Which island?"

"Somewhere in the islands south of the Wyvern's Spine and east of Minado. That's all I know. Onyx - one of the selkies - knows the name, but it doesn't sound familiar to me. He called the island we are on 'Muquin.'"

"That narrows it down to five locations." He pondered a moment. "Four. The fifth is highly unlikely. Tell me how you arrived there."

She told him, feeling more and more helpless. She had failed. The selkies might die because of it. She sank into a chair and put her face in her hands.

"Little one," the softness in his voice made her look up, "You have reached me. If you had any finer skills in this, I am certain I would have honed them so you could not miss your target." He stared at her for a long time. "You are strong, and I have no doubt I have trained you as well as I could. These hunters may be dangerous, but you are one of ours. Take them piece by piece if necessary. Wake now, and fight for yourself and your companions."

Aislinn snapped awake, shivering in the water. Damian's words had been encouraging, but she was aware her brother would not remember meeting her until too late. He had taught her that. One might meet someone in a dream, in a time out of line with theirs, but those dreams were seldom remembered. At least, not until their time had come. She feared where that would leave her and Mer and Onyx. She was shivering almost too hard to think.

"Back to land, Sea-cat."

They barely had enough time to return to shore. Aislinn helped as much as she was able, but she was near unconsciousness by the time they finally made it up on the rocks.

"Will they come?" Onyx was tired, but he worked on her injuries and this new damage from the water's chill as they lay by the waterside.

"Yes, but it will take some time. The island affects magic, he can't track me like he normally would, and we couldn't stay in the water long enough for him to try. But there's only a handful of spots that do that, so he can narrow it down." Her words felt off. She was avoiding saying something, keeping some secret. He wasn't certain what it was but he knew there was a lie there.

"Will it be soon enough?" Onyx felt uneasy, but decided to let it pass. He suspected it had not gone even as well as she said and that made him worry more than he cared to think about. He understood a lie for hope, so he would play along.

"We can hope so. In the meantime, let's get back to Mer before he eats all the food." She smiled as she spoke, but those eyes were so very sad.

When they returned to the cave, the three worked on more plans until Onyx fussed her under the blankets. She was asleep before he had finished banking the fire.

"We have a problem." Mer stood beside him.

"Ah, Mer. Why couldn't you have something to say like 'the skin hunters have left and we are all safe'?" Onyx half-smiled at him, hoping for a laugh. He had not liked the tone.

"Because the skin hunters haven't left and we're not all safe."

"You need to be more positive."

"Brother..." Mer's face held a long suffering look.

"Is this a new problem? And if it is, can it wait? We have too many already."

"Come on." Mer led the way outside. "I decided to explore." Mer pushed uphill through the forest, stopping by a pile of what Onyx took to be rocks or maybe wood and looked away.

It took Onyx a few moments to realize that the moss covered items weren't rocks or wood. They were bones. He picked one up and cracked it against a rock. Despite its age, the bone didn't want to crack, and once it did, it was easy to see how sturdy it was. Selkie bones. This island had been a stop for hunters for ages and they had left bits of their kills as thanks to the spirits for a good hunt. Onyx could now see more piles and most of them were old and moss-covered. Even the newest bones looked to have been placed several seasons past, but he still felt a chill in his heart at the presence of so many dead. He was nowhere near as schooled in magic as his sleeping dragoness, but he did not need to be told that this repository could twist the island in their pursuers' favor. The history these bones spoke of could do that. He had heard of clans and colonies on these isles in the past, but they had long since disappeared.

Onyx would have loved to be naïve and claim the lack of newer bones was because man had become kinder or wiser, but he knew the truth. When whole colonies were slaughtered, the profit in selkie parts dropped for seasons, leaving the hunters to find other, more pleasant work. Most people carried at least a few qualms about killing something that could be so human-looking. And because of slaughtered villages in the past, selkies were cautious and dwindling. Onyx tried to not to weep at the heaviness in the air as he walked between bone cairns.

"Brother?" Mer's voice sounded timid, worried. His voice seemed more pleading than normal.

"When we finish with the hunters, we burn these, Mer. For now, it will have to wait." Onyx replaced the bone he broke with a prayer and an apology. "Mer?"

"Yes?"

"Go back to the cave, keep watch. I'll be back soon. And I might be loud, so ignore it."

Onyx followed Mer back to the campsite and wandered away to where he'd covered the bull selkie's corpse with pine needles. He dragged him up to the boneyard. It was a filthy and odious job, but he felt the need to honor the bull somehow, even if he had given in to the skin hunters. Onyx wished he knew the selkie's name, he looked to be from the Crescent Moon clans, but he was not anyone Onyx recognized. Mer had been adamant his name was not Dark - names were the first thing the crew had tried to take - but the bull had refused to tell him. Whatever it had been, for now, it had died with him.

He laid Dark in the midst of all the bones, covered him again with needles, and bowed his head over the corpse. Once he was done with this prayer as a human he changed to seal and bellowed out his fury to the night air for several minutes. He moved to each corner of an imaginary square in the court of bones to shout his anger to the wind. He wasn't sure how long had passed before he composed himself.

Onyx stretched out on the moss and hummed a meditative hum, reaching out into the night to anything powerful nearby. He felt the power of the island surging and flowing through him, but couldn't quite grasp it. He sensed the trees and rocks and animals and the dark coil of death that was this mossy vale. The moss covering the bones glowed darkly in his minds' eye. There was too much death placed here, he could feel it leaving a stain in the land. He reached out further, and found Aislinn and Mer. Both were bright spots, counterpoints of life to this destructive force in the vale.

He asked for the spirits to help him with the fight, even if he could not live past it, he wanted to finish this, and they could burn down the dark stain on this island. Mer and Aislinn could escape even if he could not. Hours passed as he felt the tides of power shift about him and when he opened his eyes, he knew it was shortly before sunrise. He felt empty and defeated as the island had not responded.

Onyx ignored Mer's questioning look as he returned. He was exhausted and refused to answer questions. Sliding beneath the blankets and curling up next to Aislinn was the only thing he wanted. The thought of his companions' bright lights being snuffed out and reduced to another bit of the darkness on the hill was too heavy to bear.

Chapter 34 - Clarity

Onyx wandered off when morning came. Aislinn wondered at his reasons, but he had left with a sense of purpose so she focused on the day and time they had.

"Do you ever stop eating?" she marveled at Mer gulping down what she was almost certain was his third bowl of stew.

"Yes. When asleep." He flashed a grin at her.

"And yet you are still as skinny as an eel." Aislinn was curious about the minor wincing at the word 'eel', but let it pass. "Once you're done shoveling food in your mouth, would you like to spar?"

"With a dragon?" Mer looked at her suspiciously.

"Yes, I fully intend to change into a great, scaly, clawed beast and rip you to shreds for *practice*," her tone was as dry as long grass at high summer.

"Why blame a selkie for caution? What about your leg?"

"That would be why I need to spar. I was nearly killed by your friend when he came upon us, that should not have happened," she said. Mer looked at her, she could tell he was calculating something.

"You didn't use scales and claws on him why?"

"I have reasons. Let's just say it's difficult for me." Aislinn had actually had Onyx leave his bite marks unhealed. She wanted them as a focus. She hoped they would help her remember the shock and the feeling that had overcome her in that moment. She doubted she would ever be as smooth as Onyx, but she could at least find a way to make her dragon form as accessible as her wings. That, however, was for later in the day.

Mer put his dish down and stood. He found a spot a short ways away on the moss and stood waiting, stretching his neck and rolling his shoulders. She squared off a few paces away from him and waited. He mock rushed her. She rocked back slightly, but did not fully engage in dodging or attacking, not just yet. His real attack came with almost no warning. A small part of her inwardly complimented his skill while the rest ducked to the side and pivoted to deliver a blow to the back of his head. He had already started to turn and move to the side. He grabbed her wrist in the same motion.

And received a solid knee to his ribs.

Aislinn had put herself somewhat off balance to do so, but the knee knocked him off balance as well. Both fell and he released his grip as they instinctively rolled and twisted away from each other. Aislinn came up into a crouch, teeth bared in threat and using that expression to distract from the way the motions were tearing at everything. Mer's teeth were bared as well. By the way his sides heaved, she was guessing the damage to his throat was restricting his air intake.

"Doing well. What are you?" He managed to keep his voice mostly even.

"Direct." She let him have his banter, she needed the moment as well. "I'm someone whose work requires a certain amount of skill in fighting. I'm getting very curious on the selkie style of fighting, I might have to make a visit to the isles to learn."

"Strange female."

"Yet you trust me or you wouldn't have agreed to this." She rose slowly to her feet, keeping her eyes focused on him.

"I only trust you because he trusts you." Mer was now standing as well.

"Onyx trusts many people," she countered.

"True. But he doesn't truly trust many." Mer was beginning to move and she echoed it, circling with the conversation.

"Perhaps I'm just a very convincing liar." At Aislinn's words, Mer snorted in disbelief.

"I've seen him spot a lie from the farthest shore, but his talk of you was empty of 'she's lying, but I'm sure she has her reasons'. He trusts you." A quick lunge from him which she painfully sidestepped. Neither one of them followed up as they should have. They squared up again and Onyx was suddenly between the two of them, growling slightly. Mer's posture changed instantly – head lowered in submission. "You know I would not."

"Not. The problem." Onyx took a half step and had his hand on Mer's throat, alarming Aislinn until he spoke. "This burns, doesn't it? You can still feel that bit of leather cutting off all air."

Mer dropped his head and backed away, looking like a scolded child. Onyx kept his back to Aislinn for a few more moments. Pride told her to keep her head up, her heart and head told her to admit her mistake, a very rare match up she was inclined to heed.

"I requested the sparring. This was my idea."

"I know." Onyx's tone was hard. He finally turned around to face her. He was angry, but his eyes were wide and full of pain, tears held back. "I know you. You push and push and push. Your ribs. Your leg. Maybe other injuries. They are not healed. I know you cannot rest when the fight comes, but do not hurt each other. Rest now. We may lose each other soon enough. No need to help them by making it sooner." He stalked off towards the shore. They were both silent.

"I'm sorry. Getting you in trouble was not my intention." Aislinn glanced sideways at Mer as she spoke.

"No harm." Mer waved it off. He was calm, but looked slightly ashamed. "He's scared, not angry. And right. But you are right." Mer plopped down, crossed legged and with a bowl of food that almost appeared magically out of the air.

"His moods shift like the winds." She found her own bowl as she continued staring at the space where Onyx had been.

"Moods, yes. Heart, no." Mer watched her. "He worries. He told you why he was here?"

"A female rejected him. He got his vengeance. He feels guilty."

"That is not all." Mer sighed. "He is different, we..." He shrugged.

"Well, that part as well. I take it conformity is encouraged?"

"Yes." Mer had paused a moment before answering. His Amarantine was sharper and smoother than Onyx's but there were limits. From all she'd gleaned, she had a feeling Mer was a bit of an odd one out as well. The language hadn't really been meant for deep discussions. "That's part. Onyx tries. He never reaches what he thinks he should."

"I guessed that. He is very unique. It suits him." Aislinn was trying to ascertain where this was leading when Mer smiled and nodded at her assessment.

"We were children and hunters came. They caught another one of us." Mer stirred his food thoughtfully. "Some said Onyx's coat caught the hunters' eyes. He was blamed and it stayed with him, even though the rocks were full of unattended young ones. He tries... he tries..."

"Tries to make up for things that were not his fault?"

Mer ate in silence. It was a loud silence that stretched on for several minutes.

"You are right. It is hard, even though he keeps trying. I wish good things for him." He looked at her. "Like you. I want you to be good for him." There it was.

"That's not what's important right now."

"Perhaps. This could be easier if you were closer to the beach." Mer stared at the sky for a moment, then smirked. "The beach, it's like this place. It has a presence. It makes things simple, even when it confuses the mind. It... if you two were there, you would..." He gave up trying to politely explain and smacked his hands together, grinning. Aislinn had seen far more lewd gestures, but there was no missing his meaning.

"I doubt it, he has a lot of restraint, and I'm not a selkie." Aislinn's tone was flat. She disliked where he was going with this. She also disliked that she was having trouble not laughing. There was something honest about Mer that kept the conversation from feeling completely crass.

"Humans visited. Once. From the continents. Rich. Dunno who they bribed to visit so far into our territory. Or why. Wrong ideas, maybe? Father, mother, son, daughter, servants." Mer shook his spoon at her. "Father was chasing cows who did not want him, son discovered that his father's money would not buy a mate. Or block punches. The men wanted to leave once they learned."

"And?" Aislinn was intrigued, something in his tone left echoes of the kind of salacious story Daren would tell.

"The servants would disappear to 'pack', but were busy with other servants. Except the head servant." Mer's eyes glinted mischievously and his eyebrows raised in a way that said the next part would be particularly scandalous.

"What was the head servant doing?"

"Enjoying the beach with the rich man's wife."

"They were all human?" Aislinn was laughing now.

"All."

"I'd bet my horse the marriage was an arranged one - a very poorly arranged one. What of the rich man's daughter?"

"She was very proper. Would wear clothes in public baths with her friends." Mer took a slow thoughtful bite of his food. "A friend of mine smiled at her. The resulting pups are noisy, but cute."

"Her father must have been displeased." She wiped tears from her eyes. She could picture it. She'd known men like this: all money, no character.

"Disowned. But pups keep her too busy for worry. Also, her mother and servant. My friend is happy even though he had to add on to his family house fast. And live with his mother-in-law." He smirked. "The rich man - not so happy. His-" he waved his hands in the the air for a moment, searching for a word, "Rank. His rank came through his wife. And part of his money."

"Oh, I'd imagine not." She was laughing. She could picture everything. Mer continued smirking into his dish for a bit, before becoming serious.

"Understand, my friend will die for you. I've seen him in love."

"It's... whatever his feelings... it's not important right now." Aislinn did not like this turn. She felt cornered. "Well, it is important, but we don't have the time."

"Again. If you two were on the beach, you would figure this out. Much quicker." He raised his hands as if they could stop the retort she felt rising, but he did not stop. "Protect him, he will try to protect you. And protect yourself. He won't forgive himself if you don't survive."

"I can try. I make no promises."

"Acceptable." Mer nodded at her answer and she realized he had found what looked to be wild carrot roots and was now munching on those. "I've known of his worry for a while, but he's been strange since I showed him the bones."

"Bones?" Her voice rose in pitch. She was hoping it was some kind of mis-translation. Had to be.

"This was a hunter's stop. They leave bones from every kill to thank the powers here."

"Offerings to the spirits? And neither of you thought to tell me this?"

"I thought he'd tell you. They are up the hill if you want to see, but I think it'd be easier on all of us if you soothed your bull first."

"Not my bull." She rubbed her temples, some of the issues with dreaming made more sense. The island was not hostile, but not entirely neutral.

"Lover, partner, whichever word you use, you both know what you are." Mer shoved another root in his mouth and carefully spoke around it, pointing at her with another bit of root. "Either way, he wants you, and you want him even if you won't admit."

"I'd ask how anyone can stay friends with you, but you're loyal despite how annoying you are. I will see the bones first, and if there's time, I'll see about Onyx after."

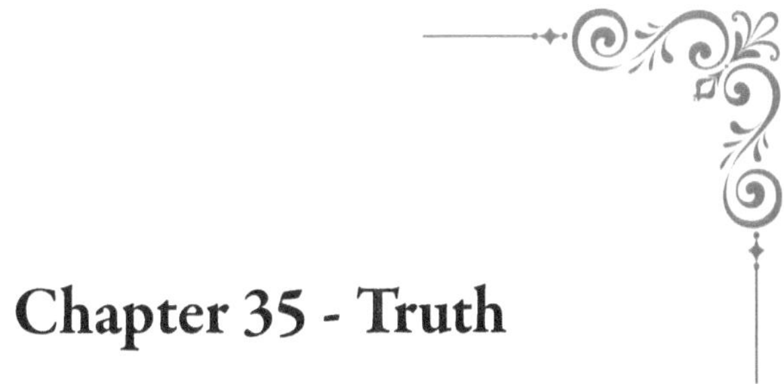

Chapter 35 - Truth

Aislinn wanted to tell the truth as she left Mer behind in the clearing. There was not more time. Nobody was coming. But she clung to the lie and the false hope it might give them. And the truth stayed in her throat when she saw the remains Mer spoke of. Hidden in the trees was the clearing with at least a dozen cairns twisting the energy of the island with the death inside them. She could smell the scent of the newly dead and realized that the selkie bull had been placed here.

"They may be more in tune with this place than we can handle." She was speaking to the air, breaking the heavy silence with her words as she examined the cairns one by one. She didn't bother counting bones. A quick look told her she was looking at whole villages stacked up on top of each other, a bone or two from each of its inhabitants.

She wandered through them, mourning silently for the endless deaths she was surrounded by. The feeling was overwhelming and she stumbled away to a mossy patch overlooking the shoreline, forgetting the other work she needed to do. Forgetting her words to Mer about soothing Onyx. He soon found her.

She heard him come up behind her, but barely glanced back to acknowledge him before returning her gaze to the waters.

"I am sorry. I did not mean to upset you, I needed to stretch my limbs and you're right, everything hurts now," she said without looking at him.

He sat down beside her in silence, his presence oddly calming. Plans had been racing through her head, but she decided to stop thinking for a moment. They only had so much time and energy to do anything with, they were worn and unable to push all day to protect themselves. If death was imminent for them, may as well throw caution to the winds.

"What would you do if I offered myself to you, Sea-cat?" Her tone was low and inviting.

"What?" His breath was ragged as he turned to face her.

"What. Would you do. If I offered myself. To you?" She eased herself over his lap so she was straddling him, holding his gaze, a teasing half smile on her face.

"Why?" He looked like he regretted his question as soon as he asked it.

"Because I want you." She felt a lump in her throat. No more lies. "And because help may not arrive in time, so we may as well have a moment in the time we have left."

She tilted her head back and breathed in the woodland mists and smoky cave scent that tangled with his rich sea smell, before looking back down at him.

"Because you want me as well. Because we're here, together, and life is uncertain." She ran her fingers through his hair. "So... what would you do?"

Onyx laid his head against her chest. His breathing was ragged.

"I wondered if they were not coming. And I do want you, Sky-cat. Not like this."

"Like what? This could be all we get."

He cupped the side of her face and brought their lips together. Once. Twice. Three times and then paused, shaking his head as if he was clearing it.

"You are only offering because the future is simple."

"Simple? We may die soon. I don't call that simple." She laughed a skittering laugh, hating the sound.

"We may. And then this means nothing." He was now staring at the sea. "Straight line. Whatever happens, it has no meaning."

"Sea-cat, nothing is certain. This has as much meaning as anything."

Silence held court for a few moments and Onyx let out a frustrated sigh. He said something in his native tongue. She slipped off his lap, and though one of his hands followed, he let her move. She hadn't been surprised by his rejection; disappointed, but not surprised. She waited to hear his reasoning, as he seemed to have more to say.

"The cow at the market. Perfect. The kind that I should want." He grabbed her hand and Aislinn bristled at the implications. This again. Desirable, but not right. But she held off saying anything as the way his fingers intertwined with hers did not match his words.

"I bought pieces for amari nodum, but they were not for that perfect cow." His eyes locked with hers. "They were for you. Want my own kind of perfect."

"Onyx, that's beyond compli-" her words were paused by him standing and putting his fingers against her lips.

"No. I won't force you to wear my jewelry or come to the beach with me. Not unless you want me. I don't seek to own you, Sky-cat." He stretched forward and nuzzled her. "Aislinn, please."

"I don't understand what you are asking."

"This is the path you assume." He drew a vertical line in the air and sliced his hand across it, indicating a sudden end. "These are the possibilities." He sketched lines fanning from the original, almost seeming distracted by the complexity of some of his imaginary lines. "Please, leave them open. I may never make you amari nodum, but..."

She kissed his palm and laid her face against his hand. Leave them open. Take a chance. She left her eyes closed for a moment. Everything was clear and on the table.

"I think your kith and kin would have issues with one of my kind being on their beach." She chuckled softly.

"They will get used to it." Onyx shrugged. "We had stranger. There was a rich man-"

"So Mer told me." Aislinn laughed again. Onyx liked the sound of this laugh and the easing of sadness in her eyes. His ears were hammering slightly with his pulse. He was a selkie, it was heading towards summer. Refusing Aislinn had been difficult. Beyond difficult. He closed his eyes for a moment and felt her move closer and lips touched his cheek.

"To possibilities, my sea-cat?" She whispered in his ear and stepped back. She held eye contact as she sat down and held her hand out to him.

He knelt beside her, leaning in for another kiss and pushing her slightly back as he did so. Then stared at the sky, counting.

"You are making this difficult."

"You are fun to tease." She smiled as she laid back, head resting on her arm. "And you have far more self-control than you give yourself credit for. Tell me tales. About your homelands, about your travels. About Dark Moon wine."

"Aren't there-"

"Better things to be doing? We're all exhausted. We can rest tonight or die from stumbling in exhaustion whenever they finally attack." She closed her eyes. "I wish they had already attacked. I'm guessing they'll be hiring a couple extra hands from the market, can't understand this wait otherwise." Her lips pursed in thought. For some reason, this expression made kissing her irresistible. She kissed him back and he ran a smattering of kisses down her neck and shoulder before they separated.

"Refusing you was not easy." His face felt hot and she laughed. He laid down beside her in the moss.

"Then, tell me what you picture in the future. And I will tell you how unlikely that is or isn't." She chuckled and tucked her face into the side of his neck, still for a moment. Then she sat up. "Have you your knife?"

He pulled it out and went to hand it to her, she shook her head.

"Cut the back of this dress. To here." She indicated a spot low on her back.

He did as he was told, quite confused. He exposed the scars on her back and touched them without thinking. He snatched his hand back when he realized what he'd done.

"If you think those are bad, you should see the other dragon." She glanced playfully over her shoulder and gave a half-smile. She reached back and grasped the top edges of the fabric, then hesitated. "I'll figure out the rest of this later."

She turned back to him and in a moment, her wings were out. She laid down on her, head resting on her arm and motioned for him to join her.

"I was getting cold." She again nuzzled her face into his neck, her breath was warm as she spoke. "Not cold enough to go back to the cave, but cold enough I needed a blanket."

"Your wings don't get cold?" He reverently touched one as she stretched it to cover them.

"Surprisingly, no. They're good at keeping heat on the inside and cold on the outside. Not sure how."

He felt content and found himself giving the slightest hum in his selkie voice. He heard the softest echo of his hum from Aislinn.

"Dragons... purr?" He traced the edges of her wing with a finger and enjoyed how her head swayed side to side with the movement of his finger. She fixed her eyes on him after a moment to respond. Her pupils were now slitted like a cat's and her eyes nearly glowed.

"Dragons have many secrets, my sea-cat." Her face was again buried in his neck. "Don't spread it about, people will forget how fierce we are if they know we purr." He could feel her smile in her voice.

They lay there, hovering on the edge of sleep for a few moments. He continued stroking the skin of one of her wings. It felt strong, but surprisingly soft, with a texture like suede or velvet. He hadn't noticed that in the early days when he'd been busy caring for her. He was surprised at the shiver that went through her at his touch and on impulse, lightly kissed her wing. A squeak of surprise.

"No." Her voice was adorably pouty.

"You don't want to give to me anymore?" He teased her as he withdrew his hand. She growled in mock exasperation.

"You made your choice. I swear when we survive our current situation, if there is ever a chance, you may explore just how sensitive they are. And the answer is very." She lifted her head to face him as she spoke. Once she spoke of the future, her gaze shifted. He could tell it was an indeterminate future that her eyes were seeing and he was not pleased that the future she saw was not necessarily one where he was. If she did not wish him to be there, that was one thing, but the sadness in her eyes said that was not what she was envisioning.

"I will live. Then, stay by your side as long as you let me. When he calls you, I'll stay behind if I must." He darted forward and kissed her throat, eliciting a surprised giggle. "But if he hurts you, I do not fear him. And I may make sure he's aware you have another lover when he forces us apart." He nipped the base of her neck playfully.

"You are a unique one, my sea-cat," she smiled and lay back again, closing her eyes. "But that is what draws me to you."

"You are as unique to me, Sky-cat." He laughed when the corners of her mouth quirked up in a smile at the name. He stared at her, silent for a few moments.

"Aislinn?" His voice was rich with selkie overtones, in a way that Aislinn had never heard before, or maybe she had become more attuned to him.

She opened her eyes ever-so-slightly, all too aware of how vulnerable she suddenly felt. There was a weight to his tone that frightened her. He could ask for anything and she would give it to him. She waited for a request for an unbreakable vow, or to run, or even for him to change his mind and claim what she'd offered earlier. She waited for him to take something from her, even as she responded.

"Yes?"

"I am yours." There was a weight to his words. She could not doubt him. The air was electric, but there was no call lingering in the air and asking for vows she was not able or willing to make. The declaration was complete without her response. He twisted about until he could lay his head on her chest, still humming softly. She tucked her wing back over him and they fell asleep, peaceful for a moment.

Chapter 36 - Planning

The ship made good time getting back to the market island; by morning they had returned to the market and by mid-afternoon they had gathered a good portion of the items needed for the spell as well as other supplies. Aarn bartered for the physical supplies needed for this hunt: things like harpoons, extra ropes, extra rations, a pair of new flensing knives. He missed his brother - in passing, he'd not dwell on it - his brother had been useful and quite adept at all parts of the hunt and trading, shame he'd gotten himself killed. Him and the few they lost to a recent storm.

Vari struck gold with a few ships docked for trading. A handful of bored men from different crews and they had more than enough for this hunt.

Dalan was having the most difficult time. He had found the items he was missing with the exception of bitterroot. It existed in the market, but according to Dalan, most everything was of poor quality. Last time Aarn checked, Dalan was aggravatedly bartering with the one merchant who had any amount of acceptable quality in stock. It was surprising that such a common ingredient was proving to be their trial. They had even found small packets and flasks perfect for spreading the oils and powders. Brother gone when he could use him, the simplest ingredient becoming the most onerous to get, vagaries of life at play. Aarn was unbothered.

Aarn filled his pipe while he waited and smoked. It was a pleasure he denied himself while he was on the hunt as the smell carried too far, but when in the marketplace, it hurt nothing and often gave an opening for bartering. Share a pipe or a little leaf and little small talk, and then on to the prices. He had spread their wares out once it was apparent that they would not be heading back this night. The island was not their best market, but it was good for questionable wares as no country owned it. Some places looked at the seal folk as natural folk and the cost could be high if one was caught with bits of selkie. Some risked it though, as the money was high. Aarn would rather sell to those fools and get coin that would not risk removing his head.

It was after sunset when Dalan finally returned.

"Did you barter your family jewels away for a few greens?" Vari asked with a grin.

"Very. Nearly." He was snappish and Aarn let him be. They wouldn't be able to get back to Muquin today anyways. Dalan's mood would improve after a few hours of toying with his newest spell.

They recouped the coin spent with a handful of patrons. There was a captain he was almost certain was going to resell the merchandise in Minado for a higher price - no loss for him, the prices paid in that port were not worth a slow drowning. He slipped most of the merchandise spoiled by Longshanks into her order. Another patron was a lovely Shay-looking girl - no, he would have to say woman for that one. Red hood to catch the eye and bosom that made the eye never want to leave. He was sorry he hadn't been able to negotiate a deal with that one. Finally, a toady little man the entire market knew too well who fancied himself a mage and bought large amounts of wares while sniveling about the high price and announcing to noone in particular that he could hex them all if they crossed him. Dalan had once opined that the man would have trouble changing cream into butter. Aarn was overjoyed to see him finally leave, after he sold him the rest of the ruined merchandise with the toad none the wiser. He then decided to close shop.

Vari was already on the ship training the new recruits when Aarn returned. Gamble had completed a thorough scrubbing of the hold where the dogs had been held. He could tell his cousin missed Dark. Gamble had been cautious, but still he and Dalan had been proud of the progress made with that one.

Aarn strode to his cabin and pulled out a map along with a bottle of wine they'd taken from Longshanks. The map showed Muquin and he pored over it, looking for the best spots for a pair of monsters to be hiding. Most would avoid the cairns at the center of the island, and they had come fairly quickly to Longshanks calls, so he was almost certain they were bedded down somewhere on the near side of the island.

He made a list of the most likely spots from map and memory with the plan being to creep up on them if possible. If not, his crew would at least know the most likely angle their quarry would attempt to ambush them from. Stanen announced that the evening meal was ready.

"I'll take mine in here. Extra ration of ale for everyone tonight." No use being stingy with new boys, it set a bad first impression.

Aarn was up late planning and studying the island until he felt he had near as good of an idea as the beasts did on where to run. They would leisurely sail back to Muquin tomorrow and train the new crew on the way and attack the following dawn. With skill and luck, they would take both of their targets, and perhaps then he could retire from this life or at least pause for a bit. Maybe find a wife, have some offspring to carry on the traditions. Life was good.

Chapter 37 - Dawning

Aislinn woke to Onyx gazing down on her.

"I don't want you to die for me," his eyes were wide and earnest as he spoke. Aislinn mused that living in a peaceful moment had ended far too soon.

"I'd really prefer you avoid it as well. Onyx..." she paused for a long time, searching for the words, "this is who I am. I will die for you. Or not. As the situation dictates. Believe me, I'm beyond stubborn, I'll try to live, but I can't guarantee everything. Someday... someday I want to have time to explain my life and my training to you. But I'm not one of your selkie wives, I can't live in your shadow, waiting for you to save me. I've tried, believe me."

"Your mate?"

"There have been others, but yes, I was in his shadow." She groaned and rolled over, slightly stiff from the cool damp air. The cave and the fire sounded welcoming, even with Mer's sarcastic wit. And food. If Mer hadn't eaten all of it.

"I won't stand back." His voice held a taut fury.

"Onyx, I know how cold the shadows are, I have no wish for you to shiver in them, even if they are mine." She leaned her forehead against his, and had an idea. She was on top of him, wings wide, pinning him down. She let her claws leave long, deep marks in moss beside him as she growled sweetly in his ear.

"I wish you happiness and I wish you safety, but I'm not a child. Nor am I weak. I am a dragoness. You've helped me remember that, so don't you forget it yourself. Fight for me, but also fight for yourself." She paused and laughed. "Also fight for Mer. I think he would kill me if you didn't survive. He's very loyal to you."

Onyx lay beneath her, clearly mesmerized and she chuckled softly. The way her fiery side drew him was amazing.

"Did you even hear a word I said?"

"Eelboy always was loyal."

"Eelboy?" She shook her head, almost certain he'd heard everything and decided to follow his tangent.

"He's so long and skinny. And he had a joke of getting eels stuck on other people's noses. It takes very good timing." Onyx's eyes had that look she knew meant mischief.

"And did you fall for it?"

"Very close." Onyx did not specify which way it was close and she did him the favor of not asking. "I may have taken the eel and let it latch on to him while he was sunning. As a human."

"Where did it latch on?" She raised one eyebrow, almost sure she knew the answer.

"Since then we call him Eelboy. He laughed at my retaliation. His family did not." Onyx smiled a sly smile. "Everything was fine. We were young. Wounds heal quickly."

"I'm sure his family was comforted by that."

"So was his future wife. No lasting hurts."

"He has a wife?" She could not keep the shock from her tone.

"He lost her to the tides five seasons past."

"Oh."

"Don't mention. He prefers less sadness. He pretends to check on me to avoid elders urging him to the beach. He loved her."

"I swear that the offspring of human nobility have less pressure to wed than a selkie." She moved and let him sit up.

"It is as we are," said Onyx with a shrug.

"In that case, I will be avoiding your homelands for a long while."

"I am very persuasive." The slightest velvety hint of selkie entered his tone before his voice lightened again. "Besides, I don't want the beach. Not for seasons. And if we did go on the beach, I don't know which of us would fight."

"I have some respect for customs. Not much, but some." She was shaking her head at him while smiling. Waves and tides, always changing.

He laughed and rested his head on her shoulder, curling into her side like an overgrown cat. She enjoyed the lightening of the mood, but realized time was fleeting.

"Mer told me of the bones. I went to see them."

"Kill cairns." Onyx's voice darkened with a new selkie tone. It felt like a bay where the water disappeared because of an imminent wave. She had not realized that his voice was capable of that. The shiver it sent down her spine gave it potential as a weapon, but with the finesse it might take, his bellows would work well enough for now.

"Once we win, we will burn bones, but now we don't have the time to do properly." Onyx's voice was lifeless and monotone.

"I promise you, we will. Every cairn and bone will be taken care of and prayed over." Her fingers tangled with his. "And we will make these hunters pay for everything that we can."

"Agreed. Can you teach me more of the skin splitting?"

It took Aislinn a moment to register what he was asking for.

"I... can try. Healing and its counter are not my area of expertise, and it is not easy. Don't hate me for what I must ask you to do," she was cursing inside, feeling she had gotten too attached too soon, even though inside she knew he would have to learn to deal with such things if he wished to remain around her. Most had little problem with her fighting skills, even Kai had been proud of those, though he wanted to keep her from the field; the problem always came when they learned her skills were functional and by necessity branched into many unpalatable things.

"I would not." Onyx looked hurt at her suggestion, then nuzzled her and wrapped his arms around her in reassurance. She edged away, wondering how he'd feel in a moment.

"You will need pieces of the selkie. He's the closest to living flesh we have and we don't have the time - nor the food with your friend - to waste hunting down substitutes." She kept her eyes on his. If she asked such a horrible task, the least she could do was meet his eyes. "I'd suggest an arm, or a leg. You can port it back near camp and there's decent bone and muscle to work with. If you can stomach it, the head is a possibility as well. You'll only get one try with most of the parts on that, but they are all useful to take out in a fight."

"Stomach it?" Onyx nervously looked between her and the hill where the corpse lay, shock and disgust on his face. That was to be expected. She was surprised when he went on. "I have to eat?" That took a moment to understand.

"Sorry, it means if you can tolerate it. I'm not asking you to eat it." Aislinn laughed weakly.

Onyx nodded, looking relieved, then silently mouthed the phrase. He opened his mouth to argue when he remembered what he was being asked to do, but he closed it before asking anything else. His lips pressed together in a thin line of determination. He nodded again, gathered his things, and trod uphill, knife in hand. This was not how she had wanted the blade to serve him well. Aislinn returned to camp. Mer was sitting just outside the cave by an outdoor fire.

"Not a word," she said to Mer.

He looked up, pretending he had no idea what she meant, but he couldn't quite hide his smug smile. He had a half dozen wooden spears he was rotating in and out of the fire and sharpening.

She sat next to him and helped him in his work, silent. For a few moments.

"Ah, my friend has disappeared. Did you kill him?" His tone was overly dramatic and he was openly grinning now.

"Nope. Just sent him to get some body parts."

Mer stared at her for a long time. He mouthed the words she said, she was certain he thought he heard her wrong. Or maybe he thought she'd used a euphemism.

She felt a mix of sorrow and pleased pride when Onyx returned quickly and carried both an arm and the head. The selkies knew how to fight, and were well aware life could be dangerous, but she hated bringing a mess like this to him. This was beyond the normal misery of life. Mer's confused expression alleviated her misery slightly.

She spent the rest of the day teaching Onyx to un-heal. Or attempting to. She could only explain the principle of it. She kept her face schooled and impassive as he tried severing various pieces. She even managed to keep calm when he forced a half-spoiled eyeball to explode. Onyx - and Mer, who was hovering nearby to absorb whatever information he could of this new idea - were equal parts fascinated, elated, and disgusted. She decided to tamp down on the elation slightly, even though she herself was feeling a bizarre pride at Onyx's progress.

"Remember, this is easier than attacking someone. Living things want to stay living. A dead thing's energy is already flowing into decay and separation." She wiped jellied muck from her cheek as she spoke. Even though he was doing surprisingly well it was not likely to transfer so well to an actual fight. Most really did not have the heart for slicing open their opponents with their thoughts, but if pain caused by a half-hearted attempt provided a moment's distraction, it could save him. A small voice warned her if anyone could find the right mindset for it, it would be Onyx. That thought was terrifying to her, but exploring that worry was a luxury. She'd taken enough luxuries recently, they could afford no more. "Never forget that you're playing with something very dangerous. A backlash of power from this may destroy you, whereas the worst a backlash from healing generally does is exhaust you."

"Is that why this is not used more often?" Onyx paused in his work.

"Partially. It wears on you in the long run in a way that healing does not," she held up her hand when she saw the barrage of questions forming in his eyes, "Normally I would not even attempt to teach you this, but it was Mer's only chance of survival, and now that you know it, there's no use pretending it doesn't exist. Once we survive, if you wish to learn more, I will introduce you to my brothers. I don't have the skills to truly teach you, so you get no more or less from me than what is necessary to NOW. And if you do not wish tutelage, I beg you to never attempt this again unless absolutely necessary."

Onyx stared down at dissected bits of selkie for several long moments, then at her. So many emotions passed across his face that she could not interpret them and then his expression fixed into an emotionless determination.

A neat slice appeared on the arm, running down its length and leaving bone bare to the sky. Onyx looked up, dark eyes earnest.

"I will be cautious. Do not be scared." He looked down at the exposed bone, shaking his head. "I won't let them hurt us."

After a while he paused to care for Aislinn's wounds as well as Mers. He was utterly exhausted after healing them, but his elation at the extent to which he did was infectious.

"It is good the careful things were done, but so strong! Mer, how does your throat feel?"

"Like it was never injured. Good work." Mer fingers examined every inch of his neck. If he could hurt his throat with pushing and prodding, Aislinn was fairly certain he was going to.

"I feel mostly healed as well," said Aislinn as she flexed her leg. "My brother calls it the pendulum effect. When you play with a power counter to your natural skills, the original is sometimes enhanced once you return to it, like the way a pendulum swings wildly back when you first release it. It evens out quickly, so don't depend on it."

"Is there anything that's not dangerous or undependable that you can teach us?" Despite the tinge of sarcasm, there was no challenge in Mer's voice. He was not blind to the realities of the world.

"Not when it comes to magic. And I've been told selkies can fight, but I've not seen much of that from you, so maybe I can give you a few lessons there – perhaps on how not to get caught by skin hunters," replied Aislinn. She stuck her tongue out at Mer and picked up a makeshift spear they'd been working on. She stepped away from the pair of them and ran through a series of practice movements, testing her body's strength and mobility. She could still feel the underlying injuries, but there was no doubt they were very nearly healed. It was more a matter of rebuilding strength now and that would take time she didn't have. It formed a weakness that she would have to be cautious of, but all in all, the practice felt invigorating. When she finished, Onyx was transfixed and Mer whistled appreciatively.

They went to bed with new hope. Mer volunteered for morning watch, declaring that he'd been sitting in a hold sleeping for days, he was tired of sleeping. By the glances between him and Onyx, Mer was volunteering to give them alone time. They used that time to sleep.

The next day, traps and snares were prepared and laid. They were limited by how much they could make and in lack of knowledge of the island. None of them could afford accidentally stumbling into one of their own traps while trying to move about.

Aislinn attempted shifting and actually succeeded in reaching full form twice. It gave her much needed confidence. If she was quick, she might even turn full dragon and destroy a few.

Onyx's practice with his new skill had been set aside until afternoon and the corpse split easier for him. Whether due to expanding skill or further decay was up for debate, but she wasn't going to point that nuance out. Despite her resolve, she must have frowned.

"Why does this magic make you nervous?"

She paused for a very long time, but decided as Mer was napping in the cave, she would share. It might also stop him from trying to practice more than she allowed.

"This goes no further than your ears, but my brother receives monthly shipments of bottled blood to feed his hunger. Another mage who attempted similar magic fell to eating livers and hearts. I heard it was tolerable... until he realized how much better fresh human organs sated his hunger." She leaned against a tree. "It's a dangerous trick. Be cautious and the effects are minimal and temporary. Forget, and you may end up forever paying the price. I don't want to be the cause of that for you."

"Your brother is a vampire? I thought those were legend." He was more curious than afraid and she welcomed that, for her brother's sake, but she wanted to scream about Onyx's self-preservation skills.

"Vampiric." She sighed and continued, not having the time to go into the precise differences between the two. "Not a vampire. Although, they do exist. Real ones are not something you want to meet with. Is that all that you heard me say?" She half smiled, half-frowned at him, already aware of the answer.

"If I'm not careful, I may end up like your brother or worse. I will be careful, my sky-cat." Onyx brushed her hair back from her face. "Why don't you use your magic? Do you not have magic for this?"

"No... it's..." Aislinn paused, "have you ever heard of conduits?"

"Yes! Old tales. They disappeared with the great magics."

"They didn't disappear. They were chained and broken or killed. Most of them."

Onyx stared at her. She could see the realization in his face.

"This place has so much raw power. You can feel it, but I can drink it in. I can pull it, but without a solid focus, or a way to turn it inward, it's hard for me to do more than a little. It's trying to get just a few drops of water from a raging flood. Who knows what I'll destroy?"

"If they are going to kill you, destroy it all." He was fierce.

"The island would fight me, and once the waves start, I can't stop them. The market nearby could be absolutely wiped clean." Her serious expression eased and she half-smiled. "Believe me, if I find a way, I'll use it. It's just finding a way. Focus on keeping yourself alive."

All of them were alert as evening moved into night. They woke before dawn and Aislinn moved off from the cave to practice with the spear again. Her body was stiff and sore, but she was certain she could survive a hand to hand battle. Several hand-to-hand battles was another question.

She sensed Onyx a moment before he was beside her, finger pressed to his lips for silence. Aislinn closed her eyes and listened carefully. She heard the slightest creak over the waves. Oars. They had come.

Chapter 38 - Danger of the Dawn

They made their way back to the cave quickly and quietly. Mer was gone. The why and where became quickly apparent when they heard splashing and shouts from the waters. Mer had upset at least one of the boats, possibly more.

They grabbed their weapons and a handful of other supplies before moving towards a point they had designated as a meeting point. Aislinn armed traps in the camp itself as they left. The hunters would have to follow through thick brush and the most reliable path held a few carefully placed traps. Birds made them aware of Mer moments before he arrived. He had a bloody bruise on one shoulder and a smile on his face.

"There's more than we planned on. I counted around eighteen. Some of them look pretty rough, but they scream like pups when they hit the water. Some can't swim."

Onyx shook his head and said something in selkie to Mer. Mer grinned back with a devilish glint in his eyes.

"If they had them here, I would."

"I'd ask, but I'm a little afraid of the answer." Aislinn smiled, well aware these might be their last moments if things did not work as planned, and savored the camaraderie.

"A trick I used as a child. They wouldn't like it." Mer's grin was almost maniacal.

The men were almost silent on the beach, but occasional shouts or the stillness of the forest near gave their locations away. There were so many.

Aislinn knew a sailor was not necessarily a fighter, but she was certain these men had planned for a fight. She would treat them accordingly. A fly buzzed and landed on her shoulder. Her skin twitched and it moved away for a moment only to land along her collarbone. She ignored it as best she could and focused on the sounds of the men while loosely coiling a piece of fabric around her palm. The quiet around them was stifling, but they could track at least one group by the sounds they were making. It was odd that there was only one group they could hear.

A sharp twang of a branch released from its tiedown and a concurrent shout warned the trio danger was near. Aislinn felt the fly bite her on her collarbone. The bite felt odd, like it had struck her while biting. Mer reached over and brushed the fly away. She stared at his fingers for a second before realizing that it was not a fly, but a dart.

Rage built inside her, she could feel the dragon coming to the fore. Dirty tricks.

"Run."

Onyx and Mer looked at her in confusion.

"Run!" She shoved them hard away and growled as she threw herself backwards. Onyx was staring, she couldn't imagine how painful the change looked as she was fighting it, but he couldn't seem to look away. She needed him gone as she had little idea how clear her head would be once the poison fully hit her system. Mer seemed to understand and grabbed his friend around the waist, lifting him up. The maneuver elicited a squeak of protest, but he had them moving. She heard a shout and the fading sounds of a scuffle. She spared another moment to hope that they would be alright; then let the fury overtake her as another dart hit her.

She lunged in the direction the dart came from. Men screamed and scrambled over themselves to get out of her way, breaking whatever shield had quieted their footsteps. One moved just too slow. Between the fangs through his side and the tree he was smashed against, it was likely the last mistake he could ever make. Ropes shot from the underbrush, attempting to entangle her. They had circled their prey better than expected. Aislinn catapulted those foolish enough to hold the ends of the rope without anchoring it out of their hiding places and lept for the sky, still filled with fury.

A well-aimed chain whizzed through the air and wrapped around her muzzle, nearly jerking her to the ground. The owner of this one had secured it to something before sending it after her.

Wings flailed against the sky and she thrashed her head, attempting to shake off the chain. Another rope twisted round her hind leg, it was also secured. Then they seemed to snake out from everywhere, wrapping around her legs and twisting about her neck, tethering her to the ground even as her wings clung to the sky. She could hear the cadence of their count and orders to heave as they jerked her closer to the ground. She fought back, one rope snapped. Others appeared in its place.

In desperation she dived, landing and lashing out at those who dared capture her. A few scattered and she threw herself into slipping those ropes, but this crew had been chosen well.

They held their ground as she fought against them. She gained enough slack to place her claws on her muzzle and slip the loop of chain off, freeing her jaws. She did not have time to feel foolish for missing that option earlier.

"Watch out! She'll breathe fire!"

She wished that trick were true, but she lacked the weapons of the wyverns. Venom, however, was in her arsenal and she gave one of her tormentors a potent dose before new bindings closed her mouth.

She wasn't sure if it was minutes or hours before they finally had her bound to the forest floor. She tried to bring her legs up under her or flap her wings to free herself, but they had her fast.

"Get the oil on her, men. We don't want her changing back when she's dead. Your pay depends on us gettin a dragon, not a woman!"

She pushed against the ropes as the men ran for whatever this precious oil was. She would use every last ounce of her spite and fury to overcome it. Most shifters remained in whatever form they died in. Dragons had a small trick that allowed them to shift after their death if being hunted. She attributed it to dragons being more spiteful than most, but that was only opinion. A half roll to escape the ropes as she hoped for the toxin that made her change originally to wear off. Some men returned, tangled in the straps of a multitude of flasks. One was so excited he tripped. The entire flask tumbled through the air, cap and all, and bounced off her scales. She managed to get enough play in the ropes to force a hiss through her teeth. If she could free her jaws, or even one of her dexterous front paws, there was hope.

The next flask of oil splashed over her and felt like the knife edge of cold. Her lungs locked and she couldn't breathe. When she finally found the air, she loosed a screaming snarl. The rush of adrenaline let her snap the rope holding her jaw.

She felt the oil holding her in this wretched, oversized form she'd wanted so much since childhood. A dream she'd come to hate so much. Her so-called true form. Her body struggled as her mind edged away.

Onyx followed Mer, smashing men that blocked their way and running blindly. He could not bring his mind to focus on anything other than the fact that he had left Aislinn behind. In pain. He could picture the forced change. The cord to the pendant he had crafted snapped in the middle of it. The last glimpse he had as Mer pulled him away was the star shattering.

They paused to catch their breath.

"Don't worry, elder brother. She'll destroy them in that form." Mer leaned against a tree trunk and gasped for air.

"She's not used to it. And we left her." The world blurred, in his mind's eye, the pendant shattered again. No tears, he wasn't crying, but focus of any sort was slipping away.

"Why- not important. She needed us to leave. We left. We'll take out these hunters - one by one if we have to - then we circle back around and help her." Mer's voice was gentle, but firm.

His reaction calmed Onyx. It was not that long ago that Mer would have tried to convince Onyx to leave her to her own devices. It felt like decades since then, but then last night was years ago and the blissful afternoon before may as well have been a dream. Onyx stared at Mer and his friend's face slowly returned to focus, along with Onyx's mind. He pushed the ominous portent of the pendant breaking aside. Attack. Destroy. Rescue. Simple.

"Yes. We can do that." Onyx focused his senses on the forest. He could hear the men around her, he ignored those. He needed to find the others. The ones who were after them. They did not need someone sticking a knife between their ribs as they freed Aislinn.

They worked together, years of hunting and herding shoals of fish as the seasons changed and diving in caves on the edges of the tideline had formed a trust and partnership that flowed smoothly with minimal communication. Mer took down the first hunter, viciously slamming his head against a rock. He stole the man's belt knife, axe, and rations. Onyx glared at him in exasperation at the last and Mer shrugged as he shoved a bit of hard tack in his mouth.

Onyx ambushed the next. First gutting the man because of the angle he had; then slitting his throat to silence him. Aislinn's blade was serving them well.

Then they were cornered by a group of four. This group worked together almost as well as Mer and Onyx. They were in trouble.

Chapter 39 - Turning Tides

Aarn watched and waited until he was certain the woman was fully dragon and going to stay that way. Stanen had shot his darts well, too bad it sounded like the beast had tracked where the shots came from before it was secured. He ordered Gamble and Vari in with reinforced spears as Dalan murmured his magic.

"Time to collect our dues."

The creature managed to find enough slack somehow to dodge their first strikes. Gamble's second strike struck her shoulder, but did not penetrate far enough to reach anything vital.

"Careful! As few holes as possible!" Aarn barked the order and held his crossbow steady. With his position, the creature wasn't giving him a good shot, despite her flailing about. She kept her head moving or out of sight and he wasn't sure enough of other targets. He did not want to enrage the creature further and the book cautioned about the hardness of their scales. It would be a sure shot or no shot. He edged forward and heard an unsteady pause in Dalan's chant.

The men pulled their ropes taut. Aarn felt the hairs on the back of his neck prickle. He spared a glance at Dalan. He was still murmuring his spell, but his eyes were open now and he looked pained. Muquin felt very awake, and for the first time Aarn could remember, somewhat hostile. The prickling feeling spread.

He moved towards the beast as fast as possible. Time to end this.

Chapter 40 - Undercurrents

She was held in her true dragon form but refused to roar when a spear pierced her shoulder. She would fight everything, even with this bulky shell. She only needed a space, a chance, a... loophole.

True form. They wanted - no, *needed* - what they thought of as her true form. But they were wrong.

Will.

The raw power of the place.

Oh, it couldn't be that easy, could it?

She directed every ounce of stubbornness and fury in her to this risky idea. She found more fuel when she looked back at the recent past. There were others here who needed her help and family not here that these men would hunt if they knew. She would not let them end her and she would not let them end it this way.

"You want blood?" She was calling to the island in her mind, feeling the power pulse around her. Calling energy was almost too easy. Ask. And offer. *"Give me a portion of your strength and I'll spill the blood of the kind that created this pain."*

Aarn entered the clearing as the beast's eyes opened fully.

He had never felt frightened on a hunt. Excited. Exhilarated. Focused. Not fear. Not since he was a small child, learning the ways of the hunt. But when this creature's eyes fixed on him, he felt a slight worm of fear threading through his gut. There was overwhelming danger in those eyes, even though he could make out what looked like glimmers of tears in them.

This ends here. She wasn't sure if that thought was her or the island.

Most mages drank a little of the power, bottles or barrels. For a conduit, it was always floodgates opening. It was like comparing ponds with oceans. She let the power wash over her - floodwaters rising. It had been corrupted, it was more in line with the man pushing her down at the moment. She could work with that though. It wanted blood and destruction, she would use it for blood and destruction, but first she needed it to bend to her will without being drowned in it. She wouldn't break the spell, a head-on attack against the same source was a waste of energy and the spell was solidly made. But it likely had been designed with a specific purpose to draw her into what they considered her true form. Nuance and precision.

"The fight in her is slacking, pull her down!" The call was followed by one for more spears. They really didn't understand the balance or the danger in the calm. They'd never fought a sky dancer, a dragon conduit. It was a risk, this moment where all power drained and ebbed away, becoming one with the mass of energy about the user.

She felt it in her claws first, rising from the ground. It was like winds and the waters of a flood rising about her, a tidal wave of magic. Aislinn focused on her true form. The delicate ear points that had been stolen. The way a scattering of scales across her body intermixed with her skin. The claws and pupils. Wings. That fight that she always had in her. She could feel the way the elements pulsed in her veins. She was full dragon, but not only a dragon. She was fully elf as well. The energy of the isle was screaming for blood, but now it was also singing. She had a moment where she was almost lost to the beauty of the song she'd not heard in ages, but that beauty gave her the final push.

One arm was freed as the ropes slackened on her suddenly smaller form, and that was all she needed. She screamed and flung the oiled ropes and chains away from her. The oil that hit her hadn't been meant for this trick, but was still oil and the ropes had been doused in it. Smoky fire ran down them, spreading out from her and filling the clearing. The men hit by the flaming restraints screamed and reeled back. Iron chains grew red hot, it was rapidly getting beyond her control. She didn't dance clear of one line fast enough, and the heat blistered and burned her leg. She barely felt it, It would heal. Once they all burned, it would heal.

She moved with sureness, knowing this body and form all too well, even if it felt new. Several of the would-be hunters ran.

Instinct warned her to dodge. She obeyed, fire licking at her face and chest for a moment before she could control it enough to force it away. She wouldn't be able to hold the flames off long and the island didn't seem concerned with them yet. Time to move.

A click had been what triggered the instinct to dodge. She knew that once she fixed her eyes on the man holding the empty crossbow. He was fumbling to reload and backing up. He was afraid, but still hunting her. His clothes, his bow, his bearing. This man was in charge. He was her main target, her prey.

She strode out of the fire towards her target. She had trained in this form since she was toddler. Learned to channel the power of a dragon with the precision of her elf and human sides. Everything she was made this form and this form made her. The man wisely backed away and ran.

Fear was new to Aarn, but regrouping wasn't. He ran, clutching his crossbow. He knew there could still be some small profit from the creature now hunting him if he could find a new place to ambush it. And even if there was no profit, he would destroy the thing.

Aislinn allowed herself to be distracted from the bearer of the crossbow by his minions when a few came between her and the man. She was brutally efficient. The knife sharp claw at the fold of her wings ripped into the jugular of one, she snapped the neck of a second. The sound was still echoing as most realized their hunt had turned and scattered. It was now pure pandemonium. They couldn't hear the island's exhilaration as she could, but some primal sense warned them they were now prey.

She could stalk them later. She had a more important target.

Pain constricted her body, someone was trying to force her back to her other form. Aislinn followed fluctuations in the island's pulse to where they ebbed and circled. She found the mage. Another target to disable before hunting their leader.

He continued trying to force her back into her other self as she approached. It was a brave but foolish move. Foolish or not, it did wear on her. She may have had more power, but he'd been using the island's power first and was more familiar with it. She braced her feet and stood shivering, trying to hold on to the truth. What they thought of as her was only a facet, not her true form. They were both playing with the knife edge of precision in spellwork, trying to turn it to cut in the direction they needed. The mage, desperate, tried to distract her by throwing a packet of powder at her face.

Unfortunately for him, she recognized the hand movement needed to throw that kind of packet all too well and flash powder was far easier than magic to ignore. And infinitely easier for her to use against him. She shut her eyes and swung her wings forward, wafting the packet back towards him as it opened and ignited. The move and sudden breeze caught him by surprise. She knew he made the mistake of opening his eyes to fend off the packet by his pained yelp and her sudden release from his meddling spell. She could also smell the slightest singing of hair and feel the brief sparks spatter against her skin. This man was pure mage. He might be a hunter, but he had not trained to blind fight, nor to deal with prey that knew his tricks better than he did. She grabbed a sturdy branch she'd spotted in the split second before closing her eyes, circled round, and connected it to the base of his skull, ending their match before he regained his sight or raised the magic again.

She sorted out her next steps in her mind while listening to the celebratory chorus from the island. She wasn't certain if the Elfsong was that loud or if the island's magic would be just as overwhelming on its own.

Most important was finding the crossbowman. He was the leader and the one most likely to get the men to regroup. Next, Onyx and Mer. Then, together they could work on finishing off any who were still attempting to destroy them. She hoped by then the remaining number would be small.

Aarn ran across two selkies on the beach fighting with his men. He was all too familiar with one of the pair. The bastards.

He was beyond furious that Longshanks was still alive. Everything thrown at that creature had bounced off. The dog changed to charge one of his sailors as a seal. As the seal paused after a successful attack on the sailor, Aarn took aim.

Mer turned to Onyx, huffing with pride at his quick takedown of the final of their quartet of sailors. Onyx was ready to respond with a quip when a stick sprouted from his friend's throat. His friend first looked confused, then terrified. Onyx was on his knees by him in a moment. Water. He needed water to assist his healing skills for something this serious. He actually wasn't sure if it was better to leave the bolt in or remove it. Mer gaped at him, helpless.

No. Nonono. Not like this. He refused to let them be picked off one by one.

Onyx was so focused on Mer he did not sense the man sneaking up on him. The sailor was down to rope, but he used it well and looped a length around Onyx's throat. Onyx twisted and turned and tried to get out of the garrote, but couldn't escape as he watched Mer's life fade on the sands, just beyond Onyx's reach.

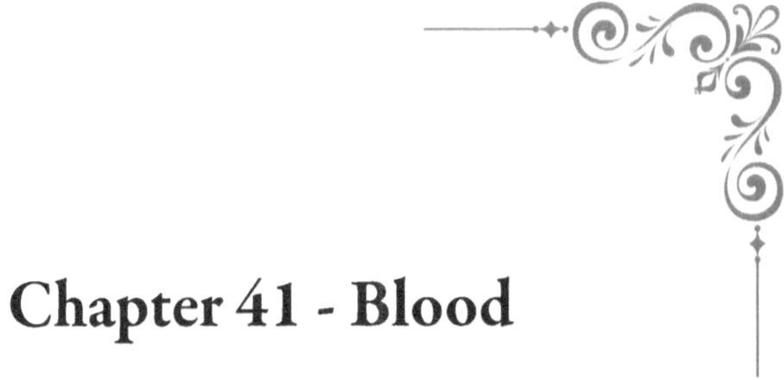

Chapter 41 - Blood

Aarn was frustrated that the silvercoat changed forms only after the sailor was between him and the animal. Lives were lost in this line of work, but he didn't want any more men dead than necessary. An arrow through one of his men was a waste of a man and an arrow. Through the man was the only clear shot he could get - from here. He was contemplating a better angle to shoot from when he felt a hand on his shoulder. He spun around and nearly brained the man with the butt of his crossbow.

It was Gamble.

"Let's go." He looked distressed. "They got Dalan. This hunt's not worth it."

"I've dropped a selkie."

"It's not worth it cousin!" Gamble hissed. "You ran when the fires started! You didn't see all that thing did. It's unnatural and it's dangerous and it wants the silvercoat. I say let the monster have it."

"All the more reason to kill them all. We don't want them reproducing."

"It's enough cousin. I'm out."

"Then stay out of my way and remember your words when you come begging for coin." Aarn turned back to the fight and let Gamble go. It wasn't worth fighting with his men when he had enough trouble in front of him. He had a clear shot for a split second.

A sudden movement by the selkie and the sailor and Aarn's shot hit near the creature's hip instead of something fatal. He cursed, but saw Vari hidden in the vegetation on the far side of the beach. His luck was turning.

Onyx felt the arrow in his side. The world was flickering slightly. He had no way out. He'd dropped his knife. Mer would die. And Aislinn... he'd not see her again.

He changed forms, returning to human even as the rope dug in more. One. Last. Shot.

He stopped trying to claw and grabbed the man's hands, picturing the corpse's arm.

The world grew dimmer. He forced everything he had into the man's hands. Nothing.

Then a scream and the pressure on his throat eased.

Aarn wasn't sure what was happening. Vari had a shot lined up and the cursed thing shifted. Then the new man let the thing go. He was holding his hand and screaming. Aarn wasn't certain if the thing had bitten him or clawed him. Either way...

Vari dove for the rope and attempted to re-tighten it around the selkie's neck. The creature rolled, snarled, and shifted again to seal, shaking off the rope as he did so. Vari was now in the way of Aarn's shot. Aarn cursed and continued moving to a better vantage point.

The seal lunged at Vari and returned to its human face. It was a quick monster with that. Quickest Aarn had seen. He settled his sights on it. Next time the silvercoat shifted, he'd be sure to get him.

He thought the thing was going for Vari's eyes. He knew Vari could dodge it; he'd have a few clawmarks running down his face. Nothing they hadn't dealt with before.

But it didn't claw. It did something he'd never seen. It took a few moments for Aarn to process the sight before him. Vari was screaming and swearing. Aarn at first thought blood was running down his face; after a second glimpse, he was almost certain it was Vari's eyes.

The thing then tore Vari's throat out. Aarn took a wild shot and then ran, regretting not listening to Gamble.

Onyx tore mercilessly at the new attacker, only returning to his original attacker once the new problem was eliminated. The first man was whimpering and holding his bloody hand, skin split to the bone in several places. Onyx glanced between him and Mer. Choices became very simple.

Onyx carefully moved Mer into the bushes once he was done healing him. His friend was unconscious, but Onyx had fair hopes he would survive. He felt a wave of exhaustion flowing over him. He licked blood off his lips and felt a bit of energy return. He remembered Aislinn's warnings. He had remembered her warnings every step of the way, but there were more men out there, he would do what was needed.

Chapter 42 - Muquin

Aarn moved towards the cairns. Dalan had been the expert on magic, but Aarn knew a few tricks. He knew how to use the strength of the offerings to the island to augment his own. He could draw upon the raw power to make himself faster and stronger. The monsters had the beach, so this was where he would run to. And he would end this.

It took Aislinn longer to find the leader than she expected; few of the sailors she came across attempted to attack her, but they tended to slow her down. A bit of posturing and even the brave ones ran away. Some even ran straight into traps they'd easily avoided earlier. She let them run. Even though the island was thrumming and insisting she kill them all, she pushed it back. For now.

She found the scent of a patch where he had paused for a bit and stumbled across the carnage on the beach. She paused, wounds of the fallen men drawing her in with their bizarre look. They did not match with wounds from teeth or claws or a normal weapon. A second look and her gut twisted, knowing they could only have been caused by one thing.

Aislinn jumped when a low moan came from the bushes. After a cautious moment, she followed the sound to where Mer lay beneath a pile of brush in his seal form. She examined him closely, finding the mostly healed remnants of a deadly neck wound.

"Oh, my sea-cat. What have you done?"

Finding Onyx was now her number one priority. The leader could wait and perhaps he would be kind enough to end himself in a trap before she could get to him. The island rebelled, attempting to overtake her, and she forced it back. She'd dealt with nature spirits before, this one wasn't sentient enough to be a threat, but she wouldn't be able to keep hold of it for long without heeding its bloodlust. Another problem in a long list. She covered Mer with more branches and roughly forced him to stay unconscious with magic. It was easy enough with his injuries. Despite Onyx's work, the wound Mer had incurred had him in slight shock. Aislinn paused, glancing between Mer and the dead men. He needed to stay warm. Nothing could keep those men warm anymore. Decision made, she stripped the corpses and wrapped Mer with the remnants of their clothing. She much preferred minor desecration to letting sentiment kill Mer. Aislinn talked as she worked.

"I swear, I will return with Onyx and we will all get out of this. Don't you dare die out of spite while I'm hunting him down or... or... I will make up the grandest tale about you dying due to getting drunk on Dark Moon wine and stupid eel tricks and spread it to your kinsfolk until that lie becomes its own truth and you'll feel the shame of it on the other side." It was a poor threat, but it was all she had.

One last look to be certain he was hidden beneath the leaves again. She glanced about the beach and saw Onyx's blade half buried in the sand. She breathed deep, inhaling slowly through her nose and mouth, tasting the air as she did so. Under all the blood, she finally found the familiar fresh sea scent, cleaner and wilder than the real thing. She'd had no fear of it eluding her, even in this mess. One day she would tell Onyx other secrets of the dragons, including how deeply they memorized scents of those close to them. If he had been in a place, even years earlier, she could trail him. She scooped up the knife and moved with purpose that her pace hadn't quite held before, letting another instinct take over. Onyx was hers and only woe befell anything that threatened that which belongs to a dragon.

Her eyes narrowed when she picked up the second scent heading the same direction. The hunter. Then she recognized their destination and decided to take a short cut up the rocky side of the hill. Wings and claws had their uses.

Onyx paused as he neared the cairns. The man could be hidden behind any of them and Onyx wouldn't notice him until he stepped out. He tried to use the magic to sense the location of the man but everything was off. Every attempt failed and woke a thirst in him.

The dead selkie was ruining any chance of finding the man by smell, as the corpse's rot now filled the air. Flies buzzed nearby and the remainder of the men yelled from far away, wrecking his chances of using sound. Onyx stood there and his caution became anger.

He was tired of being hunted and chased. Tired of being a threat to those closest to him because his coat was an odd color. Tired of holding back with the magic he felt churning inside him. Every part of him wanted to find the man with the crossbow and rip his throat out.

A slow exhalation.

All of their throats. Every last one. First the man with the crossbow, then the others scattered on the island. They would feel the same terror in their last moments that selkies had. And he could slake the irritating thirst he felt growing.

A click and Onyx dodged a bolt. Every second he was faster, more confident. More in tune with the tides of this place of death. He rushed the area where the shot had come from only to find he wasn't the only one in tune with this place. The hunter knocked him back with a well-aimed punch.

Onyx smiled. He felt the smile in every bit of his body and welcomed this fight. He really would tear this man to pieces and use every bit of what this clearing held to do so. They rushed at each other, tearing away with knives and claws and teeth and the dark cutting power Onyx now commanded. Even with the violence, it was mostly superficial wounds - testing strikes. The man was quick and strong, but Onyx trained to spot weaknesses. He could tell his right leg was stiff with an old wound.

Another rush, Onyx aimed towards the leg, and felt a bolt lodge between ribs as he did so. Tricky old man. Selkies knew how to use weapons, but it was not their forte in one on one combat. He hadn't seen that stab coming, he'd been too focused on the knife the hunter was holding to even think of the man using one of the bolts from his crossbow that way. Onyx wouldn't make the same mistake again. Also, his slashes with the dark power seemed to be half deflected by the man. He wasn't sure why, but he decided to pause in using that trick for a moment and focus on the leg.

This man was quick and clever though. He knew where his weakness was and protected it. Another fail and Onyx reassessed. He would find another opening. He recognized the knife. The knife Aislinn had taken from the first hunter. How had he gotten it?

Onyx dropped low, it looked like he had tripped and the man believed it. At least he did until he found his feet waving in the air after Onyx swept them out from under him and sent the hunter flying. Onyx pounced, covering the sudden space between them quickly, already anticipating the feel of the man's life flowing down his throat. There was only one way he would have Aislinn's knife, and the hunter would pay for that.

A blur swept between him and his prey. He aimed for the throat without taking a good look at the new interloper. He missed, but his teeth sank deep into this hunter's shoulder. They were pulling him to the ground, attempting to smother him. He fought back.

Every connection with the gods of the hunt and death felt severed three generations back as Aarn landed on his back, breath gone. His body was locked up in shock. He waited for a finishing blow that didn't come. He registered a snarl of frustration as something appeared between him and the monstrous selkie. He saw the other monster, wings wrapped around the greycoat, holding him back. He stared dumbly at the mane running down her back and the lashing tail. Her wings. He edged towards his crossbow as the paralysis wore off, limping now with the pain in his leg. He would finish this and he would have trophies to show for it, for him and the crew lost, even if it wasn't the grand payoff they had expected.

This fight felt off. Onyx had been planning to destroy anything that stood between him and his prey but everything was unbalanced in his mind. He was now hesitating. The new assailant wasn't fighting back full force, but would not release him either. The hunter was speaking, something pointless. His jaws released their grip on the shoulder and he tried to get space, or more blood, he was still caught up in some sort of binding and he tried thrashing his way out of it.

"LOOK AT ME CURSE YOU!" The yell cut through his senses in a way calmer words had not.

"Aislinn." All fight dropped from him when he recognized who it was before him. She looked less human, more feral. Like the creature he'd found on the beach so long ago, but freed from all the riff raff and trash that had held her down back then.

"Idiot. I warned you. You just had to push it." Her wings had been holding him back. She dropped them and wrapped her good arm around him. Aislinn slumped forward, head on his shoulder. He didn't know how to respond. He felt completely drained this time and she was injured. He laid his hand on a dark slash he had left. She nuzzled him slightly. "Calm, my sea-cat. I've survived worse."

He felt the growl in her chest before he heard it.

"You have one chance to live, hunter. I suggest you take it." She turned her head, looking back as she spoke. The man almost had his crossbow again. Onyx tensed when he saw that, and Aislinn continued speaking. "I will finish this if you shoot, sir. For you and everyone on your crew this will be finished."

"You don't have it in you, beastie."

"Lift your weapon if you truly believe that."

They rolled as he shot. Onyx thought the bolt missed them completely until he saw it caught in her wings.

Aislinn plucked the bolt from the skin of her wings, tossing it aside and mentally throwing her pain along with it. She wasn't sure that exercise would work long, but it was time to end this game. Not by running, not by rushing, none of them had strength left for that. Even the island was holding back and waiting now, trying to decide who would feed it better. Or maybe it was busy finally dampening the fires she'd lit in the clearing, either way, she was fine with that. It left them on a more even field. She moved steadily towards the man as she twirled the scrap of fabric she'd somehow managed to keep on her hand through all the fires and changes. She didn't know she had prepared it for this. One last trick. One last fight. She palmed Onyx's blade in amongst the fabric.

He was reloading and she let him, tensing and waiting for the moment he'd let it fly. She opened her wings, making herself a bigger target but effectively blocking Onyx from his sight. The tip of her tail twitched in anticipation as she neared him. She would have far less time to dodge any shot at this distance.

"Last chance to run, old man." In the air hung an unspoken plea. *Please, walk away and let it end, we are all tired.*

The inevitable came, with a slow and graceful precision. Aislinn took the shot in the same shoulder Onyx had torn into. The same one hit by a spear. Training let her know nothing vital was destroyed, even though it couldn't stop the pain. Training also let her use the momentum of the striking bolt to her advantage.

Her left shoulder was pushed back, and she twisted with the motion, bringing her right arm up and loosing the scrap of oiled cloth in his face. It was a focus for the last bit of island's power that was moving wildly through her. Fire flashed from spark to inferno. Her tail whipped around, completing the circle and smacking against him one of the cairns. The bones caught like the cloth had.

She shifted - ignoring the pain of the bolt digging further in - and lunged, pushing his body deep into the pile of bones and fire he was trying to escape. She pushed the dagger in with the same motion, pinning the wick in him. She held the hunter down for another moment until the flames became too strong for her to hold back from herself. She reared up against the sky, giving him one last view of what he had foolishly decided to chase, then fell back on her haunches and crawled away from the pyre, shifting back down to her two-legged form. She could not go further than her half form.

She lay in the moss, chuckling weakly and unsurprised that the loophole she had found carried unexpected costs. She rolled and tried to push herself up with her good arm.

Onyx scrambled to her side, attempting healing. The bolt wound tore open further instead of closing. His magic was all mixed up inside of him and he could no longer sort one from another. Aislinn laughed fondly.

"It will return to you. It doesn't really hurt right now." She touched his face. She was soothing him. He had injured her and she was soothing him.

He looked at her, frightened by her words. Lack of pain in a wound like hers was not a good sign. Her eyes were unnaturally clear as she looked at him.

"We've survived." Her head was on his lap now and she raised her good hand to his face. "I'm not going anywhere. Nor are you. Nor is Mer. We. Will. Be. Fine." He could almost feel her willing it to be so. Aislinn's eyes closed and Onyx drew her closer, hoping that he and the nearby flames could keep the chill of death at bay and wishing he could do anything to fight it off.

He felt a shift in the air of the island as she grew still and reached for anything he could to keep her alive.

Chapter 43 - From the Ashes

Aislinn stood, head held high, watching the first of many pyres burn in the darkness before dawn. She touched the jeweled headpiece pinning her hair up and adjusted the gown's high silk-covered collar so it was sitting properly. She had grown unused to starched satins and silks during her sojourn on the islands, but she was glad this gown was here. Arguing with Kaienar was easier when properly clothed. Also, fiddling with the adornments kept her from touching the newly returned points of her ears. That motion and distraction tended to undermine her fury.

"I will not be returning with you." Her response was firm and automatic.

"Aislinn -"

"The answer is no, Highlord Bryndagr. Perhaps you haven't heard me before, but you will hear me now. I will not be returning." She moved to the second stack and lit that as well.

"You nearly died. Be reasonable. My lands are closer than your homelands, you can rest there." He attempted, for what seemed like the hundredth time, to take the torch to light the fires. That angered her more. This was not his place, there was someone else who should be here helping her banish the pall that hung over this clearing.

"I've been more than reasonable, especially to someone who did not show up until long after my corpse would have been cold."

"You told me to stay away."

"And you didn't do that either. If you're going to ignore my wishes, the least you could do is be useful rather than coming after the mess is cleaned up and pestering me to follow your wishes. Also, how do you think this new look of mine will go over with your people?" Her tail lashed slightly. She was trying to keep it in check, but she was beyond irritated that he appeared two evenings back. Fortunately, the twins had also arrived by then and formed a dragonic wall between her and Kaienar. Until today. The cairns could not wait any longer and since Onyx could not do it, she would.

"You may still be able to fully shift back to human after healing, all will be well."

"Part elf." She moved to another cairn and lit it with the torch she carried. If she could, she would return to her wingless form. Her wings felt heavy and Kaienar was enough of a weight at the moment, but what was, was. And she wouldn't trade the elfsong for all the shifting ability in the world. "I won't perform for your court any more. I'm not your wife, I'm not your lover and I'm neither human nor dragon nor elf. That being said, we have a son together." She saw him relax, that would soon be remedied. "You will find a way to let him know that I am alive."

"Aislinn! We agreed that-"

"I did not agree. The ONLY thing I agreed to is that he was to be raised as your heir, not that he should be raised in lies. You're the one who decided that you needed to lie to him to save face." She was angry, but she finally felt steady in this anger and her calm tone reflected that.

"Aislinn..." Kaienar paused, she could tell he didn't know what angle to come from. She was ruining his strategic skills again. Good.

"I'm not telling you to have a town crier announce your folly or hand out papers announcing all you did. Our son will know I'm alive. I will be allowed to see him." She felt a pull then. He was manipulating the bond, trying to force her to follow him or manipulate her emotions. She let her aura flair a challenge.

Kaienar actually backed up a step, unused to this calm fury from her. She saw his guards that were in sight but out of earshot shuffling nervously as they felt the challenge. The only one within earshot, Eingeir, half-nodded; likely approving this turn. Kai's brother had often urged a more direct approach, but she had not had the strength nor focus for it.

"You may decide how best to tell the truth and save face. I know you're clever enough to find a way to do both. For now though, you and your entourage will leave." She let the air crackle for a bit longer before letting the energy drop.

"Aislinn, you cannot fight me, you know this." Kai's voice was low and worried. He was used to her somewhat backing down after a day or so and she hadn't.

"If it came to it and we found a way around the 'no pain' caveat, you mean you cannot fight me. The mating sparring was a draw. You may be a weaponsmaster, but in the day to day, you sit making the policies." As she spoke, Kai's face clouded and she saw Eingeir slightly quirk an eyebrow. This was obviously new information to Kai's brother. It was disappointing, but unsurprising, that Kai had never shared that outcome. Such a fragile ego. She pushed further and continued keeping her voice low, she had no intention of embarrassing him in front of his people unless he gave her more of a reason, but she wasn't about to let this drop.

"You sit in audience with your councilors while I bleed. Since that sparring match, I have stood against wyverns and worked from the shadows and, most recently, have been the terror of a relentless crew of skin hunters, so do not patronize me and do not underestimate me. It may take time, but I will find a way to fight you if I must because I would rather die than let you continue to use me for your pleasure." She actually touched her eartips for emphasis.

"And I know it would only be a matter of time before you stole what I restored."

"I will not make that mistake again." His voice was earnest.

"Then you'd make worse, for the same reason, but I've no plans to allow you that chance and I am done with letting you control access to our son." She paused, searching for her next words and realizing she'd said all she needed to say. "I'm done arguing. I have far too much to do to continue repeating myself. Remove your people and yourself. Either at my behest or at my brothers' insistence."

"Our people will withdraw as instructed, Lady Bryndagr. Unless my lord needs our assistance?" Eingeir smoothly cut in before his brother could speak any further and bowed low behind Kaienar. He was also loud enough the others could hear.

She did not have the authority to order Kai gone, but she did, technically, hold some authority over Eingeir and the soldiers, so long as she held the position Kai claimed she did. She was laughing inside at the delicate trap Eingeir had placed. To deny the order was to either deny her station or claim weakness as there was no reason for the soldiers. Though Kai kept a calm face; she knew once the two were out of earshot, Kaienar would thoroughly reprimand his brother and general. She wished Kaienar had backed down from her, but she would take this win.

"That will be fine. Considering all that has happened, I will let this matter rest for now." He walked away with a minor measure of dignity intact. It wasn't long before their silhouettes rose against the grey pre-dawn sky. She could tell by their flight path that they were not returning to Minado straight away, but they were no longer her concern.

She lit another pyre and let her legs take her to the ground. A presence that had been hanging back the entire time Kai was with her drew near.

"Thank you for bringing my ceremonial clothes, that would have been far more awkward in rags. Or nude." She smiled over her shoulder at her brother.

"Intuition mixed with faith in you. You were in danger. There were those attempting to kill you. I assumed you would return the favor preemptively and wish to honor even the dishonorably deceased." Damian handed her a cup filled to the brim with herbs and hot broth. "It seemed a reasonable addition to the supplies we carried."

"My brother knows me well. I suppose the nearness of Minado had something to do with it as well?" Aislinn watched him as he moved to the next pyre, taking over where she had left off.

"Perhaps," he replied. One fluid hand motion and Damian had the stack of bones alight. She let him assist without argument, sipping the bitter liquid he'd handed her. Her brothers had taken part in the battle of the island, or at least the aftermath of it. He was still not the one that should be here, but he had more than earned his place. And she'd already been having trouble keeping the cairns lit with the misty air of the island.

"I'm still surprised you found us," she spoke, needing a slight break from the medicinal drink.

"One can, if one is of sufficient skill, force dreams to return when necessary. It is an imprecise method and we were very fortunate. If it had returned too early, the memory would have scattered, leaving nothing but dread. Too late, there may have been more bodies on these pyres." Another motion with his hands, another pile aflame.

"How long ago was the first time you dreamt it?" She was trying not to envision the selkies burning in the flames.

"Mere days before we first met you. I was focused on meeting an old friend and calming prior animosity, as well as cautious about his mysterious new sibling." Damian lit another stack. "Likely that focus on you and Edorian are what drew you to that moment. I have questions about some of what has happened, and about future alterations to our lives with your ultimatum to Lord Bryndagr, but most can be postponed. Particularly considering your injuries and the vexation from the Bryndagr whelp."

She snorted. Trust her brother to call Kaienar a 'whelp' and reduce the situation to 'vexation'.

"And the questions that cannot wait?"

"Most concern the selkie."

"My relations with him or his magic?"

"I have no desire to delve into your relations with him. I already know far more than I wish in that regard." His tone was dry. One of his specialties was sensing auras and emotions in folk as well as the connections that ran between them. It had proven awkward at times. And she could not picture the selkies being difficult to read, at least not in that. Damian went on. "As to his injuries, his abilities have stabilized and the destructive and healing magic are separating. There will be no long term effects. This time. I recommend he not try again, but I am as familiar with the temptation as I am with its outcome. If we returned him to his homeland, his temptation would be lessened."

"That is true. And if we didn't or he didn't want to return?"

"I would be willing to take him as an apprentice. He has potential." The last was high praise from Damian.

"I will inform him of the possibilities." She looked away and brushed moss and dirt off her hands. It had only been a few days and moss had already covered most of the bloodstains. It was even beginning to regrow in her scorched clearing. The island hadn't let the fire get far. She wasn't certain if the island was reclaiming itself from the travesties inflicted on it in the past or if it was hungry for more blood. Nature's logic was beyond her ken.

Once Damian was done lighting the final fires, he returned to her side. He knelt for a moment, eyes closed and hands raised in silent prayer to the elements. She watched the fires burn, feeling oddly detached. She had no need to commune with the spirits or the island at this juncture, she had played her part and fulfilled her promise. The hunters' corpses had been buried in the cold ocean by Daren over the past few days. Their bones would not be allowed to rest with those they destroyed. He had towed the burnt remains of the ship over to where they lay as well.

The twins had arrived at the wrong time for passage through the fogs, but made use of that time by attacking and clearing the waiting ship. They looted the ship before burning it, setting the remaining bits of selkies in a lifeboat. Those remains were now burning on the cairns.

Damian's prayer was soon over. He examined her wounds yet again, noting aloud that the burns along her arms were healing nicely and frowning at the slow progress on the bite wound. She waited patiently while he worked, understanding he had something more to say.

"He is waiting. Daren kept him occupied while you and Lord Bryndagr discussed arrangements."

"Thank you. I'm still not sure how Kai found me."

"Your bond and there being someone in the port on Bryndagr's payroll. He informed them once Hanjib's ship anchored there."

"I've asked for-"

"As I mentioned, I am aware. We can discuss your son's care at a later time. Perhaps on the voyage home?" Damian was standing now, one eyebrow raised.

"Am I allowed to finish a sentence?" She was amused at the implied order to rest.

"Until you are further along the path of healing, all unnecessary activity is to be avoided, including pointless conversation."

"And with your far more advanced age, you of course know exactly which conversations are necessary and which are not." She had missed this.

"Lord Bryndagr was barely necessary, any conversation we may have can be set aside for the time being. The selkie is another matter. I need to know what direction our good captain should direct the ship when he reaches the market in a few days time. And as he is also my patient, I cannot ignore the good your conversation does him." Damian stared at her, expression too bland and almost innocent. He was enjoying bossing her around.

"To think I missed you while I was running for my life." Aislinn smiled, held out her hand, and let him pull her to her feet. She found the selkies and Daren near the shore. Mer spotted her first, raising a hand and yelling out a greeting. They had enough near death experiences between them to be good friends, or at least that was how she decided to translate his new-found openness to chattering.

Onyx sat on a log, facing the ocean. He turned to look at her for a moment, nodded, and turned away. She sat beside him, back to the sea, facing him. Damian was right. She needed to get to the bottom of this odd mood.

"We could use some fresh fish, and I know I could use a swim," Mer loudly announced, in fluent Dawnlands. He was moving towards the sea before he finished his statement.

Between her brothers' language knowledge and Kaienar's appearance, they had realized they were all reasonably fluent in Dawnlands. She'd not realized it was close to their selkie dialect, so selkies found it easy to learn. She guessed Onyx had never tried speaking it to her as she looked nothing like the people of the Dawnlands, though he wouldn't admit that. And she had never bothered mentioning Kaienar's full title, so Onyx hadn't connected Kaienar with the lord of Minado.

When they discovered this, Mer had given a long suffering sigh and acted as if he was tasked herding idiots, though he had chosen to speak Amarantine to her up until then as well. Mer's mood passed quickly after she and Onyx had spent most of yesterday asking him how to do the simplest of things. It had been an odd spot of levity in the past few days and brought a small smile to her face as she thought of it.

"I've fished with a half-selkie before. I think I'll tag along with a real selkie. I'd like to give her tips to help better her skills," said Daren.

"You'd best brush up on dodging the blunt end of a spear if you're planning on telling Laira how to fish." Aislinn's retort earned a winning smile from Daren and a snort from Damian.

Unlike the others, Damian simply left without announcing his departure, leaving Aislinn alone with Onyx.

Onyx was relieved when the interlopers finally left. He and Mer had been kept separate from them by Aislinn's brothers. By Daren's rapid Dawnlands, dragons were territorial and the one in charge of the handful of dragons that appeared too late to help fight was the one that considered Aislinn his territory. Daren had informed them in a rather light tone that murder was not uncommon if someone else tried to get between mates, while also clarifying she was that dragon's mate only by technicality. And he also threw in more than a few insults towards the other dragon.

Onyx had stalked the elegant lord from a distance and made faces at him from the waves. He should have been afraid of the sleek blue dragons, and maybe at an earlier point in his life, he would have been at least intimidated, but they didn't have the same presence as his beautiful brown-striped dragoness. And they lacked the quiet command present in the stockier blue dragon-forms of

Aislinn's brothers. Onyx's surreptitious mockery was still a foolish move, but Aislinn had shook her head and smiled at him the one time she'd caught a glimpse of him. That moment was the only smile he'd seen on her face while the overgrown blue carp was in her presence.

Onyx had wanted to be present for the lighting of the pyres, but the bones clawed at his heart and the lord had not seemed willing to leave. Damian had also advised against going near the cairns, as the air of that place twisted what was injured in his magic and set back the healing. So he'd reluctantly requested Aislinn to do it in his place.

Aislinn looked irritated and exhausted and beautiful when she finally strode into sight. Her tail twitched - much like the cat he called her - betraying her frustration. Wings shook slightly and settled back into place, he wasn't quite sure if that had meaning yet, but he couldn't stop watching all the tiny little movements, as he was entranced anew with her half form. That was how she first came to him, but now she was full of life and healed. Mostly.

The burn wounds still visible on her arms made him wince. He couldn't see the bite marks he'd left, but he knew they were there as well. He turned back to the sea, disquiet in his heart. That attack felt too close to striking the bull on the beach. He was dangerous and his new magical discoveries made him more dangerous. And useless. His ability to heal was compromised and he was useless for a while longer yet.

It left him at the worst time and he couldn't remember when or how he stumbled back to Mer and half-dragged him to the knoll where Aislinn was. The powers here hadn't answered his pleading to save Aislinn, so he piled clothes and bedding on them and attempted to keep everyone warm and alive. They waited for hours like this before he hazily remembered the twins appearing. He'd made several weak attempts to attack them before the pair managed to calm him.

The snarl of healing and destructive magic were now mostly untangled, thanks to countless poultices wrapped about his arms. Poultices that turned black. Poultices that Damian burned downwind from their camp. The magic and the caution of the cure made him uneasy, but part of him wanted to know more. He'd learned so much of magic and healing over the past few days and his brain felt on the verge of bursting, but it still wasn't enough. Then he'd catch glimpses of Aislinn's wounds and hesitate.

Onyx had barely responded to her sitting down. Aislinn removed the stiff leather gorget and pauldrons that made up the collar of her outfit. Silk covered or no, they were not meant for long wear.

"This gets so uncomfortable." She plopped it on Onyx's lap as she spoke, startling him.

"Is this customary for your people?" Onyx asked.

Aislinn felt she had cheated by using curiosity to draw him out. She was not sure why he had been so distant since the battle. She would have blamed Kaienar - still did ever so slightly, on principle - but Onyx had been edgy before her former mate made his unwanted appearance.

"No, it was my choice. Silly child me." She traced the patterns in the silk covering the leather with her finger. "Damian drank from a tainted batch of blood when I was a child. He didn't realize it until he was suddenly starving. I was right there, playing, and he had to explain to me later why Daren rushed me away for no reason. I got my first outfit for official meetings shortly thereafter and decided it would be a good idea to have a collar."

"You were protecting yourself from him." Onyx's tone was empty.

"That was his thought too. I very firmly corrected him while that dress was being made. Pretty sure I thumped him with a folding fan.

I was avoiding distracting him by covering my throat. He told me his responses were not my responsibility, but children have peculiar ways of translating things and I was adamant. I keep the style now because we have enough enemies who wouldn't mind ripping my throat out," she noted his twitch at the phrase and continued, "And because it reminds me that there are those I trust to never do so. I was never afraid of him hurting me, just afraid of distracting him at a crucial moment."

"I am not him." Onyx looked pained. There it was, the blame was back.

"If you were my brother, our relations would be beyond awkward, Sea-cat." She tilted his head towards her and kissed him. He didn't pull away after and she rested her head against him. "I know you're upset. If I thought it was the least bit intentional... I saw your eyes Onyx. I know blind bloodlust and magic gone wrong. I knew I was going to end up bleeding when I dived in, you don't break up cats fighting and expect to escape without a scratch. I also knew what would have happened if you hadn't been stopped."

Onyx murmured something under his breath.

"What?" she asked.

"It will take time."

"For?"

"Me to trust myself." He looked away

"If it helps, I trust you every bit as much as I trust Damian. And much more than Daren." She smiled when the last earned at least a brief laugh. In only a few days, Onyx had been around her brothers enough to understand that at least. "With what I know... you'll not lose control like that again. Especially if you're under proper tutelage. Which he offered."

"Sky-cat..." His eyes said it all. He was leaving. For her safety, for his peace of mind. This was not a path she had imagined. She inhaled even though she could not breathe.

She considered begging, arguing. Trying to keep him somehow, but she was well aware of the cost. A fiery cold calm fell over her. She would not beg, but she would not let him go until she was certain it was what he wanted. She wanted him to understand. She half turned away and rose from the log.

"Aislinn…" Onyx trailed off as she stood. He could feel the pain he was causing her, but he wanted to make it easier on everyone. He couldn't make himself say the words though. Especially not after the offer of training from her brother. The things he could learn! And he'd be in Seacove, with her. Maybe it was the home he'd searched for.

"I release you." Her words were a low but firm whisper. He stared at her in confusion and felt like he'd been stabbed. She turned back to him; something new crackling under the surface in her eyes. "You are mine. You said it yourself. If you wish to go, I release you from that. Be safe. Be well. Find happiness. But before you go…"

The air was electric and felt like the moment prior to a lightning strike. Onyx wasn't sure what was happening.

"I'm not afraid of you. I'd say you should be afraid of me, but I know you aren't." She stared at him, that dangerous feeling still buzzing in the air. "I think you've forgotten what you found."

"Never," Onyx tilted his head back slightly, basking in the feeling and watching her through nearly closed eyes. She was beautiful, he could not deny that in this moment if he'd wanted to. Something about her fury… she was a flame and he was a moth. He was on his feet and drawing closer to her.

"You said you wanted to see where this went; I don't want this tale to end here." She knew three words that could stop him, but refused to manipulate his feelings. Especially when her heart couldn't fully feel those words. Not yet. She was still healing.

Onyx watched her closely, and she saw thoughts flickering across his face, but had no idea what they were. He closed his dark eyes.

"You want me to stay so much?"

"Yes." She didn't hesitate. "I washed up on these shores broken in so many ways. You healed more than the storm's wounds. You've helped me remember who I am. There's... there's so much I want to show you. Bits of the song. Libraries in Seacove. My crazy half-selkie friend."

He laughed slightly at that, but eyes remained closed. He was trembling, clearly torn. She reached out and laid a hand on his cheek. He leaned into it with a small whine.

"Promise me you will fight if I attack you again." His dark eyes opened and stared deep into hers. "If bloodlust takes over, attack me. No holding back. No talking. Stop me."

"No." Her voice was strong, sure.

"I don't want to hurt you like that."

"If you don't want to hurt me, don't leave. Stop running. Face these mistakes and maybe find some rest." She clawed the shoulder of her dress, exposing the bite and its still raw and angry-looking edges. "Look at this. It's healing - slowly - but it's healing." More fabric tore, exposing the other shoulder and a slightly older bite mark. "You helped save your friend with this one."

Fingers touched his chin and she turned his face so they were looking directly in each others' eyes.

"I will *never* promise to attack you in those moments. And I won't promise to save you. If you can't see the other side and I can, it's foolish to blindly promise anything. I fought the sea, I can fight you if I have to. If you don't want to be with me, you can go and go now.

If it's only fear, rethink, Sea-cat." She was fury and passion contained in the shape of Aislinn. "You said the tale of us could go a myriad of ways, I repeat: I don't want this to end. Not yet. Maybe not ever."

"Brown." He spoke without really thinking.

Her mouth opened, but no words came out. She raised an eyebrow, asking for an explanation.

"I wondered about the color of your eyes when you were sleeping." He touched the side of her face, aware she was waiting for more of a response. "I noticed it before now, but the fire in them; I'd not expected that." He kissed her deeply, using that distraction to return something to her.

Aislinn felt a light weight settle around her neck as they kissed. They parted and she saw the necklace he'd made, intact again. He had somehow found and repaired it.

"I won't accept this if you're leaving. I have memories of our time together, I don't need mementoes." She felt wary and did her best to keep hope in check.

"Keep it." He brushed strands of hair back from her face as he spoke. "Though I must leave."

She caught the spark of mischief in his eyes, but her heart still fell. It was a poorly timed joke.

"Only for a little!" It came out almost as one word, as Onyx tried to compensate for the failed teasing. "I will come to Seacove as soon as possible. I must gather things from my home in the Spine and let my family know that I will summer and perhaps overwinter in Seacove."

"My brothers will insist on taking you part way, but yes, I can wait for you in Seacove." She leaned her forehead against his. She felt a giddiness she thought was dead though she couldn't completely shake her trepidation. Her past had a part of her convinced this choice could only end in pain, but she refused to turn aside.

Her heart calmed when Onyx spoke again. His voice was laced with soft and sensual tones of his kind.

"I am still yours, Sky-cat."

Don't miss out!

Visit the website below and you can sign up to receive emails whenever J. M. Gordon publishes a new book. There's no charge and no obligation.

https://books2read.com/r/B-A-MXSTB-FNSRE

BOOKS 2 READ

Connecting independent readers to independent writers.

About the Author

J. M. Gordon currently lives in the southern US and is the servant of three cats, only two of which are hers. The third belongs to a housemate but insists she deserves an equal share in all treats.

Read more at https://deavaric.wordpress.com/.